Women of Consequence

Gregory Wolos

Regal House Publishing

Published by
Regal House Publishing, LLC
Raleigh, NC 27612
All rights reserved

Printed in the United States of America

ISBN -13 (paperback): 978-1-947548-49-7
ISBN -13 (epub): 978-1-947548-50-3
Library of Congress Control Number: 2018951843

Interior, cover image and design © by Lafayette & Greene
lafayetteandgreene.com

Regal House Publishing, LLC
https://regalhousepublishing.com

For Stephanie

Contents

Queen of the Waves

The vehicles in the eastbound lanes on the Massachusetts Turnpike have stopped dead: dozens—no, hundreds or maybe even thousands—of cars and trucks are bunched up in front of me. Steel and glass glitter in the morning sun like the scales of a mile-long snake dozing between snow-covered hills stippled with black, bare trees. This shouldn't be happening here, halfway between Boston and Springfield, midweek in late winter.

I'm stuck in the passing lane, and a tractor trailer on my right blocks my view of the shoulder. The guy in front of me is already out of his van, standing on his tiptoes near the median guardrail, gazing at the double line of idling vehicles that disappears around a bend far ahead. In my rearview I watch the woman directly behind me busy with her cell phone, texting, calling. I turn on my radio, search a few minutes for news, catch instead some pop, some classical, some country western.

I know why we're stopped. Things don't come to a total halt like this because of roadwork. There's no traffic approaching us from the westbound lanes—whatever has stopped traffic in both directions is certainly fatal.

I settle behind my steering wheel and turn off the ignition. The woman behind me is now using multiple phones, has propped a folder open on her dashboard. The trucker next to me swings open his door and climbs out of his cab, a tiny

1

dog in a flannel coat under his arm. He places his leashed pet on the pavement and follows it behind the car in front of him, which has a dented rear bumper and, across its back window, a college sticker I can't make out. This car's driver, a young woman with blonde hair tied back in a pony tail, sticks her head out of her window. She says something to the trucker, who stops and nods. His dog, eager to get to the shoulder, pulls the leash taut, and his owner follows him to the other side of the truck.

A band of sunlight warms my lap, but it's chilly outside. If we're stuck much longer I'll have to start the car for some heat. Daylight Savings Time stole an hour this weekend. I've heard that there's an increase in accidents on Mondays following the time shift. It's hard to adjust. I look for the trucker and his pup, but they're not back.

At Mom's funeral the sun was bright like it is today, but that was January, and my teeth ached from the record cold. The crowd joining me at the cemetery was pretty thin. No relatives attended—there is no family. Mom was an orphan; I never knew my father and have no siblings. And none of Mom's fellow patients from her psychiatric facility would have been permitted to attend—not that she had any friends there. The director showed, and the chaplain, who offered a few words intended to comfort.

Because Mom was a veteran of the Coast Guard, a uniformed representative of the military came. He draped Mom's coffin in an American flag and thanked her for her service. Then he raised a bugle, keeping it an inch from his lips because of the cold, and flipped on a little recorder, which played a wispy "Taps."

The one stranger in attendance turned out to be a lawyer. She nodded sympathies after Mom was lowered into the ground and stuck a business card into my gloved hand. Her high heels rang out on the cemetery road as she hurried back to her car, trailing a frozen rope of perfume. The official report was that Mom's fall from a fifth-floor window was accidental, but there was a question of negligence on the part of the staff—Mom had been on suicide watch since she'd begun her long commitment. I never pressed the negligence issue. I wouldn't exactly call her death a comfort, but it was good to know she had no further to fall.

Though I was only five, I remember my first day of school—Mom shook off my hand to take my new teacher's. Mom wanted to tell her that I was special.

"My boy was born without a sense of smell," she said. "Congenital anosmia.

Please avoid activities that might exclude him."

She told me she first noticed I couldn't smell when she read me *Pat the Bunny*, the little board book for toddlers. "At six months old you rubbed your hand on the bunny's fur, and you felt the father's scratchy face—it was a bit of sandpaper. You'd lift the bit of cloth to play peek-a-boo with the little boy in the book, Paul, and you waved bye-bye to him and his sister Judy. But you wouldn't sniff the flowers—there was perfume infused in the page. I'd get so frustrated, I'd try over and over, but all you did was slap at the book so I would turn the page. When I realized that you didn't have a sense of smell, I felt so guilty that I couldn't sleep for weeks. 'My poor baby,' I thought, 'my poor, poor baby.'"

Mom conducted experiments to confirm her diagnosis: "I tried everything, hoping for a reaction," she said. "Lemon, orange peel, cedar wood, perfume-soaked cotton, banana, coffee, dirt, vanilla, onion, mint, vinegar, moth balls, rose flowers, ginger, pencil shavings." She nodded as she ticked off each item as if reciting a prayer. "I held each sample under your nose—but you didn't twitch a nostril. I kept thinking about that French writer who remembered the smell of a cookie from his childhood and it inspired him to write thousands of pages about his life. 'If my baby can't smell,' I thought, 'he won't have a past.'"

But when Mom listed the items she'd stuck under my toddler-nose, my head filled with a kaleidoscope of images—soaked cottonballs, Dixie cups, paper plates—and I could hear her voice: "Try this, now this, how about this." I told her what my inner eye and ear were seeing and hearing, but she just squeezed my shoulder.

"It's amazing how the brain learns to compensate," she said. "But none of that is real."

She bathed me twice a day. "Thank goodness you can't smell yourself," Mom frowned, raising her voice over the gush of steamy water filling the tub.

There were times I thought I could smell: the lilacs in the neighbor's yard (we had no flowers, only shrubberies); my shit; Mom's cooking, particularly when she burned something. On what turned out to be my last day of elementary school,

I excitedly told her about an experience I had when we were led back to the classroom after gym: "Before we opened the door," I said, "I knew there was going to be popcorn—I had a feeling in my nose and a picture in my head. I think I smelled it."

"Popcorn?" Mom's eyes drilled into mine. She sat me down at the kitchen table. "Honey, it's time we had an important talk. The truth is, I can't let you call what you're doing 'smelling.' We'd just be fooling ourselves. The sense of smell is a miracle you're just not capable of experiencing. Smell has *dimensions*." Her gaze dropped a moment. "I might as well try to describe color to the blind," she muttered. She raised her eyes. "Listen—it's like you only smell the skin of things—you're missing the blood and bone inside. You can try and try, but you'll never get it. Everyone else takes the miracle for granted. I'm not going to allow you to lie to yourself. You're going to need a particular kind of education," she said, "and I don't think the schools are prepared to give you the attention you need."

I jolt awake, see the double line of cars in front of me, and jab for the brake pedal with a panicked foot. But the exterior world is as still as a photograph. I remember I'm in a traffic jam. Where's my steering wheel? And what's this folder on my lap full of papers covered with unfamiliar charts and columns of numbers?

"I don't know how long—" The voice of the woman beside me quivers with frustration. She's not talking to me—she's holding a cell phone. "So *change* the schedule." She looks toward me—through me. I'm in her passenger seat. It's the woman I'd seen behind me when traffic first came to a halt. Through her windshield I see my car—those are my plates.

"Hello," I say, but the woman turns away. She has no idea that I'm with her. I might as well be a ghost. This has happened before: overtaxed senses sometimes invert, I've learned. I feel like a cramping fist, but my guess is I become like a black hole in space, where the pull of gravity is so powerful it won't let light escape. My senses suck me into myself until I'm invisible.

Though she can't hear me, I talk to my host. "Do you know what my mother told me about my lack of smell?" I ask. "She said, 'You may lack the miracle, but you also avoid the misery. Depths of pain you'll never have to worry about. Look at the faces of those around you. Everybody's suffering.'" The woman next to me keeps texting. Is that a tiny picture of a baby I see on the screen of her phone? She twists suddenly, grasps for a briefcase wedged behind us in a child's car seat, but can't dislodge it. I keep talking: "Mom said, 'You can try to pass as a "smeller." You can learn to mimic those faces. But the little whiffs you say you get will never be anything but fool's gold.'"

The busy woman slaps her cell phone onto her lap and lets her head fall against her window. I look past her—the westbound lanes across the median are still empty.

"I was homeschooled," I tell my companion. "There was a lesson Mom and I kept coming back to, reusing it for history, for science. It was about a hurricane they had over a hundred years ago that destroyed most of Galveston, Texas. There was an orphanage run by nuns, right on the coast. As the winds blew and the water rose, the nuns tied themselves to the children with ropes, eight or nine kids per nun. The nuns and orphans sang a French hymn, 'Queen of the Waves,' right up until the orphanage gave way and sank and they all drowned. I don't know who heard them singing, but that's how the story goes. They drowned because they got tangled up in the ropes." The first time Mom told me the story she gave me a look that still burns inside my skull.

"Mom said," I tell the woman beside me, "'Whenever you wish you had the same sense of smell that normal people have, imagine that you were part of the crew that came across those dead orphans and nuns, all twisted up in ropes the way they were, after their swollen and rotting bodies washed up on shore. Imagine the stench of death and sadness, and ask yourself if a sense of smell is worth having.'"

My overwrought host's attention is riveted on something out her window—I hear it, too, and now I see it—a helicopter, flashing into view above the trees, startlingly black against the blue sky. Its shadow passes over us like the blink of a god.

After Mom withdrew me from school, she began her attack on my remaining senses. Color first, then sound.

"Find the number," she said. I was staring at a swarm of colored bubbles on the top card of a stack Mom held on her lap. "You're supposed to see a number in the bubbles. *I* do. *Everyone* does. If you can't see the numbers hidden among the bubbles, then you're colorblind."

There were forty cards, and I failed every one. I didn't see

7

a single number, even when Mom traced the digits with her finger. "I can see that there are blues and yellows and reds and greens," I said. "Purples, too. Just not any numbers."

"Well, it's obvious that whatever you think you're seeing is different than what the rest of the world is looking at. You're missing virtually everything." Her eyes gnawed at my face. "It's not going to be safe for you to drive a car, you know—how will you tell the color of traffic lights? And that's the least of it." She gathered the cards into a neat stack. "This is as bad as smell, you know. Your world is even smaller than I thought."

I cringed, suddenly claustrophobic—it was as if I could hear the walls of our house scraping against the floor as they closed in on me. What an incredible place the world I was missing must be.

I'm talking now to the trucker driver—I'm sitting beside him in the cab of his truck, and, like the busy woman I visited earlier, he doesn't seem to know I'm here. He's fiddling with his radio. But his little dog stands between my feet and stares up at me with Raisinet eyes.

"Mom told me winter would be my easiest season," I explain. "Snow and slush, black trees, gray skies. 'Spring and summer people will have moods you won't understand—because they'll be absorbing the smells and colors of flowers and lawns,' she said. 'And in autumn—those red, yellow and orange leaves, like the trees have burst into flame. Don't worry—all the leaves will crumble into dust when it gets cold. The snow will cover everything. I should move us to

Alaska, that's what I should do.' She stripped color from every room of the house, explaining why as she hung black and white photographs on the walls, deleted the "color" setting from our desk-top computer and cut color pictures and charts from my homeschooling textbooks: 'I'm creating a safe environment for you,' she said as I watched her replace bedroom curtains I knew were blue with gray ones. 'At least at home you won't have to worry about what you're missing. You won't be straining yourself to feel something you're incapable of feeling.'"

"Music came next," I tell the trucker. "When I couldn't name all the instruments in a CD of Beethoven's *Ninth Symphony*, she concluded I was tone deaf. She outlawed singing."

The trucker finds a country western station. Guitars twang. The singer laments his losses. As a child, I rarely thought of my father. The idea of him was like another sense I didn't have. The trucker closes his eyes and tilts his head back. A tattoo of a dragon runs up his neck and disappears into his beard. Covering his thick forearm there's another tattoo that looks like a maze. At its center is a name I can't read. And just above the middle knuckles of his hand are tattooed musical notes, one note per finger. I wonder if they're part of a melody or a chord. What would hitting someone with his fist sound like? From his cab we've got a bird's-eye view of the stalled traffic. I can see that the sticker on the rear window of the car in front of us reads "Framingham State University."

"I taught myself to whistle," I tell him. "Like colors and

9

smells, whistling was something that I read about in books and wasn't sure I understood. But I practiced at night, and I figured out how to make a sound. Mom heard me, of course, and came to my bedroom door frowning. 'What are you doing?' she asked. 'You can't possibly know how horrible that sounds. Thin and weak. An insult to music. Don't.'"

The tattoo I'd like would cover my chest—instead of an inked outline, it's a movie, an old newsreel clip Mom made me watch on the computer. The brief clip shows a crew of twenty men trying to anchor a huge blimp. They hang onto ropes, but the blimp drags them down the airstrip. One by one, the crew members let go, and the blimp soars into the sky—but two men hold on, and the camera follows them as they're pulled into the air. A few hundred yards up, one of them loses his grip and, kicking and flapping, drops out of the picture. The other manages to wrap his arms and legs around the ropes. The blimp keeps ascending, and he's still rising with it when the clip ends.

"He hung on for hours," Mom said. "The blimp's crew pulled him in as they floated along, so high up he must have been just a speck to those on the ground. It took hours." She shut off the computer. Her eyes were shiny. She patted my chest. "Whatever you're feeling this very second, that's probably as close as you'll ever get to what real senses are like."

It's impossible to describe how much the crazy sky-dance of the guy who gave up means to me.

I'm in the backseat of the young woman's car now, the

one with the Framingham State University sticker. If she sat up straight, I'd see her reflection in her rearview mirror. But she's leaning on the door, so I'm staring at the back of her head and her blonde ponytail. All I see in the rearview is the college sticker.

"I don't know why Mom brought me books," I say, "since she assumed my failed senses kept me from understanding most of what I read. Was she encouraging me to create some kind of shabby half-world so I could limp through the real world everyone else enjoyed? I was nearly a teenager; I had powerful longings I couldn't identify. And I fell in something like love—with myself—with my own touch. Morning and afternoons I peeked from behind my gray bedroom curtains at the kids my age on their way to school. At night I remembered the girls. And then one evening, as I forked through my plate of sauce-less pasta, I asked my mother if I could go to public school."

The young woman straightens and grips the wheel as if she's steering us somewhere, though no one on this road has moved for hours. I'm nothing to her, but now I see her face in the mirror—a tear sits on her cheek like a jewel. Maybe she's missing something important at Framingham State. I keep talking.

"'Public school?' Mom glared. 'The kids would eat you alive. You haven't got the senses. You'd understand nothing and have to pretend everything.'

"I was shaking—I had never contradicted my mother before. I couldn't speak out against all the evidence she'd accumulated. And I couldn't describe my nighttimes of fingering and palming myself, envisioning tall school girls leaning forward under their backpacks, tossing their hair, gossiping and laughing with open mouths. How could I tell my mother that touching myself released the same feeling I had when the blimp crewman lost his grip on the rope. 'I *do* feel,' is all I said.

"'Oh—' Mom stuck out her jaw. '*That.*' She sighed. 'That's nothing. Your nocturnal emissions? *Those* are no secret. Who do you think washes your sheets and socks? You don't dream you're experiencing a tenth of what it's possible to feel, do you?'

"My face was hot," I tell the young woman. "'This is something else, Mom,' I said. 'I want to be with people. I can do it.'

"Mom lifted her eyebrows. Her smile looked more like grieving. She reached toward me, as if she was going to lay her hand on mine, but instead her palm fell flat on the table. 'Phantom limbs,' she said. 'Your sight, your smell, your touch. You *think* you have them—something in your brain tells you that you do. You're like an amputee—people without legs and arms swear they can wiggle their toes and fingers, swear that they've got an itch where there's nothing.' She settled back in her seat, took her hand off the table, folded her arms over her breasts. 'Son, I thought you had accepted your limitations. I thought we'd come to terms with that. There's no reason you should suffer through those urges of yours. They're a nuisance, really—messy. We can make something for your hands, thick mittens. And we can rig up something thick and tight under your pajamas that will prevent the touching. Let me think about it.'

"Later that night Mom came to my room with mittens as broad and stiff as ping- pong paddles. They had Velcro straps. And she brought a woman's girdle. Mom tugged these on me, fastened them, and left me in my bed. 'I guess you can't turn pages. No reading yourself to sleep,' she said. 'Or maybe you've had enough reading. Too confusing—what could it be for you besides frustrating? Better to accept your boundaries and stop pretending.'"

The young woman suddenly strikes her steering wheel with the heel of her hand. Was she aiming for her horn? Why now? We're no less stuck than we've been for hours. A sketchpad sticks out of the backpack beside me, and I slide it out. It's folded open to a penciled caricature—it's the young woman . . . a self-portrait? She's smiling in the picture, but tears splash from her eyes. There's a black cavity between her breasts—her sweater is torn around the wound. And she's holding her heart in her hand, severed arteries and veins writhing like eels.

I tuck the sketchpad back in her bag. "That night," I tell the young woman, "after Mom left me trussed up in my bed, swallowed by darkness, I thought about the world she'd imprisoned me in—a world in which scents, colors, and now touch were as distant from reality as dragons, unicorns, and witches. Then I heard a low, sweet sound—there'd been so little music in our home I didn't recognize it at first as singing. The muffled voice was Mom's. I couldn't hear her distinctly, but I knew the words and recited them in my head: 'Queen of the waves, look forth across the ocean/ From north to south, from east to stormy west/ See how the waters with tumultuous motion/ Rise up and foam without a pause or rest.' The words were from a hymn sung by roped-together nuns and orphans who drowned in a hurricane long ago. Mom made me memorize it years earlier for a homeschooling assignment.

"The girdle must have been cutting off my circulation, because my feet were numb. What if I lost them? How could I follow the school girls? As tightly bound as I was, I needed Mom to set me free. And it was her voice and song that drew me all the way to her closed bedroom door. Light seeped beneath it. Mom still sang, but much more softly. I knocked with my mitten and called for her, but she didn't answer."

There's a cool breeze—has the young woman opened her window? I catch my breath—her blue eyes, brimming with woe, fill the rearview mirror. But she couldn't be looking at me—it's the name of her college or the grill of the truck behind her she sees. Her self-caricature—am I sure she held her heart? Was the cavity in her upper or lower abdomen? Did the bloody thing in her palm wave tiny arms and legs? Might one of the severed arteries have been an umbilical cord?

"I fumbled with the doorknob," I continue, "and pushed the door open, preparing to argue for my life. 'Mom,' I said to an empty bed. Where was she? She'd taken off her robe and hung it on the hook of her open closet door. And then I saw that she was *in* the hanging robe, swaying slightly, that her wrists were cinched behind her back, that her bare feet twitched a dance six inches from the floor, just above the shoeboxes she must have stood on and kicked aside. Her face was pressed into the door, and the cord cutting into her neck was stretched tight over its top.

"I lunged for her, embraced her—she was soft and heavy in my arms—and I yanked her sideways until the cord, fastened to the knob on the other side, slipped off the door. Mom collapsed on top of me, her purple, swollen face inches from mine. Her hair smelled of her shampoo. There was a dreadful rasp as she struggled for breath. I lay still a moment under her body, feeling our intimacy, before I shrugged myself clear, tore the Velcroed mittens off with my teeth, and dug my fingers under the cord around her throat. Her flesh felt like dough against my knuckles. I dialed 911 from the cell phone on her night table."

I'm back in my car. Unless it's an illusion, traffic has begun to move. Exhaust drifts from the tailpipe of the van in front of me. The truck beside me inches forward—the angle's too steep for me to see the driver. The truck follows the car with the Framingham State sticker. My car starts up as if there'd never been a delay, and I slide the gearshift to "drive." I creep with the flow of traffic. In my rearview I see the busy woman I'd visited first. She chokes her wheel at nine and three.

After Mom was evaluated and declared unfit for parenthood, I became a ward of the state and lived in a group home for teens, where I kept to myself. I attended a public high school and earned a scholarship to the state college. Mom's hospitalization became permanent.

15

"Munchausen syndrome by proxy" was a diagnosis repeated to me again and again in therapy. I was told that there was nothing different about any of my senses, that there never had been, that I had been a victim of my mother's delusions. I was told that I was a completely normal boy, young man, man, in every way.

The power of my senses was not a subject I ever broached with Mom during our short, supervised visits. She was always heavily sedated, nodded as I told her about school, raised her eyebrows and clamped her mouth shut as if stifling a yawn as I spoke. And each time I left her, she gave me an unmistakable wink, as if we shared a secret no one could possibly understand.

Traffic moves along the Mass Pike like a funeral procession. For a while, the lane to my right outpaces mine, and I feel like I'm losing part of a family. Far ahead, the young woman's arm—red sleeve and white hand—dangles from her open window. The rear door of the trucker's trailer asks HOW'S MY DRIVING? and gives a phone number that's now too distant to read. The woman behind me stares at her cell phone while she drives. Is she looking at the picture of her baby?

The smell hits me the second I see the flashing lights where the state cruisers wave traffic off the road onto the shoulder, and I'm not sure if I'm imagining the odor—in spite of years of therapy, I don't trust my senses. Denial has become ingrained, and who can measure overcompensation? My eyes water from the foul stench, but I see that the young woman hasn't rolled up her window—I catch a last glimpse of her arm as my lane funnels into hers. I glance behind me and see with another pang of loss that the busy woman has been replaced by a white-haired couple in an SUV. I'm surprised she let anyone slip in ahead of her.

The smell intensifies as we come upon the site of the accident, but it's become less noxious. In fact, it's as if the terrible odor has been peeled away, releasing a sweetness at first ambrosial, then more lightly aromatic. I see crushed and twisted metal—cars and guardrails, a tractor trailer on its side with its cab smashed into a grinning skull. Lights riot from firetrucks, ambulances, police cruisers, tow trucks. Grim officers in broad hats and high boots wave us forward, and we slink by, one witness at a time. The pulse of the lights is saturated with the sweet fragrance, and the voices of children and women rise from the wreckage: "Queen of the waves," they sing, ". . . the waters with tumultuous motion rise up . . ."

We drift past, car by car, and we're directed back onto the open lanes of the highway. The sweet smell fades. I move to the fast lane and before long pass my trucker. His windshield is shadow and glare. Is that the busy woman hunched over her wheel, accelerating past me on the right? I don't recognize her from this side. I look for the young woman, for the college sticker—I don't know if she's ahead of me or behind, whether I should speed up or slow down. Had I made it clear to her that the ropes the nuns hoped would save the orphans drowned them instead?

17

An Oofy Baby Sees Fortunato's Side

The sweating teen boys with the basketball sit at a picnic table in the far corner of the park's only covered pavilion. They drink sports drinks they bought from the refreshment stand by the pool, which is hidden behind a fence. I can hear kids frolicking, water splashing, shouts, the shrill blast of a lifeguard's whistle, a hoarse command to "stop running."

I eat my lunch and eavesdrop on the boys' talk. Is it sports? It's got to be sports, though I'm not connecting it up yet, waiting for a recognizable phrase, like "slam dunk" or "home run." Their voices are low and serious. I'm eating a chocolate pudding cup with a plastic spoon. This is Mrs. Cuchinello's pudding. When I dropped off her "Meal on Wheels," she didn't notice that dessert was missing. If she complains tomorrow, which she's never done, I'll *tsk-tsk* and tell her I'll inform Administration. Mrs. Cuchinello isn't a caller. Only three of the eighteen people on my list would call if something was missing from their meals, and I keep them off my "special rotation."

"Implications of gestational location . . ." My head snaps up when I hear the phrase from the shorter of the basketball boys. His baggy shorts and tank top hang from him like hand-me-downs from a giant, and his yellow wristbands match the sweatband crimping his black hair. The boy and his lanky

18

friend, whose blue jeans are fashionably torn at the knee, glance at me before I duck back down to my meal. Does my thinness confuse them as they measure my age? Am I as old as their mothers? A big sister?

Pudding done, I move on to the entrée—Mrs. Poulter's chicken broccoli alfredo with bowtie pasta. The tiny widow flutters around her living room to music she plays so loud her windows vibrate. I could probably take her entrée every day without her noticing, but that's not how my plan works. Mrs. Poulter will lose her entrée no more than once every three weeks, like everyone else in my special rotation. She still got her garlic roll, pudding, and three bean salad. This afternoon I've already eaten the roll I took from Mrs. Wong. It was soggy with alfredo sauce.

Gestational location? That's not sports talk or kids' talk. Did I hear right? Maybe it was rap lyrics, like *"just take a vacation."* Maybe I'll try Mr. Silberbach's three bean salad before the pasta.

"It's called 'extra-uterine fetal incubation,'" Yellow Bands says. "They can grow a baby from scratch, outside the mother. E-U-F-I. 'Oofy'."

"'Oofy'?" Blue Jeans has got their basketball pinned under his arm. "That's goofy."

The boys snort ragged laughs at the rhyme. But which do they think is goofy, the name or the idea?

I never take more than one item per five day week from my fifteen non-caller Meals on Wheels patrons, and I rotate through their bread, vegetable, entrée, and dessert. Every weekday I wind up with a completely free, multi-course

19

meal. The kidney bean I stab at with my plastic fork slips off, and I chase it across the picnic table where I finally spear it. The boys are too involved in their conversation to notice. I nip the bean and wince—it's too vinegary. Mr. Silberbach is lucky I've taken it off his hands. He was today's last stop. Before I carried his meal to his front door, I hunched down in the driver's seat of my car and pinched back the foil on his plate, then scooped all but one kidney, one wax, and one green bean into my Tupperware bowl.

My car has a permanent smell like boiled cabbage. At night sometimes when hunger nags, I sit in my car, inhale deeply, and pretend I'm eating.

Mr. Silberbach greeted me with his usual stained-dentures smile. "I'm hungry," he said. "You're late."

"Only five minutes," I lied—it was more like fifteen. Today being a Monday, I was fighting the headache I get from weekends without eating. On Saturdays and Sundays I only drink water. On Sunday nights I dream about food.

It was Mrs. Poulter's fault that I was late to Mr. Silberbach's.

"Come in, come in, I want you to listen to this," she said through her door. The music flooding past nearly pushed me off her stoop. Every day she listens to something from *Man of La Mancha*. Today's song, like on most days, was "The Impossible Dream." The singer's voice was muffled as if he had a pillow over his head. Mrs. Poulter looked at me slyly.

"It's Hungarian," she said over the singing. "This is from the performance Peter and I saw in Budapest in 1987. They were selling cassettes in the lobby, so we didn't have to use the recorder I had in my purse."

"Hungarian, nice," I said, hyperventilating slightly as I raised my voice. "Better than the Japanese."

"Not better than the first of our three Japanese versions, the one from Kyoto. Have I told you that we saw *Man of La Mancha* over two hundred times? In seventy-seven cities on five continents? Peter and I would play a game where we would try to remember a detail from each different performance, and we almost always could. Since he's been gone, all but the special ones are muddled together."

"Mmm." Of course she'd told me. Mrs. Poulter's meal, even without her pasta, felt like a lead weight in my hands. Stars swirled when I blinked. "Gotta go," I said. "Hungry folks are waiting."

Mrs. Poulter's head swayed to the familiar tune and its incomprehensible lyrics. With her eyes shut she mouthed the words in English: "'This is my quest, to follow that star, no matter how hopeless, no matter how faaaar...'" Then she squinted at me with a suddenness as sharp as the swipe of a knife. "You look so pale, dear. And you're nothing but skin and bones. Would you like something from my lunch?" She clawed at the box, which, of course I couldn't surrender—if she opened the meal she'd certainly have noticed the missing entree. I clung to her meal.

"You know what I'd like to hear in Hungarian?" I asked. "That song about the prostitute. The part where she says she was left in a ditch after she was born."

Mrs. Poulter's frown of concern lifted into a smile. "Ah, 'Dulcinea': 'Naked and cold and too hungry to cry,'" she sang creakily. She pivoted and, with a slow motion prance, headed for her cassette player across the room. While she had her back to me, I tossed the meal box onto her foyer table and hurried down her walkway to my car. "The Impossible Dream" halted abruptly behind me. I knew from experience that she wouldn't miss me.

Dark clouds blot the sun, and it's so dark in the pavilion I can hardly make out what's left of my meal. Rain would make basketball impossible. The boys are still discussing EUFI: "Oofy." The lives of boys who talk about extra-uterine fetal incubation are a mystery.

"There's *implications*," Blue Jeans insists. His knees poke through the holes in his pants. He's tucked the basketball inside his T-shirt and slaps it while he talks. Is he mimicking pregnancy on purpose? "If the baby's not inside, how does it get the mother's, you know, juice*s*?"

Juices?

Yellow Bands is drinking his blue Gatorade when he hears the word. He wipes his mouth and frowns. "There's chemical fluids that supply those, whatever they are," he says. "Who knows what the set up would look like? It doesn't have to be a replica of a woman's..." He pauses, searching for the word, which is funny, since he knows "extra-uterine fetal incubation." I grin into my Tupperware bowl, pry a green bean from under a limp bowtie.

"Womb," his friend with the basketball belly supplies after a few seconds, though at first I worry that it's me who's answered. Do the boys notice how *womb* rhymes with *tomb*?

"Womb, right. Nothing has to look like a real womb.

Probably something like a fish tank hooked up to a computer. There'd be tubes and wires. You'd see a wall of tiny babies in aquariums, like tropical fish in a pet store. Things will be rigged up to get them all the juices they need."

"But aren't the *real* mother's juices special?"

"How?"

"I don't know," Blue Jeans shrugs. "Maternal instinct? Isn't that a thing?" I think he's just realized he looks pregnant.

"That's mental. It's not juices. How do you *not* get attached to the thing that fills you up for nine months? But all the baby needs is, like, food and shelter. What, you think there's some kind of 'maternal instinct sauce'?"

The boys laugh.

I'm always famished on Mondays. If I were alone in this pavilion, I'd lick the alfredo sauce from my Tupperware. On weekends I look at food pictures in supermarket ads, but they don't fool my stomach as much as the smell inside my car. Meals on Wheels pays me fifty-five cents a mile for gas, three times what I need, but most of what's left over goes for rent. I could probably afford a box of crackers once in a while, but I don't want to create a dependency. There never seems to be as much money as there should be, though toilet paper I get from stalls at McDonalds, and I haven't needed tampons in a while since my period stopped last winter. I've stopped producing eggs. I'm empty. What would my Oofy boys think about that?

There's an ozone smell that comes before storms. The kids at the pool are whistled out of the water. Lightning flashes, and I get an idea—I could double my income with

23

a second Meals on Wheels route! It would have to be at another location, because eighteen clients is the maximum for each driver. The boys are staring my way. Have I said something out loud? No, they're looking past me at the rain that's suddenly spattering the pavement outside the pavilion.

Two routes. There's an hour to deliver the meals, noon to one, and only one me. Impossible, right?

Mr. Silberbach's the one who got me thinking about time. He didn't really mind that Mrs. Poulter's Hungarian "Impossible Dream" made me late. Half a minute after I showed up at his door, I sat next to him on his sofa, looking at pictures of his granddaughter, who's with the Peace Corps in Madagascar, where she's teaching villagers how to raise bees.

"She's about your age," Mr. Silberbach said, though I'm sure I'm much older. Being starved-skinny makes me look like a kid. When I first volunteered at Meals on Wheels they checked my license to confirm my age. To my great relief, they didn't notice it was expired. Renewing a license is expensive.

When Blue Jeans stands, the basketball slips out of his shirt, and he dribbles it on the pavilion's concrete floor. There are two echoes with each bounce, a loud one off the roof of the pavilion, and a tiny buzz inside the ball like there's a bee trapped inside it. It's raining steadily, and thunder rumbles overhead like someone moving furniture. If I leave the shelter, I'll get soaked. My clothes will take forever to dry, like they do on Saturdays when I rinse them in the sink.

I spend most Saturdays naked and waiting.

"There wouldn't have to be abortions," Yellow Bands says. The beat of Blue Jeans's dribbling slows. "Why not?

"Because instead of throwing the baby away, you can just grow it. People need babies to adopt. They wouldn't have to go to China or Russia. There'd be tons of fresh ones."

Bounce-pause-bounce-pause . . . *Tons of babies. Don't throw it, grow it!* I snap the cover onto my empty Tupperware container and stare through the foggy plastic, half expecting to see a bee. How do I drive two routes at once? How does a body decide to stop making eggs?

"But is that it—is that all abortion is?" Blue Jeans holds the ball. He doesn't look at his friend. "Isn't there more to it than that?"

"Like what? If you're throwing the baby away anyway, what do you care what happens to it?"

"I don't know—just more." He stops dribbling, spins the ball like a globe on his index finger. "Maternal instinct sauce," he says, pronouncing each word like he's sharing a song title.

I feel the boys' eyes suddenly stuck on me like the mouths of sucker fish. I stare into my empty container. There's no genie inside, or even a bee, just bits of clotted food.

"You must be tired, all that driving."

Mr. Silberbach's words came to me out of a black void deeper than sleep. He thought I'd dozed off, but I'm pretty sure I passed out. Just for a second though, because I still held the picture of his granddaughter in Madagascar.

"You want to see something?" Mr. Silberbach asked. He

took back his photograph. He rocked himself to his feet, his body hunched in the shape of a question mark. I rose like a lifting fog and followed him to his kitchen.

"Here," he said, stopping beside the kind of kitchen table I'd seen in Salvation Army stores. He was so stiff, he had to swivel his whole body to look me in the eye. "Did you ever read 'The Cask of Amontillado,' by Edgar Alan Poe?"

"Armadillos?" I knew what they looked like—rat-sized, armored rodents that could roll themselves into a ball. About Poe all I knew was that he wrote spooky stories.

"No, *Amontillado*. It's a kind of wine. Poe wrote about a man who feels insulted by an old acquaintance, so the insulted one lures the insulter, a man called Fortunato who's a very heavy drinker, down into the cellar deep under his house with the promise of some very special wine called Amontillado. Then the insulted fellow chains up Fortunato to a wall in the corner of the cellar and quickly builds a brick wall in front of him so nobody would ever find him. Fortunato is left there behind the wall in the dark. Forever."

The hair on the back of my neck tickled like someone was blowing on it. Very creepy. When I looked warily at Mr. Silberbach, he was gesturing at his kitchen table.

The rain drums on the roof, hissing on the concrete and grass outside the shelter where puddles are forming. A narrow stream leaks into the shelter from a big puddle like a finger sticking out of a palm. The boys have stopped looking at me.

I peek at Yellow Bands, who rubs his chin. "You think

they could grow meat like that? Outside the cow? Could you pull out the calf right away, when it was just a couple of cells, and start growing it on the outside, and then get the cow pregnant again, you know, like, the next day? And then the day after that and the day after that? No waiting around for a birth. There'd be big warehouses with tanks where Oofy calves grew to birth size, and when they were ready, they could be harvested for meat."

"Does a cow have a cycle like a human woman?" Blue Jeans asks. "Does it get new eggs once a month? Or does it take a cow longer because it's a bigger animal?"

I wince, expecting the suck of their mouth-eyes, but feel nothing.

"Well, it's got to take less time than a whole pregnancy."

"And I bet you could speed things up by injecting the cows with hormones or something."

"I think they call them steers when they're for food." The boys speak quickly, excited by their idea.

"Whoever works it out, they'd be billionaires," Yellow Bands says. "But you've got to be an expert on how a cow's body works."

Cows have more than one stomach. Would the boys want to know that?

And then the boys do look at me again, though I'm sure I haven't spoken. I focus on the splinter of wood I push at with my thumb. I'm trying and failing to force it through my skin. *I'm no expert at cow anatomy,* I want to tell them. *I don't even have a period. I don't eat enough.* Are they worried that I might steal their idea?

27

"The hell—" Yellow Bands mutters. "All of this Oofy technology won't be ready for decades, anyway." He catches the ball Blue Jeans tosses and rubs it with his palm and stubby fingers.

"Nope," Blue Jeans says. "Probably not. But this meat talk is making me hungry. I could use a double cheeseburger."

My shrunken stomach growls, even though I've filled it with a Meals on Wheels lunch.

"This is a model for a life-sized sculpture," Mr. Silberbach said. "If I get the materials, I'll build it in the yard. I thought of the idea one night when I couldn't sleep. I'm no artist. I was a school teacher."

The "model" on his kitchen table was under a dome—a turned-over glass mixing bowl, actually.

"I cover it with a bowl because of ants," Mr. Silberbach said. "They smell everything in the summer. They're after the dried apple, which I used instead of clay. My daughter was supposed to bring me some clay, but she kept forgetting. She's worried all the time about Sarah in the Peace Corps. There's no clay sitting around at Meals on Wheels is there?"

"None that I've ever seen," I said.

The apple part of Mr. Silberbach's sculpture model didn't look dried. The puffy brown lump sat in a pool of leakage. Mr. Silberbach lifted the dome with two hands, as if he was removing the crown from a king, and the sweet odor of rot hit me like a punch. Backed up against the rotten apple was a pink plastic doll. I rested my hand on the table's sticky surface and bent over for a closer look. It was one of those troll dolls—I hadn't seen one in years. Mr. Silberbach's bug-eyed, grinning troll stood naked and with open arms, like it was waiting for a hug. But the thing I remembered most about trolls was the long hair that burst from their heads like colored fire, and this one was completely bald. There were dots in its scalp where the hair had been pulled out. Had Mr. Silberbach found the troll like this or plucked it clean for his art?

Then I noticed that the doll was wired to the rotten apple: paper clips had been twisted around each spread-eagled arm and jammed into the rotten apple. And then I saw the wall of dominos stacked like bricks a few inches in front of the troll. I gasped, tasting a hunger burp.

"That's right," Mr. Silberbach whispered, admiring his own work. "It's Fortunato. He's been chained up and walled in by Montressor, the man he insulted. Fortunato will never escape. He would have been in total darkness, but we have to pretend that the light shining on him here is the opposite of light."

"The light is the dark?" I asked.

"If it was actual total darkness, how would we see him? You'd have to take my word for it. Besides, Fortunato eventually took care of the light. I call my sculpture 'Fortunato's Side.' Because we're on *his* side of the bricks. Edgar Alan Poe didn't write about that. But this became Fortunato's whole world."

The basketball boys don't mention that there could be Oofy piglets or lambs, too. Any kind of meat could be grown. If I was a vegetarian and chose never to eat the meat from the entrees I deliver to my Meals and Wheels clients, I'd probably starve to death. The life plan I stay faithful to doesn't leave me much of a margin.

The snickering boys sit together now. The rain has thinned to a drizzle. These are not kids I would have known when I was in school. These boys would have been in different classes, the ones for smart kids, classes where topics like "extra-uterine fetal incubation" came up. They would have eaten lunch at tables far from mine and taken school buses to and from homes on streets I never knew existed before I started driving for Meals on Wheels.

"One business not to put your money in would be rubbers," Yellow Bands says. His big grin and squishy body remind me of Mr. Silberbach's troll. "Everybody could have sex all the time and not worry about it. Women could sell the little embryos. Now *that* would be a business to get into."

I blush. I'd been looking at the puddles and thinking of the wrong kind of rubbers.

"Wouldn't the embryos belong to the men, too?"

"Maybe women would keep it secret and take all the money. There'd probably be legal hassles. Women." Yellow Bands shakes his head, looking more like a troll with every word he speaks.

"It would be the same thing as with the cows, anyway, wouldn't it?" Blue Jeans asks. "The technology won't be around for years."

The boys are quiet again. There's just the rain. I'm picturing a huge building with row after row of incubating human fetuses lined up in thousands of tanks: Oofy babies arranged in order of development, so if you ran down a row a long, long way it would be like time-lapse photography. You could pretend you were watching a single baby grow from something the size of a pea into a fully ripe infant. In the very last tank in the row, I picture a full-sized baby troll, as bald as Mr. Silberbach's Fortunato.

"This is Fortunato after Montressor, the insulted man, left him chained up and walled in," Mr. Silberbach said. "But what Montressor didn't know is that Fortunato didn't die. Nope. At first he was terrified, alone in the damp, cold blackness. Who wouldn't be? But then Fortunato figured it out. And after that, he lived a long time, relatively speaking. As happy and fulfilled as any human being has a right to be."

"What did he figure out?" Bent over and dizzy, I resisted resting my chin on Mr. Silberbach's dirty kitchen table. My gaze stuck on the bald, grinning troll doll's whiteless bug eyes.

"Out of the silence and darkness, Fortunato heard a tiny buzz. He wasn't alone—a fly was walled up with him. What did he know about flies? Not much, he'd never thought about them except to swat them away from his food. Minor nuisances. He listened to this fly circle his head, and he tensed—*all* of him tensed, his muscles, tendons, bones, even his skin. He was waiting for the fly to land on him— to touch his flesh. Where would it make contact? He was certain it would settle on his face, and his eyes and nose and lips twitched with anticipation. And, oddly enough, chained there in total blackness, Fortunato *felt* his features for the first time in his life. Because his face, his body, his senses—these were all he had."

Riveted to the face of the troll doll, my dry eyes burned. "What happened to Fortunato's fear?"

"Fear was a feeling too, just like his other senses. Feelings were all he had. They were his treasures, he realized."

"Fear was a treasure?"

"Fear and everything else he felt."

"And when did dark become light?"

"Ahh—" Mr. Silberbach reached out and floated his palm just above the doll. "Light is supposed to come first, but it didn't for Fortunato. First came *time*—he was thinking about the rest of his life, and he measured it against that buzzing fly's. Neither had more than a day or two left, but to the fly, that day or two was a lifetime. And this was Fortunato's triumph. Chained up and walled in down in Montressor's cellar, he determined that he would live out his remaining time with the sensibility of a fly. If every breath was a week, if every heartbeat a day—I've figured this out—forty-eight hours times sixty minutes, times an average heart rate of sixty beats a minute—Fortunato had forty-seven years of fly life left—he'd die at a ripe old age."

I shivered. I no longer felt my legs. I stood up straight, but it was like I was a pencil balanced on an eraser. The slightest nudge would have toppled me. Did troll-Fortunato wink at me? I tried to imagine living forty-seven years in the dark.

"The light?"

"Simple. Fortunato had so much time, he invented it." Mr. Silberbach swiveled toward me, pointed at his head, and squinted one caterpillar-browed eye. "With the power of his mind. It didn't take him long. A thousand heartbeats, maybe—less than three of his years."

I heard my own heartbeat, which sounded like a dripping faucet.

"What did he eat?" I asked.

"Eat? I thought you were worried about the light. What did he eat? He licked the sweat from his upper lip: water, salt—plenty of nutrients to last forty-seven of the kind of years that were his to live. But the light—that he molded out of darkness. Like a bat's echolocation. You know what that is? Echolocation?"

"No."

"I told you, Fortunato had his *feelings*. He threw his treasure at his world, and what there was to see, he saw. He 'saw' the bricks a few feet in front of his face, and he saw the mortar between them. He saw the grains of sand in the mortar, the flecks of light in the mica. And you know what? He looked so hard, he saw the history of each rock and pebble and grain of sand—he gazed into the past, for millions of years, from when the rocks were bubbling lava that swelled into mountains and hardened. And then he watched as the mountains were worn away by rivers, wind and rain, then pounded into beach sand by waves. Fortunato saw the first creatures crawl out of the sea. On Fortunato's side of the brick wall he saw forward and backward for as long as there was time."

Mr. Silberbach's tongue slipped up to the little groove under his nose. When he pulled it back in, the skin over his lip glistened. "Fortunato was a god," he said. "And he never would have known it if he hadn't insulted somebody and gotten himself imprisoned in a cellar wall."

Then I must have fainted again, or fallen asleep, because I dreamed I was in a tent in Madagascar, and a young woman I understood to be Mr. Silberbach's granddaughter was talking about honeybees:

"When their hive is attacked by a Japanese giant hornet, the sting of which is fatal to bees, the entire population of honeybees surrounds the invader. And then they vibrate—a mass vibration that produces heat at a level that honeybees can stand, but that's intolerable to the giant hornet, which melts to death from the inside out. As if it was microwaved."

I heard singing—a familiar tune in an odd language, and then I saw Mrs. Poulter and a smiling old man sitting in folding chairs in another corner of the tent. They wore matching safari hats and bobbed their heads in time to the music.

"'The Impossible Dream' in Malagasy," said the man with Mrs. Poulter, who clasped a cassette player to her chest. Someone passed me a Meals on Wheels food container.

"We're going to have hornets for lunch," Mr. Silberbach's granddaughter said. "Toasted hornets. Yum."

I woke up sitting on Mr. Silberbach's sofa. I held a glass of water. How did I get there? He couldn't have carried me. Dust filmed the glass. Particles swam in the water. I held the cool, smooth glass against my forehead, then peered through it— walls and furniture were warped like reflections in funhouse mirrors. Did I dare look at Mr. Silberbach through the glass?

The rain has stopped. The sky is so white it hurts to look at it. The pavement around the pavilion is steaming. I suck at the thick air, pretending my shallow breaths fill me up. The basketball boys rise from their table and rush toward me as if riding a wave. As they come at me through the shadows, I see that they're younger than I thought—maybe late elementary school. The holes at Blue Jean's knees look less fashionable than worn from play. Yellow Bands' troll features are baby fat. Driven by hunger, they sweep past me without even a nod, still boys I wouldn't have known who'll become men I won't ever know.

I hear their ball smack wetly on the pavement, but I don't turn to look. They're no more attached to me than any of the thousands of warehoused Oofy babies would be to the mothers or fathers who spawned them. No more attached to me than they are to each other.

They're going to eat. My stomach makes a fist, gives a small cry. I take another breath. Nobody hears that cry but me. The cry is triumphant. It announces the fulfillment of the life I have chosen to live. My plan. My creation. Like Mrs. Poulter's Hungarian "Impossible Dream" and Mr. Silberbach's sculpture and his granddaughter's Madagascar bees. Everything is so clear under Fortunato's light.

Doctor Moreau's Pet Shop

Is there such a thing as being 'fresh out of rehab' when it's your sixth time?" Annabelle asked as she settled into the bucket seat of her convertible, coaching the B-list reporters who followed her after she'd signed herself out of the facility. "Maybe say 'rotten out of rehab' or 'spoiled.' Or 'stale'. . . 'Stale out of rehab Annabelle Hadley.'"

Which, in her condo, where an odor of something neglected in the refrigerator lingered, was exactly how she felt: stale, and detached from the thickened figure facing her in her bedroom mirror. She wouldn't even try to lose the rehab donut weight this time. There seemed no point in whittling herself down to a self so easily condemnable. With less effort she could crop her hair, maybe brutally short; the new look would match the voice that countless cigarettes had scrubbed into a growl.

Annabelle's court-ordered abstinence from outside communication was over, and her agent had left word about a job on her voice mail: "P. P. Frederico is remaking *The Island of Dr. Moreau* as a full-length animated feature. He wants you to voice a character named 'M'ling.' I told him you'd be thrilled."

Annabelle hadn't been so sure. She'd seen enough has-been actresses lose themselves in the world of animation: usually they'd be animals—gloriously feathered and distinctively beaked birds, sinuously-waisted minks, cobras hooded like Cleopatra—that were all sad memorials to faded careers. She'd be turned into a cat, Annabelle guessed, with huge green eyes, a whiskey purr, and a slender body. For a cartoon no one needed to trim down, either by exercise or diet pills or a finger down the throat.

A *Moreau* script was delivered, but Annabelle didn't bother to read it. She knew the story—a crazy doctor on a remote island operates on animals, trying to turn them into human beings. Her character's name, M'ling, hinted at a wickedly seductive antagonist, maybe with a vaguely threatening Middle Eastern allure. Too late in the arc of her reputation to give her voice to a heroine.

It wasn't until the telephone interview arranged by the studio a week before recording was to start that Annabelle discovered what she'd gotten herself into. The interview began with the usual questions about her rehab stint and her legal trouble. Did she think she'd stay sober this time? Would she think twice before again leaving the scene of an accident? Would she consider an apology to PETA and the vegan coalition she had enraged with her observation that "only stupid people don't eat meat—meat, including brains, is brain food. Even zombies know that." Curled up on her bed in sweatpants and a too-snug T-shirt from her own "Scaredy Cat" line for tweens, she watched herself yawn and smoke in her dresser mirror as she asserted her "every confidence and hope" that her new sobriety would lead to better future decisions. Annabelle considered herself adept at deflecting awkward questions provocatively yet insubstantially; when asked what she thought PETA's take on her involvement with Frederico's *Moreau* project would be, she saw the languorous drag she took from her cigarette and the careful way she patted the bed around her hips for the Snickers bar she'd half unwrapped before the call. She could still mesmerize herself with her own eyes, though at the moment they were no more bewitching than frozen peas. And when had her chin begun to melt into her neck?

"It's just a cartoon," she said. "No animals, I can assure you, will be harmed during filming."

The reviewer chuckled. "Right. But since Frederico has already commented on his intentions of releasing this as the first graphically violent cartoon in the history of cinema—"shocking," I think was the word he used, do you get the feeling you were cast *because* of your comments on meat?"

Annabelle watched her brow furrow, thought "worry," and deepened the frown. Cigarette ash dropped onto her chest into the open green eye of her T-shirt's winking "Scaredy Cat" logo. The identical logo was tattooed in color on the small of her back.

"You mean do I think it's unusual for a filmmaker to inspire interest in his film by introducing a note of controversy?"

"Animals surgically altered—torn apart by Dr. Moreau and reconstructed as humanoids—deformed, suffering creatures treated first as experiments, then as slaves by the evil doctor." The reporter seemed to be reading this from a press release.

"What cartoon doesn't tear apart animals and make them half human? Mickey Mouse and Goofy and Bugs—they're *freaks*, right? Talking biped animals. Bipedophiles—is that a word?"

"No—but the film's theme seems to glorify suffering—"

"It's a *horror* cartoon. And I like meat."

"Hmm. Well, are you put off by the absence of a female presence in the film?"

"I'm M'ling."

"Right." The interviewer waited. Annabelle traced a circle around her reflected face with her cigarette butt. She imagined herself with a snout and protruding yellow teeth, shivered, and looked away.

"Well, I'm sure that some suppressed sexual tension will bubble to the surface—isn't that what horror films are all about these days?—red-lipped vampires burying their fangs into the necks of— "

"Of course, but how do you feel about the fact that M'ling is a male?"

"Excuse me?"

"How do you feel about the fact that for your first role in almost four years, you've been cast as a male?"

Annabelle pictured her script, still in its Fedex envelope in the center of her black granite kitchen island. "Um—" She wouldn't surrender the truth—that her career was in the toilet and this was the only job she'd been offered. "—I'm sure it's integral to the film. Mr. Frederico is an artist, and a certain liberation from convention should be—expected. Are we almost over? My publicist is pointing at her watch. I think I have an appearance at a charity event scheduled." Annabelle watched the figure in her mirror tap her wrist.

"Just one thing more. How do you feel about the fact

that Carl Walchuk is responsible for the screenplay? You know the *Moreau* project originated with his father, right? The production is something like a memorial to Raymond Walchuk. He gave P. P. Frederico his start, after all. Do you know Carl?"

"Not really. Maybe we met at some child star thing twenty years ago, before he quit acting. I don't remember if he was on the set of *Svidrigaylov's Dream*, if that's what you're getting at. That whole mess with his father got settled, and everybody involved moved on. Raymond Walchuk died years ago. I've really got no comment beyond that."

After the interview, Annabelle shrugged back on her pillows and shut her eyes. Raymond Walchuk, the filmmaker responsible for *Svidrigaylov's Dream*. Who would try to make such a movie? Who would cast an eight year old as the object of a perverted Russian noble's nightmare, choosing the little girl whose features were most precociously adult? It hadn't been difficult to transform her into a dream-whore. But what responsible director would emphasize to the child that the goat-bearded character imagining her was "thinking fucky-fucky"? All done for the sake of art, Raymond Walchuk argued when her parents brought a civil suit against him for attempting to corrupt a minor. The settlement and publicity had ruined him, and, paradoxically, launched Annabelle Hadley's career. She had been the winner. There were long stretches, months at a time, when she didn't think about being the little girl of *Svidrigaylov's Dream*, the movie that was never finished; but, when she *was* conscious of *being*, she was never anyone else.

The chicken or the egg? The life that followed—a few family movies and teen romps, G and PG, then a love affair with drugs, with older actors, male and female celebrities of similarly tattered reputations, raunchy paparazzi photographs, moments when she glimpsed her own mascara-ringed eyes or caught a whiff of her cigarette breath or the fermented smell of bodily fluids she only half-remembered sharing. It hadn't taken long for the butterfly to revert to a worm that had a love-hate relationship with the spotlight's shriveling heat.

Her parents should have known, Raymond Walchuk maintained. Had they been so eager for their daughter to succeed that they had at first ignored the obvious subject of *Svidrigaylov's Dream*? Hadn't they read the script? Weren't they familiar with *Crime and Punishment*? And now Mom and Dad lived snugly and advice-less on the edge of a Palm Springs golf course, while Annabelle found herself marooned on *The Island of Doctor Moreau*— in another of Raymond Walchuk's fantasies.

◄⑤►

Annabelle finally read the *Moreau* screenplay. There was a note that the description of her character M'ling had been transcribed directly from H. G. Wells's novel: "a misshapen man, short, broad, and clumsy, with a crooked back, a hairy neck, and a head sunk between his shoulders. He...had peculiarly thick, coarse, black hair...the black face was a singularly deformed one. The facial part projected, forming something dimly suggestive of a muzzle, and the huge half-open mouth showed…big white teeth."

The story seemed pointlessly grim and violent—live animals torn apart by Moreau and reconfigured as gruesome humanoids. It was a story of degeneration and madness; there wasn't a shred of redemption or hope in it. As a cartoon, maybe it would develop a cult following among the morbid, but it was nothing but a grim, gratuitously violent slaughterhouse, in spite of its Victorian era pedigree. When Annabelle called her agent to tell him she wanted out, he pooh-poohed her.

"Classy author, classy connections. You need a touch of class. It's P. P. Frederico! And now is not the time to quit smoking, if you're thinking about it. Your voice is your signature now. There's a fortune in cartoons and commercials."

∾

Annabelle's dangling legs ached, and her ass had cramped from sitting for almost two hours on a rung-less stool. Her headphones pinched her ears, and her scalp was sweating under her new buzz cut. On the screen in front of her, a human-ish blob haunted a glimmering vacancy. Her voice would aid its transformation into M'ling. She wouldn't see the completely realized character until the film's premiere.

She had just delivered her sixteenth take of her first line: "They—won't have me forward." M'ling, the only one of Moreau's "transformed" animals to be trusted as a house servant, was being abused by sailors on a ship transporting fresh animals to the mad doctor's island.

"Ms. Hadley—" P. P. Frederico's words buzzed like hornets in her headphones— "according to Mr. Walchuk's faithful transcription from the original text, M'ling should deliver this line 'slowly, with a queer, hoarse quality in his voice.' You've captured the 'hoarse'—but that's just your natural rasp. Where's the 'queer'? Once again, please."

Annabelle craved a cigarette, but no break seemed imminent. "They—won't have me forward," she said for the seventeenth time.

"Ms. Hadley. Annabelle. What does 'queer' mean to you?"

"'Queer'? Annabelle had made a dozen films and had never repeated a line more than four times. And this was just a goddamn cartoon. "For Wells it would have meant 'strange,' right? 'Weird.' But there's a lot of 'weirds.' I think you need to tell me a little more of what you're after."

"'To you, to you, to you. To you. To. You—' I said. M'ling's words don't belong to H. G. Wells any longer. They're ours, and we're in the twenty-first century. What does 'queer' mean *to you?*"

"Hunh," Annabelle sighed. *To-yoo-to-yoo-to-yoo.* Frederico, the bird man. If she turned she'd see him through the glass wall of the control booth, his face surrounded by feather-petals, pecking at his microphone with a tiny beak. On the screen in front of her the gingerbread man blob standing in for her character floated impassively, waiting for her voice. Queer? A YouTube video gone viral flashed through her mind: a kiss—less kiss, really, than glottal assault—she'd shared with a one hit pop nymphette. Annabelle remembered the video clip, but not the actual kiss. She looked at the

M'ling-blob waiting for her answer. "'Queer' means 'gay' to me," she growled into her microphone.

"Exactly! Could you lend something of your new understanding to your characterization, please? Oh—wait a minute—visitors—take five. Hello, Carl—and how's our little man?" Annabelle heard a click and dead air. She plucked off her headphones and slid from the stool. She stamped the pins and needles out of her numb legs before hurrying out for a cigarette.

❦

They won't have me forward. Annabelle sat on the hood of her lipstick-red convertible in the parking lot of the sound studio, trying to enjoy a second cigarette she'd lit from her first. Her fingers shook from nerves or anger or nicotine. *I'm keeping my voice in shape*, she thought as the smoke burned through her throat and filled her lungs. She'd been sober for weeks. Two. The truth was, cigarettes were her only craving. She tried to remember what her other urges had felt like. A haze Annabelle imagined rising from the united efforts of all the city's smokers absorbed the distant hills. *Queer* wasn't one of her words—it didn't measure her liberal attitude toward her own sexual proclivities or history, clips of which swam through the stew of her memory along with the YouTube kiss.

Annabelle thought harder, surprising herself with a desire to understand P. P. Frederico. Her character M'ling had been carved by Moreau into human form from what? A dog? He'd suffered a kind of extractive rape, torn from one body,

44

one species, into another. Forced to fit an idea of "human." Dragged from a natural self into an isolating "otherness." *They won't have me forward.* Annabelle felt an unexpectedly sensual swelling behind her eyes—she wasn't far from tears. Poor, queer M'ling. How cruel of Moreau to have thrust him into the human condition.

"P.P. says you're doing great." A young man pushing a blond toddler in a stroller had passed through the glass doors of the sound studio lobby and now stood squinting at Annabelle through the milky sunshine. Not eager for company, she pretended that it was the child who had spoken. The toddler was sunk deep into the stroller's seat, and his limp arms and legs hung from his stubby torso like the appendages of a sock monkey. He'd fixed her with a pale-eyed gaze that seemed to insist on an apology. What if, she wondered, what if this little boy was dying, what if his brief life was ebbing away with each heartbeat? She mewed with relief when the child hurled his doll, a naked, flaxen-haired Barbie, toward her. It was a healthy toss. The doll struck the headlight next to Annabelle's knee and fell face down onto the blacktop. Annabelle caught her breath and choked up a cough that turned into sobs. Two heaves, and a third, before she bowed into her shoulder, smothering her tears. "Sorry," she said. "Wrong pipe."

The young man, who was not robust, had rolled the stroller closer, leaning on it as if it were a walker. Though his hair and eyes were dark, the shape of his head and the tilt of his posture were identical to the child's. "Pipes can be ornery," he said. He waited for her to compose herself. "P. P.

isn't always able to communicate his needs. He wants me to tell you to give M'ling a little lisp. He thinks it'll get audiences to think about a dog's inner life."

Annabelle's nose was full. Without a tissue, she snorted back her salty mucus and swallowed demurely. "A dog's life?"

The young man's dark curls receded like an eroding coastline; he would probably shave his head before too long. Annabelle shielded her eyes with her cigarette hand as if his cranium already gleamed. With sudden dexterity he bent, caught the child under the arms, and swung him out of the stroller. The clean, white rubber bottoms of the toddler's tiny sneakers flew past Annabelle's head. Set on his feet, the child tottered toward his doll, picked her up by one of her long, flesh-toned legs, and flipped her into the parking space beside Annabelle's convertible.

"Careful for cars," the young man warned, though Annabelle's was the only vehicle within a hundred yards. "Careful. Yeah—" He kept the corner of his eye on the toddler, while shifting the bulk of his attention to Annabelle— "so P. P. sees each species as having a kind of 'hook'—something subtle about them that the change into human form exposes. I can't tell you about the other animals, because he thinks too much information will muddle your performance. But he wants his dog-people kind of fey."

"'Fey.'" It was an odd, antique word. Annabelle doubted she'd ever spoken it.

"P. P.'s approach to creating a film can be idiosyncratic." The young man's tone and expression begged for patience— or was it with Annabelle he was showing patience? "His idea is to keep all the parts separate until they meet in the final cut. Like a recipe where the ingredients don't mix until they reach your palate. Or a painting where each brush stroke is a distinct entity. When you see the whole, you also feel the impact of each separate part."

"Hmm," Annabelle said. She threw her cigarette butt to the pavement on the opposite side of her car from the busy child, who had squatted and was marching Barbie along the yellow parking line.

"It's like he's arranging flowers," the young man continued. "P. P., I mean."

"Okay, so which is he? A chef, a painter, or a florist?"

The young man smiled; his patience had been for Annabelle. "He's a magician."

"Fay-Fay-Fay!" The little boy had picked up his doll and was banging it into the door of Annabelle's car.

"Hey!" she yelled, and slid to her feet. She almost stepped on the child. His shortness surprised her. She wanted to grab his arm, but couldn't remember ever touching a toddler and didn't know how to go about it. One of her legs trembled. The child paused in mid-blow, Barbie suspended like an ax, and his gaze boiled at Annabelle. Two teeth from his thrust jaw bit into his upper lip. His sudden ugliness froze Annabelle. When the young man whisked the toddler from the pavement and settled him upon his narrow shoulders, the child's mouth dilated into a cavernous *O*. He wrapped one arm around the balding head and drummed his heels against the man's concave chest while clenching Barbie around her thighs and whipping her long hair in circles as if she were a

47

pole dancer. The young man eyed the car door.

"I'm sorry. He hasn't had his nap." He held the boy's ankles firmly with one hand while he ran the other over the glossy red finish. "You better take a look. Wray-Wray, say you're sorry to Ms. Hadley. I like your hair short, by the way."

"Thank you." She smoothed a hand over the door. "Nothing here."

The child squeezed his knees against the young man's neck and continued to whip his doll in circles. "Fay-Fay-Fay—"

"Probably has to pee. Do you have to pee, Wray? You might not get an apology. I'm not sure I ever taught him 'sorry.' Hey up there—have you got a 'sorry' for the nice lady?"

What did Annabelle know about children? Didn't they all have syndromes these days? Aspberger's or ADD or something. What had she heard about babies on the news? Mothers had six or seven or even eight at a time; toddlers tumbled from windows or into tiger pits at the zoo. Sometimes they were found, alive or dead, in dumpsters. Annabelle's thoughts spun as if she were the doll the little boy—Ray-Ray?—continued to whip in circles, and she tried to spot a focal point like a ballet dancer. The child rested his chin on the fringe of the young man's disappearing curls, and their heads, one atop the other, reminded her of a totem pole.

"You're Carl Walchuk—" she blurted. She supposed she'd known all along: Carl Walchuk, screenwriter of *Doctor Moreau*, erstwhile child star, and the son of Raymond Walchuk. Why hadn't they met decades ago on the set of *Svidrigaylov's Dream*?

Had he seen her wearing all that makeup? "—and this is your little brother." *Not* his son. She'd seen it on *E News* a couple of years ago: how, after Raymond Walchuk had been dead for years, his ex-wife used his defrosted sperm, over which she still held custody, for the *in vitro* fertilization of her eggs. After seeing a zygote implanted in a surrogate's womb, she'd died of cancer before her second child's birth. Which left Carl to inherit the infant—a surprise little brother, a quarter of a century his junior.

Carl Walchuk smiled like someone accustomed to deferred recognition. "This is Wray." He dipped the boy toward Annabelle. "—with a *W*. He's named after his father, homophonetically. His initials are W. W. People usually use initials to make their names easier to say. Like P. P. Frederico—his real name's unpronounceable. But 'W. W.' is six syllables. Remember vets referring to 'double-ya-double-ya-two'? The abbreviation takes twice as long to say as 'World War Two'—it made the war shorter and longer at the same time—a love-hate relationship for the greatest generation. My grandfather spent that war on a Pacific island—the same one that P. P. is from. I've been there, but I forget its name. My dad made *Son of Kong* there. Oh—and the doll is Fay. Her *name* is Fay. I don't know how she identifies herself sexually; I don't believe lesbians use 'fey,' but I'm no expert."

"Wray and Fay."

"Embarrassing, I know. Really, on his birth certificate it's Raymond. After our father, like I said. You and I could have met a long time ago, but we never did, even though I told my friends for years that we were thick as thieves. I even told

49

them you kissed me. On the cheek. Under mistletoe—on the movie set. They say we dig ourselves in deeper when we elaborate lies, but I think a good lie is in the details." He shifted the child on his shoulders. The boy made a *V* of Barbie's legs and wedged them around his throat, aiming the prone figure at Annabelle like a divining rod. "He really loves this doll. I tried a GI Joe, but he didn't take to it. He didn't like his stuffed Kiko either—remember the white monkey they marketed with *Son of Kong?* We've still got dozens of them at home spilling out of closets. You want one? Mint condition, wrapped in plastic, probably worth something on eBay. I don't know at what age Wray will identify himself as a particular sex, or if it's happened already. The *W* will help if he's transgendered, though, don't you think? 'Wray'— that could be male or female." If Carl was joking, his expression didn't belie it.

"I had a Kiko. The little white ape." Annabelle hadn't thought of Kiko in years, but suddenly she could almost feel his soft weight in her cradling arms.

"Sure you did. Every kid had one after *Son of Kong.* That doll kept my dad out of the poorhouse."

Annabelle looked at the toddler perched on his brother's shoulders. "You're raising your little brother."

"Mom's dying gift to her soon-to-be-orphaned elder son," he said. "The beauty of an indestructible egg, a surrogate's wholesome womb, and Daddy's frozen sperm. Whenever I think of little Wray's origins, I picture a strawberry daiquiri." He jostled the little boy. "How's Fay, Wray?"

"Fay-Fay-Fay," the boy muttered, then began to chew

Barbie's foot.

"We're quite a novelty act," Carl said. "Little guy's the Ninth Wonder of the World. I pretend I'm the Empire State Building. We're on constant lookout for biplanes. I suppose one day he'll find out Kong's son never made it off Skull Island. We should all know our personal histories, right? You ready to go back to recording? Trust P. P. and fey it up. It may seem simplistic and offensive, but he's got amazing instincts—or incredible luck. I told you your hair looks good short, right?"

Usually a man would compliment Annabelle's eyes, and then his gaze would melt over her breasts like sculpting hands. She patted her head, felt its contour under the bristles and, when her palm passed over her face, sniffed her breath— tobacco scented, but not foul. "You did," she said. "Thanks again."

∾

The lilting sibilance she gave M'ling's growl struck the right chord, and P. P. Frederico approved Annabelle's delivery of her first line on the twentieth take.

"Your breakfast, sir," she recited next, to P. P.'s immediate satisfaction. Though M'ling was present in most scenes, he spoke rarely. Most of Annabelle's contribution consisted not of words, but of background gutturals that P. P. Frederico insisted be precisely matched to a setting that existed only in his mind's eye. Annabelle locked her gaze on her character's featureless blob as if it were her reflection and listened to P. P.'s directions ("try a long 'grrr,' almost a whimper, here—")

while her thoughts wandered. She fancied a pair of lips on the blank face whispering "Kiko." She'd loved *The Son of Kong*. She'd made her parents take her to see it in the theatre three times, and the video and doll had been birthday gifts. The giant juvenile ape was so cute, and heroic, too. She agreed with her parents—it would be fun to meet the man who'd made her favorite movie. She'd brought Kiko along to the first day of filming on the set of *Svidrigaylov's Dream*, coddling him like a nursing infant, as if Mr. Raymond Walchuk himself were to confer a personal blessing on the ape-doll. But Kiko had been left with her mother on the other side of the lights, while Annabelle's child face had disappeared beneath the brush strokes of Raymond Walchuk's makeup experts.

"He's thinking fucky-fucky," Raymond Walchuk explained to Annabelle, who was waiting beneath her transformed features. She hadn't understood. "You're the dream Svidrigaylov can't help from happening." Annabelle had cuddled in the bed Raymond Walchuk lay her in before the cameras, the first bed she'd occupied without her Kiko in months. She'd smiled with her made-up face the way he told her to, purred a laugh, and licked her lips as directed—she had never forgotten their sweet, slick taste, remembered it with each of ten thousand adult applications. From time to time she heard rumors that rough cuts of her scene from the unfinished *Svidrigaylov's Dream* survived, but Annabelle knew the dream belonged only to her.

Annabelle wondered how much of *Svidrigaylov's Dream* lay

between them during her first night in bed with Carl. He'd been an attentive, even fastidious lover. She couldn't recall fucking on cleaner sheets.

At the end of her week as the voice of M'ling, Carl had invited her to share a meal with "les frères Walchuk," and she'd accepted, although she might have begged off if she'd known how trying the last recording session would be. The script finished, P. P. Frederico requested "a treasury of utterances" so calling back Annabelle wouldn't be necessary if a particular effect were required. For half a day she fulfilled his demands for snarls, snorts, barks, whimpers, and an array of howls in different pitches. Most harrowing was the last vocalization P. P. solicited: a long wail broken by a string of sobs and ending with a strangled cough.

She left the studio drained, responding with a grim smile to the director's observation, "Now that was cathartic, wasn't it?"

But a meal with the Walchuk boys had been salubrious. The three of them had shared a spaghetti dinner around the kitchen table of Carl's Studio City home. The toddler ate with his fingers the strands his big brother had cut into bite-sized pieces, and soon his cheeks, T-shirt, and overalls were sauce-stained. "Submersion-emersion!" Carl announced, which Annabelle discovered meant a raucous, splash-filled, pre-bedtime bath that included the vigorous scrubbing not only of Wray, but also his ubiquitous Barbie. "Pity," Wray-Wray said about the plastic figurine at one point, quieting down amid his bubbles and inserting Barbie's head into his mouth. "He means 'Pretty,' I think," Carl said. The doll's wet hair must have been soapy, because Wray-Wray jerked her out and spat, then held her at arm's length and gazed at her. "Fay," he'd sighed with such exaggerated rue that he might have been acting.

Carl's baby, Annabelle thought as she held the wriggling child out for him to towel dry. Then Wray, freshly pajama-ed, had curled between them on his over-sized bed. He lay facing Carl, who read *The Cat in the Hat* with excessive passion, both brothers lost in the destructive hijinks of Thing One and Thing Two. Wray had drawn up his knees fetally and planted the soles of his small feet on Annabelle's breasts as if he were preparing to spring off them toward his brother. But he wasn't exactly Carl's baby, was he? Had Carl been such a disappointment to his mother that she'd felt the need to try again with a test-tube pregnancy? Yet she'd chosen to duplicate her first child's genetic code with Raymond Walchuk's dangerous sperm.

With a formality Annabelle found charming, Carl granted her permission to smoke in his bed. It was a sentiment she knew she'd never before applied to a sex-partner.

"So what the hell are Thing One and Thing Two?" he asked. Annabelle lay with a wineglass-ashtray, its stem sticky with diet Coke, perched on her belly. She'd spilled her cigarettes over the sheets, and Carl played with them as if they were Leggos he'd just discovered at the bottom of a toy chest. He sighted her down the line of one of them and waited for her to reply.

"What do you mean? They're 'Things.'"

"Well—where'd the Cat get them from? Who are their

parents and why didn't they give their children better names? Maybe they came from Doctor Moreau's pet shop." He raised his eyebrows. "Do you think I'm screwing up my brother?"

Annabelle hesitated. He'd baited the nature vs. nurture trap, and it was a discussion she wasn't eager to have with the son of Raymond Walchuk. "I don't think so," she said, "But I don't know anything about kids."

"Who does?" Carl put a cigarette between his lips, then a second and a third. "We're all novices," he mumbled.

"I'm not a novice," Annabelle said. "I'm just not in the game. I don't qualify at all."

Carl spit out the cigarettes. One clung to his lower lip, and he left it there. Annabelle watched it bounce on his chin while he spoke until it finally dropped to the bed: "How do I know if there's something wrong with the kid? What if he's autistic. Or maybe he's got infantile Tourette syndrome. Is there such a thing? Obsessive-compulsive disorder? Ecolalia? You see him with that doll. How do I even know if he's a boy or a girl inside—or something else entirely. You have to admit, he lacks coherence."

"He's a baby, Carl. It seems to me you're doing a wonderful job."

"But you've declared yourself unqualified. And I will brook no platitudes."

"He seems happy. I think he's happy—at least not unhappy."

"I'm remarkable, I know. Heroic. Maybe I'll get nominated for bro-dad of the year. I like to make it awkward for people not to compliment me. But I've got a bigger question." He was playing with the cigarettes again, throwing them like darts at Annabelle's hip—no, at her ass, and she imagined him impossibly lodging one between her cheeks and grinning over his achievement. Given the indulgences she'd allowed her flesh in the past, Annabelle's modesty surprised her. She shifted the target out of Carl's range, careful not to spill the soggy ashes from her wineglass. But Carl's big question. It would have something to do with Raymond Walchuk—the conversation was inevitable. Annabelle was startled by her sudden certainty that while she and Carl had been fucking, he'd been envisioning her as that leering child-whore his father had turned her into so long ago. Sex under the shadow of Papa Ray's tombstone. He was the pimp of her history. Maybe she had screwed the son to make his father's ghost jealous. Demanding the Bic lighter, lost somewhere in the sheets, Annabelle ran the hand holding a fresh cigarette through her brush cut and felt the shape of her skull. During the one month of public middle school she'd tried before retreating permanently to on-set tutors, someone had slipped an envelope with her name on it into her locker. She'd torn it open excitedly—maybe it was a secret admirer's note, like the one she'd gotten in her last movie, *Poppy Starlight, Girl Astronaut.* Instead she found a photocopied picture captioned "Parisian prostitutes shaved bald for associating with Nazi officers." "WHORE!!" had been printed across the picture in red marker, obscuring the women's faces.

"You had it last, M'ling. M'ling One," Carl said. He was watching her closely, and she saw his father's eyes in his; Raymond Walchuk was in Wray-Wray's eyes, too, and she heard the three Walchuk men whispering in chorus, "He's thinking fucky-fucky." Carl stretched his leg beneath the sheet and found Annabelle's thigh with his foot. She remembered the feel of his baby brother's soles on her breasts. "My question is," he said, "who was afraid of women, Moreau or H. G. Wells? There are barely any in the novel. For the first movie they invented Lota, the Panther Woman. Jesus—she might have been my first love! I remember getting nauseous when they showed she had claw-hands, and you figured out she wasn't human. I'm pretty sure the Panther Woman was the whole point for my father. But P. P. insisted I strip the screenplay down to the original male-fest."

Annabelle sucked sharply on her cigarette, and her eyes watered.

Carl made a show of checking his arms and shoulders and craned his neck to get a look at his back. "You didn't leave scratches, did you? Am I bleeding? It's okay if I am. I don't mind."

Not Lota—Kiko, Annabelle wanted to say, but the name of the little white monkey stuck in her throat. She exhaled gruffly, beginning to believe that Carl would dare to embrace her again. "You're 'M'ling Two,'" she said.

Wray-Wray Walchuk nearly died on a Saturday evening West Coast time while Annabelle was on her way back from New York, where she'd flown to discuss a theatrical role: Boo Boo Tannenbaum, a young mother, in an adaptation of J. D. Salinger's short story, "Down at the Dinghy."

"Really, the play's about the entire Glass family: Seymour, Franny, Zooey, Buddy—Buddy Glass narrates like the Stage Manager in *Our Town*," she'd told Carl before leaving her hotel for the airport. She read the script this time, and had accepted the part after a second lunch with the director. "They didn't even ask me to read. P. P. apparently said some pretty nice things about my work ethic. Wray-Wray was napping, Carl said, and would be sorry that he missed her call. "Tell him, 'It wasn't the planes—it was Beauty killed the Beast,'" Annabelle said. Maybe, she fantasized, the Walchuk boys could relocate to New York City for the run of "Dinghy," and she could show Wray the real Empire State Building.

At JFK, conscious of heads turning toward her, Annabelle waited for her return flight and thumbed a message to Carl: "I love you." She'd hardly the time to marvel at the words she'd texted before a young woman in military fatigues asked for an autograph and echoed them. "I loved you!" she gushed. A small fever sore cracked over her upper lip. "Back when you played those triplets in *Switcheroo*. For years I thought there were really three of you."

"Just me," Annabelle said, as she signed what looked like the back of an official military communication.

Minutes later, settled into her seat on the plane, Annabelle caught her breath when her phone revealed a new voicemail from Carl. She cupped it to her ear, anticipating anything but what she heard.

Carl's voice, raw and electric: "You must be in the air. I'm at the hospital. Don't worry, everything is okay. Wray choked—he bit the head off Barbie. I called 911, but he turned blue, and his eyes were rolling. I Googled 'tracheotomy.' I stabbed him in the throat with a shish-kebab skewer, where the picture showed, between his—I forget what they're called. Oh, God—blood spurt out, not much, and bubbles. I stuck a soda straw in the hole like it said to do, and I held him on the kitchen counter with a dish towel under his head and my hand on his chest, and he looked at me, like, 'What the hell are you doing?' but he didn't move, and the paramedics showed up and took over and said I saved his life. But it's okay. I did okay. Wray's going to be okay—I—we're—at the hospital, LA General, I—"

The call ended abruptly, as if Carl had dropped the phone or it had been snatched from him. Breathless, barely able to hear because of a ringing in her ears, she listened to Carl's message a second, then a third time. Finally, unable to wave off the flight attendant bowing over her—the time for shutting off cells had long passed—Annabelle gave up. She shut off the phone, tucked it in her bag, and showed her empty hands to the attendant, who winked and moved down the aisle.

Annabelle shrank back in her seat. How could news be delivered this way? It was as if an old-fashioned postcard, one with a picture of a monument or tropical sunset, had been blown onto her lap through an open window. As if its message were addressed to somebody else, and by reading it Annabelle was somehow trespassing. Carl's voice—it had been his, yet more than his—triumphant—tragedy had been averted. How had he done what he'd done? Little Wray's limp body in his arms—skewering the baby's throat—a *soda straw*! When, Annabelle wondered, had she entered Carl's thoughts? Had he cleared her out as he dedicated himself to saving his baby brother? How long before she reappeared?

Maybe he'd read her text just before—maybe he'd lingered over it a moment too long while Wray bit the head off his doll. Carl had been about to say *what* when his message was cut off? Annabelle felt like a victim and was angry at herself for it, but that anger was inside a greater anger she couldn't name. But—Wray was fine. Thank God.

With horror she remembered an early date with Carl at a restaurant where he'd been certain they'd be safe from prying eyes. That night she'd fantasized about choking, because she *had* choked, just for a moment, on a clot of the melted cheese smothering her French onion soup. She'd strained for air with a rush of panic before clearing her throat, then wondered how the man across from her, his eyes on his own plate, would react if she really were choking—would he rescue her? Would he wrap his arms around her and try to squeeze the death out? Why hadn't she been the one he'd saved?

The flight attendant offered a beverage, and Annabelle asked for a scotch, and when it was brought, immediately ordered a second. Responding to Carl's message was impossible—they'd ascended into turbulent skies, and the signs prohibiting electronics remained lit. Carl was a hero. There would be publicity. Layers of privacy would peel away like old wallpaper. Carl would be the toast of Hollywood. Carl Walchuk: son of Raymond Walchuk; savior of his test-tube brother; lover of Annabelle Hadley, rehab slut—it was too soon for her to be redeemed, no one would believe she'd earned it.

She hated jets, but on her flight to New York Annabelle had been so busy reviewing the "Dinghy" script that she hadn't bothered with the Xanax prescribed for her. Now she gagged down a double dose with her second drink. The cabin seemed to shrink. The jet struggled against the storm, and Annabelle imagined the fuselage gripped by a gigantic hand before she plummeted into a tormented sleep. She dreamed she saw Carl's back as he stood over a black granite counter. The perspective shifted, directly overhead now, just as Carl raised what looked like a silver spike and drove it downward into the small figure sprawled across the granite. It was Wray, she knew, but it was also a little white monkey, and its limbs jerked when the spike pierced its throat. There was no blood, just a gust of warm air against Annabelle's face. Carl yanked the spike out, and Annabelle saw only the bloodless wound, like a rosebud mouth, glistening pink and red against the white flesh and fur.

Then it was dark. Annabelle knew somehow she stood behind a curtain on the stage of a theatre, heard a distinctive voice she couldn't place—but there was no doubt that it issued from the lips cut into the pale throat. She heard "Moreau" and "M'ling One" and "Walchuk." Then she heard her name—she was about to be introduced! Annabelle reached reflexively for her face, but her fingers couldn't find her features. Instead, she smeared makeup, like a child finger-painting, and knew she wore a mask. She heard the rosebud lips on the other side of the curtain whispering into a microphone: "and Annabelle has come a long way from the little girl of Svidrigaylov's dream . . ." There was a thunderous roar. It could only be applause. It was thick with expectation. One finger on those lips would hush them. She could feel the suction on her fingertip as she plugged the straw's open end.

Interstate Nocturne

I'm driving down Interstate 81 into the blackness of well past midnight. Driving alone, to keep an appointment I have in Knoxville tomorrow morning at nine thirty with a man I barely know about some numbers I've compiled concerning his liquor business. The figures are in a briefcase in the trunk of my car; I haven't thought about them in miles. The car's a rental, a white Honda Civic, 6138.7 miles. I wouldn't dare drive my own car on a long trip, especially late at night. I know too much about what could go wrong, what has gone wrong. I picture us—the car a lifeless chunk of metal, me hovering beside, dumbfounded, while traffic whizzes by at speeds that threaten to suck me off the shoulder through the holes they smash in the air.

I'm smashing my own hole through the star-freckled night, nothing around to be sucked into my trail except a few small animals that trickle out of the humps of forest the highway splits. They squat on the pavement, transfixed by approaching headlights. Assuming that only humans can contemplate their own mortality, I imagine the deaths of these creatures for them. The radio wrings only static from the air. I have no CDs for the CD player, but its slot reminds me of the black boxes salvaged from the wreckage of downed aircraft, the mystery of "what happened" locked within.

The engine hums through the night air. My headlights

63

cast an apron of light that extends my isolation only about a hundred yards against infinity. The broken white line flashes from the darkness like grains of rice. With each slight bump the blue digits on the clock trace a blur in the air.

Without warning, I am weightless—falling or flying. The humps of forest have collapsed, and the chill black sky is now beside and beneath me. Balancing on the broken white line as if it's a high wire, the Honda carries me from stripe to stripe. I flatten the accelerator, desperate to cross a bridge I can't see. The hairs at the back of my neck tingle at the rumble that follows me. The car and I dive for land, and the forest's solid darkness embraces us again. I'm convinced that the bridge I've crossed has disappeared.

"FFFF . . . ." A sigh of relief from the figure in the passenger seat—the ghost of my mother. Occasionally she joins me for stretches of time along the night highways. The bright numbers of the clock frosts her in blue. She clutches her sweater to her throat.

"These bridges, Jackie," she sighs. She is wearing one of her better wigs. "When are they going to stop frightening you, hmm?"

"I don't know, Mom." I sigh too, partly out of relief, partly at having to admit my fear to my mother. I don't know how her ghost winds up in my car. Strictly speaking, it couldn't be her ghost, since she's not dead yet, which may be why her appearance never frightens me. She doesn't acknowledge these nocturnal visits when I see her and Dad three or four times a year. "Why don't you fly?" she asks then if I complain about my lonely drives. My mother's ghost would never ask such a question. Flying is even more frightening than crossing bridges—it's a long, long trip over a bridge of air.

Ghost Mom is wearing her glasses, the wig, and a wool suit she reserves for special occasions. Together we glide along the highway.

"Nice car," she says. "When did you buy it?"

"Never," I answer. "Rental. You know I rent for these trips." She's got something else on her mind, I can tell.

"Of course you rent, dear. That just makes you a little harder to find is all." I don't ask why.

"It's chilly in here." She gathers her sweater more tightly about her with bony fingers worn so smooth they reflect the clock's blue glow.

"Air conditioning, Mom." She and Dad hate air conditioning. They claim it makes their noses run. "Do you want me to shut it off?"

"No, no. Don't make yourself uncomfortable on my account." I turn off the air conditioning. I roll down the window, and the blackness slops in, splashing onto my lap like warm ink, puddling around my feet and the pedals. Darkness pours over my crotch, and the puddle rises over the edge of my shoes. My legs become sluggish. Mom dabs at her nose with a lace handkerchief.

"Aunt Anna died," my mother says. I barely remember my mother's aunt. When I was a child she was already so old that I was more annoyed than embarrassed about accidentally walking into the bathroom when she was on the toilet. She'd already stopped counting, even to children.

"She was ninety-seven," my mother says. "Died in the nursing home. They say she was senile." My mother speaks the word in a whisper, rhyming it with "kennel." Mom mispronounces many words that make her uncomfortable, like "gynecologist" and "semen." "Isn't it a shame she couldn't have lived another three years?" Mom asks. I don't answer. The question feels like a trap.

Black air rushes through my window and down my neck and chest. The tail of some slippery night creature smacks my jaw, flops in my lap, and joins its mates below my knees. Now and then one rubs against my calf like a cat.

Outside, the dotted line penetrates our apron of light like a cartoon gamma ray. Inside, my mother's glasses absorb the clock's blue light. Her legs stir the deepening night; it splashes faintly against her door.

"Your father read an article to me about a bridge," she begins.

"Mom, come on . . ." My hands crowd midnight on the wheel, fists together, index knuckles targeting the pulsing white line.

"Now, dear, there's nothing to cross between here and Marion, for goodness sakes," she says. Then, comfortingly, "Don't I feel what you feel, honey? And please don't roll up the window. The air feels nice. I really don't know what air conditioning does to my sinuses."

The black tide rises above my seat and leaks under my thighs, soaks my butt cheeks and edges up my spine.

"Some major highway somewhere—not too far away, I don't think—" Night, warm and tasteless, lolls beneath my lower lip; a swell covers my mouth, and another takes my nose and ears. Finally, my eyes. Submerged, I peer at Mom, who's also under, all but the very top of her wig. She glows blue in the night air. Tiny bubbles of light shimmer off her lips when she smiles.

The white line, now blue, strikes relentlessly. Gliding shapes leave trails of iridescent bubbles about my face. Everything seems soft and comfortable in the night air.

Mom settles into her story, I think of the books she read to me when I was little, how I recognized the letters and studied the pictures, but only her voice gave them meaning. Something like that is happening now.

"There was a bridge, an overpass, above a little stream. With all the rain, the stream swelled and weakened the supports that held the overpass up. Then, just like that"—she snaps her fingers with an explosion of bubbles—"the bridge collapsed! Just dropped straight down, maybe fifty feet, right into that flooding stream." The lenses of her glasses throb with blue light.

"Right off the bat, about ten cars drove in, nine cars and one tractor trailer. Seems like only one car tried to brake; only one set of tires left marks."

I am inside each of those cars, falling, wondering, screaming.

"Somebody watching from a local road down by the stream—it was just about a river now, roaring right along— he saw what happened and rushed up to the highway and started waving at traffic. On his way up he saw two cars plunge in."

I see a heavy man in a plaid shirt and worn overalls waving at me from the side of the road, and I worry at how desperate he looks and I consider stopping to help him, but I don't.

"The troopers took days to find the bodies because the water was moving so fast. They're still only 'reasonably certain' how many victims there were."

I see pictures, as if from a children's book. The cars are vintage, red and blue and mustard yellow. The truck is a moving van driven by a man in a neat uniform who a few pages previous would have carefully packed a worried child's teddy bear in corrugated paper. The warning man is a round-faced farmer whose grandson and granddaughter, waiting safely on a high bluff, had earlier in the day learned about chickens and milk cows and who will, by their story's end, receive the kitten of a farm cat to take back to their suburban home.

"The police waited to get word of missing people—folks who didn't get to where they were supposed to or return from wherever they'd been."

A slender blonde woman wearing a blue apron holds a telephone to her ear. One of her penciled eyebrows arches. A blonde, pink-cheeked girl wearing an identical apron frowns at her mother's side. She holds a blonde, blue-aproned doll under her arm.

On the facing page is a bald man with a black mole centered on his forehead. Bristles protrude from his wide nostrils. His upper lip sweats. He also holds a telephone and glances through thick glasses at his wristwatch. Beside his desk are boxes marked with the brand names of vodka.

The headline of the newspaper on the desk has a single decipherable word: "BRIDGE."

"Your father said it was a good thing the bridge didn't go down at night. Nobody would have seen the stream then, so there wouldn't have been any warning. Cars from both directions might have kept driving off until dawn. Your father said that after a while the cars would have piled up so high that maybe folks would be able to drive right over them instead of falling in. Isn't that a terrible thought?"

"Mom," I whisper, "that's enough."

"You're probably wondering about the police," Mom says. "Your father thought about that too—if this had happened at night, I mean. Maybe the toll collectors would have noticed that nobody from past a certain point was coming through, and maybe they'd call the troopers. So a few police cars from either direction would be sent. And they'd fall into the stream! When they weren't heard from, a few more would get sent. Same result. Then so on and so on until morning, when someone finally noticed."

The round-faced farmer and his grandchildren stare at a glittering mound of automobiles towering over the level of the absent bridge. Cars spill onto both sides of the highway. Here and there men and women jut out form the wreckage, unbloodied, Xs where their eyes should be. A few wear police caps.

"Oh, it's just your father's morbid story—something to pass the time." Mom's sweet, youthful voice reaches me in popping bubbles. The steering wheel squirms out of my grasp and loops around my wrists. I squint against a blue glare. My mother is no longer visible. I feel her, though, as if I'm an egg waiting to hatch. We fly backwards on the highway: the car spits blue-white dashes into a single beam. My eyes close. I'm floating. My knees bump my forehead.

"Mom!" I cry, "What about Aunt Anna?" But I lie in the soft curve of time's arm, my words lost in a baritone lullaby, and I am one rock-a-bye away from sleep.

Refugees of the Meximo Invasion

The tall, pregnant woman with the dark curls spilling around her pie dish face sat alone in the back row of the chairs arranged for Leonard's Barnes and Noble reading. In front of her an audience of a dozen tired mothers and wriggling children watched and listened as the author read from *Mend My Tail, Doc*, the latest in his series of *Emergency Vet* picture books. He'd retired from his veterinary practice and now lived a nomadic life on the road promoting his stories. Leonard displayed the illustrations: here was the cat being fitted for a prosthetic leg; here, the pig with its snout stuck in a peanut butter jar; here, the monkey with its hand super-glued to its tail.

The expecting young woman remained for the question-answer period.

"How long did it take you to make the pictures?" a chubby boy asked around the finger in his mouth.

"I don't do the illustrations. We have an artist for those," Leonard explained.

"But how long? And what's the matter with your eye?"

"*Shh*, Jake, be polite," his mother hushed.

"It's okay, ma'am." Leonard was walleyed. He'd been born with the imperfection his mother had reassured him a thousand times was "slight." Frown lines framed her smile whenever she patted his cheek and called him "my handsome boy." Leonard's gaze flitted to and from the pregnant woman.

71

She wore a yellow raincoat. "I keep an eye pointed to the side so I can see if anyone's sneaking up on me," he told the boy. "Did you know that a chameleon's eyes work independently? Can you imagine looking at two different things at once?"

The boy blinked, spun his eyes around the room, shook his head and groaned.

"Do you have a pet?" a little girl called from her mother's lap.

"Nope," Leonard said. "Traveling around to talk about my books, I can't really keep an animal. Sometimes I think a companion for the road would be nice, though."

"What about children?" It was the pregnant woman. Leonard flinched when she batted her eyes at him: on one of her lids, the left, an extra eye had been tattooed.

"No children, no pets," he said. "I'm not married."

The pregnant woman stood nearby as Leonard signed his books for mothers whose children were tugging them toward the exit. Her belly swelled out of her yellow raincoat, stretching her orange maternity shirt as smooth as a pumpkin. She held a large paisley bag by its strap. When he finished, she approached. She was tall—taller than Leonard.

"Your book title's a pun." Her hands slid over her stomach as if she were polishing it. "Doesn't docking a tail mean to cut it off? Like for cocker spaniels? So, 'doc' is a pun, right? You can't mend something and cut it off at the same time."

Leonard wagged his head, a nervous habit. He was trying not to stare at her eye tattoo. "The publisher titled it. But good catch. You're the first to notice."

"I saw you on *Denver Today* this morning. You told the monkey story. *Loved* it! Would you want to get some coffee? If that doesn't cross some kind of author-fan boundary. Not here, though—somewhere more private. You drive us, and I'll treat. It's hard for me to squeeze behind a steering wheel these days. I'm Mindy." She held out her hand, and Leonard shook it. It was dry and cold and strong.

❧

When they'd settled into Leonard's Escalade in the mall parking lot, the sun was setting. Mindy rummaged in her bag and pulled out a pistol. She held it by her belly so it couldn't be seen through the SUV's windows and angled it at Leonard's face. "I'm afraid I'm going to have to ask you to give me everything in your pockets," she said. "Keep your keys for now. But I want your phone, wallet, everything else." The gun didn't look like a toy. "I'm not joking, Doctor Friedman."

"You're robbing me?"

"No. You won't lose a thing. This isn't a robbery. It's a kidnapping. Or no, a *doc*-napping." She paused, licking her lips as her attention dipped to her swollen stomach. "Though I guess it *is* a kidnapping, too. That depends on who you think this baby belongs to." Her eyes flashed at Leonard, and she grinned. "I'm a surrogate mama," she said. "Somebody else's zygote has grown to full term inside me. But I'm calling it mine. I've got a promise of fifty thousand for it in Mexico City. That's double what my contract here calls

73

for." She extended a palm toward Leonard. "So the wallet and the phone—and whatever else you've got that identifies you. Keep the keys in the ignition. Start up and get us out of here—take the Interstate south." Without lowering the pistol she took in the SUV's interior. "Nice car. How's it on fuel? It's about ten hours to the border and twenty more to Mexico City."

Leonard couldn't think of the questions he knew he should ask. He tugged his wallet out of his back pocket and his phone out of his front and placed both in Mindy's hand. He started the Escalade.

"So—you want me to be your chauffeur?"

"Oh, you'll be that and maybe much more, Doctor. I'm going to call you 'Doc,' okay? Listen, I could have picked anybody to drive. But I chose you after I saw you on TV and heard you were going to be reading right here in town. What you are is my insurance policy." She glanced around the parking lot, clutching the gun like it was a small animal needing restraint. "Just get us out of here. We'll get food and gas on the road. There's a long way to go. I pee often, by the way."

An hour later, Mindy pinned her gun between her knees while she peeled the plastic wrap from the sandwiches she'd bought with Leonard's cash. It had gotten dark. The only light in the SUV was the luminescence of the dashboard and the occasional swimming beams of northbound cars and trucks.

"Do you ever use your four-wheel drive?" she asked with a full mouth.

"No," Leonard said. "I don't even know how it works."

Mindy swallowed, then rested her sandwich on her belly. "You got what I meant by 'insurance policy,' right? You understand your purpose?"

Leonard wished he was taller—long-legged Mindy had pushed her seat back to its limit, and, because his right eye was weak, he had to screw his head like an owl to see her face. He hadn't much of an appetite for his sandwich and chewed mechanically. He'd been thinking about a coincidence: Mindy was a surrogate, and he had once attempted to donate his sperm.

"Is it because being in the car with a celebrity will help if there are border issues?" he asked.

Mindy laughed. "You're not *that* well-known, Doc. You think customs guys read? I guess they might watch talk shows, though. And they are trained to recognize faces. But, no, don't you get it? You're a *doc*, Doc! I'm due any second— what if my time comes before Mexico City?"

"I'm a veterinarian, not an obstetrician."

"A baby animal is a baby animal—a delivery's a delivery. I've got towels and alcohol and scissors and a threaded needle in my bag here. I hope we don't need them. There's a clinic waiting for me in Mexico City—if I hold out that long."

"You could just take some of my money for a plane ticket," Leonard said.

Mindy patted his shoulder—he felt the thrum of each long finger. "That's a nice offer, Doc. Really. But why would

75

I pass up an opportunity to travel with the Emergency Vet? I love your stories! The truth is, I've got passport issues. As in, maybe I've misplaced mine. Or I never got one, I guess. Besides, air travel's unsafe this late in a pregnancy."

"You'll need a passport to drive into Mexico, or a passport card. I have one in my wallet."

"We'll cross that bridge when we come to it—so to speak. It's funny—we're sneaking somebody into Mexico when everybody else is sneaking out. But keep both eyes on the road, Doc!"

Leonard had edged onto the shoulder and eased the SUV back into the center of the lane. "I've got a problem with my eye," he murmured.

"Yeah." She purred a laugh. "I saw. For a minute there I thought you were getting a little crush on me, sneaking peeks—getting a little Stockholm-ish. You know, Stockholm Syndrome? Everybody falls in love with their captor, right? I've got an eye thing, too—this extra one on my eyelid—I got it when I was fifteen. It's supposed to be spiritual. Hey—" She touched Leonard's shoulder again. "—we could get matching eye-patches. Like a couple of pirates. Ouch!" She wrenched herself back in the seat, and her huge stomach rose beside him. The gun was still between her knees. "Christ, it's hard to get comfortable." Her pale hands floated like lily pads on her belly as she settled herself.

They drove in silence through the tunnel of light the Escalade's headlights cut through the darkness. The tattooed lid made it impossible for him to tell if Mindy slept. An excess of stars swam through the sky—like crystallized sperm, Leonard imagined. Would he share the story of his failure on the long drive to Mexico City? He'd been warned by the clinician: "Only five percent of potential donors are approved. Frankly, most are college students, much younger than you." Leonard had continued doggedly through the process—physicals, paperwork, interviews. One night he dreamed that he'd been chosen: he'd been ushered into a gleaming white bathroom where, with the aid of *Penthouse Magazine*'s Miss October—a petite redhead wielding a glass dildo—he'd ejaculated into a plastic cup. Upon exiting, product in hand, he'd been greeted by a crowd of a thousand children, boys and girls who resembled his third-grade photo—the one his mother had framed because his eyes were shut. He'd awoken full of hope, only to receive his blunt rejection in the morning mail.

Mindy's voice startled him. "This little monkey inside me is a blondie."

"Excuse me?" Leonard shivered himself alert. He'd need to rest soon.

"This baby I'm carrying—there are rumors about him," Mindy said. "I'm not supposed to know who the parents are—sometimes that's part of the agreement. But I heard nurses talking at the fertility clinic. Sperm from a dead actor, they were saying. I didn't recognize his name, so I Googled him. He was old—he died two years ago. But he was blond and very handsome when he was young. I never saw any of his movies. Wikipedia said he was married to a model I never heard of either, much younger than him—also a blonde—natural, I think. I read that she had cancer, but recovered. I know chemo makes you sterile, so I figure she had her eggs harvested first—then they cooked up a zygote for the widow with her husband's sperm, and voila!" She patted her stomach. "But this one's mine now. She's got more frozen zygotes, I'm sure. I wish I could advertise this baby as Hollywood royalty. Can you imagine what he'd be worth?"

Leonard shrugged.

"I saw the way those young mommies were looking at you in the bookstore," Mindy teased. "Is that what you're thinking about? Can you tell which moms are single? Or don't you care?"

Leonard face warmed. His head wagged. "Never—"

Mindy sighed. "Doc, here's what's going to happen next—" She hoisted herself up as if she were pinned under a boulder, and when he glanced over, he saw that she again aimed the pistol at his head. She cupped it in both hands as if it were a kitten. "The next cheap motel we come to, we're going to get a room. Both of us need to sleep. I'm going to handcuff you to the bathroom sink. Underneath. Don't worry, I'll give you a pillow and some blankets. It'll probably be a little uncomfortable—sorry in advance. I'll be stepping around you to pee in the middle of the night. Or maybe I'll need you to deliver the Hollywood royalty. That'd be a riot. Think I can keep the gun on you while that's going on? This is my third pregnancy, you know. First one I gave up for adoption. The second was a surrogacy like this one. But that baby had something wrong with it— they never told me what. I did my part—and was paid in full even for a defective—" The sudden illumination of a carcass on the side of the road stopped her short. "Ugh—what do you think that used to be?"

Leonard blinked at the body as they flashed by—only a long torso, really, its head long gone, its legs crushed to a ruby froth. "I don't know," he said. His joints ached—he'd be sleeping on a bathroom floor? But escape was out of the question—he was too weary. "A coyote, maybe. An antelope?"

"Save *that* one, Emergency Vet." Mindy yawned. "Yuck."

The Blue Daisy Motel had one room left with a private bathroom. In it, Mindy offered suggestions for Leonard's comfort: "You'll have to lie on your back, and we'll cuff your right wrist to the pipe. Wedge your pillow in the corner there. See—you can stretch your legs around the toilet." The cuff she pulled from her bag and snapped around his wrist pinched slightly. She grunted as she kneeled to fasten the other end to the drain pipe. "My stomach's in the way," she puffed. "You do it." After Leonard locked himself up securely, Mindy lurched to her feet. A meaty odor wafted from under her skirt and mingled with the cool air beneath the sink. Leonard stared up at the filthy underside and closed his eyes—how many more bathrooms before Mexico City?

"I'm leaving the light on and the door open. I'll try to tiptoe around you," Mindy announced. Leonard could only see her legs. Her blue running shoes looked new, and her ankles were swollen and chafed. A quarter-sized bruise yellowed on her shin. The bed springs squeaked under her weight. "Oh—"

she called, "if you need to go, just give a shout. I'm a pretty heavy sleeper, though. Maybe you'd better hold it."

∽

Leonard woke, stiff, unsure of where he was. His wrist touched something cold and metal, and he jerked it, thinking *gun*—and he remembered that he was chained up and why. He strained for sounds of Mindy's breathing, but heard only the faucet dripping above him. Mindy liked his stories, she'd said. He imagined that she couldn't sleep and called to him: "Tell me a story about a time you wanted to save something but couldn't—or you *didn't* want to save something, but had to." Leonard thought hard. Absent from *Mend My Tail, Doc* were the more lurid stories he'd been saving for an adult version: a frantic, semi-carved steer savaging a slaughterhouse; a manatee with an anchor through its head; a shih tzu and an eagle locked in a thousand-foot death plunge. Then he remembered a rural emergency from his internship—a distressed cow with Madonna eyes suffering through a breech delivery. The cow stood trembling, and the twig-legs protruding from the leaking opening beneath her tail shook with her.

"Pull!" Leonard's supervisor had shouted, and Leonard had grasped a warm, slick leg and yanked. The calf slid free, and as he and the newborn slipped to the floor, he'd hugged it to his chest. The smell of blood and raw flesh washed over him. Then his supervisor and the dairy farmer swore at the same time: there was a second calf, a twin, left in the womb. "Stillborn," his supervisor had determined with a plumbing arm. The cow and the senior veterinarian struggled to deliver the dead calf while its sibling shivered next to Leonard on the barn's dirt floor, waiting for its mother to lick it to its feet.

❧

Mindy's legs! Her greeting dropped from above: "Morning, Doc. You sleep okay? You were dead out when I came through to pee. Both times. I'm going to wash up, then I'll give you the key so you can free yourself." She straddled his hips. Water hummed through the pipes and splashed in the sink over Leonard's head. A hand descended with a wet washcloth, and she washed her legs. Her skirt rose and fell with each stroke. He caught a glimpse of her pale underbelly and closed his eyes, opening them when he heard the jingle of the handcuff key.

By the time Leonard released himself, Mindy sat on the edge of the bed, watching him. He craved a long, groaning stretch, but resisted, unwilling to admit his discomfort.

"Hurry up and do what you've got to do," Mindy said. She clasped her paisley bag under one arm. "Leave the door open, please. Any funny business and you'll be sorry for it. I'll shut my eyes—that's the best I can do for privacy. What're you staring at?"

The tattoo of the eyeball was missing. There was only a dark smudge on Mindy's lid. "Your third eye—it's gone."

She snorted. "Oh—yeah—that was washable marker. You don't think I'd really tattoo something on my eyelid, do you? Who'd do that to themselves?" She picked up her gun and looked at its muzzle. "This is all the 'third eye' I need, right,

Doc?"

Leonard didn't answer. He washed his face and rinsed his mouth, then used the toilet, peeking now and then at Mindy, who, to her word, didn't open her eyes. A smudge instead of a tattoo on her lid was a disappointment—no twin patches; no pirate gang.

᪥

Back in the Escalade, Leonard behind the wheel, they breakfasted on Twinkies, corn chips and Mountain Dew from the machines in the tiny lobby of the Blue Daisy Motel. The morning sunlight sharpened the borders of the black highway that sliced through parched land. The broken white line leapt at them like machine gun flak as they made their way south, and the blue sky spread over them as if they were in an enormous tent. Mindy's thumbs fluttered over Leonard's phone.

"I'm going to crack your access code," she said. She bent over her beachball belly, her unwashed curls hiding her face. "What's your date of birth?"

"Why don't I just tell you the code?"

"No—I want to figure it out. I'm good at it."

"My birthday's June 28, 1970."

"6-28-70—no—no—" she grunted as she tested permutations. Leonard peeked at the gun in the folds of her skirt. "Hey—that's tomorrow! Happy birthday, Doc."

"Thank you," he said, surprised. He searched for a birthday memory, but found nothing. Instead, the moment when he realized he'd never marry rose: he'd just finished neutering a ferret and was transferring it to a recovery pen. Its limp body hung from his gloved hands like a necktie. He'd looked at its tiny, shut eyes and thought, "I will never have a wife." The words struck him like a chest punch, and he'd had to sit down, the ferret still dripping from his hands. His failed sperm donation had come soon after.

"I'm in!" Mindy laughed. "Wow—'628vet.' I'll check your messages. Then I'll send some. I'll tell all your contacts that you're on your way to Alaska. Okay, good, the GPS works—I see where we are and—there's Mexico! I love the GPS! It's like a big eye in heaven that's picked us out of nowhere. Mmm—looks like no text or voicemail messages for you, Doc."

❧

"Thank God for air conditioning," Mindy sighed. Even with open vents blasting at full power, she was flushed and sweating. They weren't far from the Mexican border, according to the last highway signs they'd seen, a fact corroborated by the GPS. The blue had drained from the morning sky, leaving a pale midday haze. Leonard suspected Mindy was planning their assault on the border, and his heart beat faster. She'd been texting busily for an hour—his phone hummed like a jar of bees in her hand. Now and then she mumbled or laughed at something she read without telling him why, and he wished she trusted him enough to share. It had been years since he'd been in the company of another person for so long.

"I have an idea," Mindy said. "Let's pretend we're refugees.

We're on the run—"

Weren't they? Leonard wondered.

"—There's a joke my father used to make—I think it's from my father—I heard it when I was little. Whoever it was said that Mexico and Canada were planning to attack the United States together. There'd be Eskimos attacking from the north, pulled by sled dogs and waving harpoons. Riding up on horseback from the south would be Mexicans with big floppy hats and rifles and those bullet belts crossed on their chests."

"Bandoliers."

"Right, okay. They were going to squeeze in on us from the top and bottom. They'd call themselves the 'Meximo Army'—Mexicans and Eskimos, get it? You and I are running away from them. We're refugees of the Meximo invasion!"

"We don't use 'Eskimos' anymore," Leonard said. "It's 'Inuit.'"

Mindy hesitated. "That spoils the joke. It's so easy to ruin a joke. What if—" she began matter of factly, "what if my mother died giving birth to me?" Leonard pictured his own dead mother and the *handsome boy* lines that marred her smile. Did he owe Mindy a "sorry for your loss"? But she'd only said "what if." Condolences for a hypothetical didn't seem appropriate. Mindy patted her belly and huffed: "Woof. Sometimes I forget what I've got going on here. But never for long. If I had no mom, that would explain why I lack a nurturing impulse—no maternal role model. Incubation would be my limit. Would you please pull off here at this exit? Take me off the Interstate. I've got to pee before our next move."

❧

Off the highway, they headed due west along a narrow tar road. Weeds grew in its cracks. The dry land, the sparse brush, the gullies and arroyos, the distant hills and cattle fences looked the same as they had from the Interstate, but Leonard felt different, as if the scene had swallowed them, and they were seeing things from the inside. He wondered how difficult it would be to engage the four wheel drive. The Escalade's owner's manual was in the glove compartment. Would they have to ford a river? Would there be a border patrol that shot first and asked questions later? He sneaked a look at Mindy. She had picked him, something no woman had ever done before. Though they weren't pirates, they shared something. They were pioneers of modern survival. Leonard had been rejected as a sperm donor, but Mindy had given him a new purpose: she was an incubator in need—an *entrepreneurial* incubator—and he was a deliverer.

"Here is good," Mindy said when the road cut through a sandy stretch along a dry creek bed. Leonard slid the SUV to a stop, the tires crackling and shushing. Mindy still toted the gun, but Leonard doubted she'd force him to follow her while she went off to squat behind a bush or outcrop. She probably wouldn't even ask for the keys. After she did her business, they'd plan the crossing—from north to south, right through the southern outpost of the Meximo Army.

But Mindy didn't budge. "I think I just saw an animal in distress," she said, staring straight at Leonard, her face as

85

cold and flat as a china plate. "I did. Definitely. Down that empty creek bed. It was limping." Leonard peered past her, to the right and left. There wasn't a sign of movement, and he could see for miles. "It was a burro, I think," she added. "Probably escaped from a ranch. Poor thing. A burro or a mule. What's the difference?"

Leonard focused on the gun, which seemed to have woken up and taken an interest in his chest. Mindy braced it on her belly next to the phone. He choked the wheel. "A mule is the offspring of a horse and a donkey," he said. "Mules are sterile."

Mindy shook her head. "I meant what's the difference *what* it is? You've got to investigate, right? You're the Emergency Vet." She started a deep breath, then cut it short. "Doc, there's no Mexico City. I couldn't drive that far in my condition. But we're less than an hour from the border now, and my associates are going to meet me when I cross. I'll flash your passport card. Believe me, nobody'll give it a second look. We kind of resemble each other, in a way."

Leonard's thoughts unspooled—he felt light-headed.

"No contractions yet," Mindy said. "I don't need insurance anymore. But it's been nice talking to you. What I would like now is for you to get out and walk down the creek bed—off the road a ways, please. Leave the keys. Just right there in the ignition, thank you. This is a beautiful vehicle. Real value." Mindy gazed up and down the road. Leonard noticed for the first time that her eyes were the color of lilacs. "Let's go, Doc. Think of that suffering creature out there. Who's going to investigate if you don't?" She gestured with the gun. The phone hummed, but she ignored it. "Go on—open the door and step out."

Leonard lost his balance as he swung the door open, staggering as he set his shaking legs on the baked ground. Fresh tar oozed from the cracks in the road. The air above it shimmered with heat in both directions. His cheek muscles tightened, and he held his hands out to his sides as if he'd dropped something. His gaze swept across the terrain to the horizon. There was no injured animal.

"Which way did you see it go?" In spite of the dry air, his voice came back to him as if he was underwater.

"It doesn't matter," Mindy said. "Just start walking. And don't look back. That way, I guess, off the road. Hurry up." As he shuffled around the Escalade, Leonard heard the passenger window whine open. He kicked up dust on his way to the creek bed and glared at his feet: his brown moccasins looked new—when had he bought them? Where? He passed rocks and pebbles striped with glitter. When he was a kid, he would have collected stones like them, pretending they'd make him rich. Maybe it had been a hundred years since anyone had looked at these. Maybe they'd never been noticed by a soul.

"Keep going!" Mindy's voice sounded as if she were just a few feet behind him, but he'd walked at least thirty paces. He shivered a breath. His shadow leaned away from him, and he watched it pass over larger rocks and the shriveled bushes that would become tumbleweeds when they broke off in the wind. A half-hope rose in his throat—maybe Mindy didn't mean to shoot him. She wouldn't have to—she was going to Mexico. His elbows brushed his hips; he regretted never having learned to walk proudly, and he tried to stand straight. But he didn't want to march. He waited for an instinct to tell him to run. The Escalade started, and the drone of its engine rolled out to him. This would end up no worse than a desertion, he reasoned. He'd need water.

What if Mindy's water broke? What if, as she lowered her smudged lid and tightened her finger on the trigger, she suddenly exploded? The water would gush between her legs and flood the upholstery. Her dress would be soaked. Contractions would begin. Driving would be impossible, and she'd need her insurance policy once again. She'd call Leonard back to the Escalade, but he would plant his feet in the dust, fold his arms over his chest, and wait. Until she begged. Time would crawl by. He'd outlast her. Where are your associates now? he might chide. Leonard would have to deliver the baby.

There might be complications. The newborn, a fine boy, would slip into Leonard's steady hands, but Mindy, lying back on the reclined passenger seat of the Escalade, might hemorrhage uncontrollably. He'd drag her bloody and unresponsive body from the car while the infant squalled. Leonard would cover the young woman—she'd either be dead or the next worst thing—with brush and rocks and sand. Then he'd drive south overland while the phone buzzed with orphan messages and all of nature drew toward Mindy's body. Scavengers, sun, and wind would pick her clean until her bones merged with the country.

The boy belonged as much to Leonard as to anyone. Years in the future, Leonard would share with the handsome child the true story of how they came to live in their villa. The Meximo invasion would have dissolved all borders, but Leonard would faithfully describe the world as it had been: he saw himself flipping through a picture book, lingering over each illustration, pointing out details.

But each turn of a page was a scuffed step into the plain, and, as Leonard edged further from the SUV, a question rose like a monument—would he hear the shot before he felt it?

Cherish the Muffin Top

Becca opened one of the hard lemonades they'd brought for the Saturday night party the GPS couldn't locate. They were looking for a farmhouse ten miles deep in the dairyland outside of campus. She took a sip and offered the bottle to Danielle, the driver, who waved it away. Katie, lounging like Cleopatra across the backseat of her own Toyota, waggled her fingers for the drink. She always surrendered the wheel when the three roommates drove to parties because she liked to get high before they started out.

Becca opened a second lemonade. "I've seen that barn. We're lost, we're going in circles. We're going to die."

"This isn't *The Blair Witch Project*." Danielle let the car glide to a stop in the middle of the road. "I need to know where the shit we're going."

"*Re-dy-recting*," Barry, the Australian GPS voice, insisted. "*Re-dy-recting*."

"You can't just stop," Becca said. "We're going to get rammed from behind." She looked back over Katie into the darkness framed by the rear window. "Some farmer is going to smash into us with his hay wagon."

"I've got the flashers on."

"A 'combine.' Isn't that some kind of farm thing?" Katie yawned. "We're going to get crushed into a bale by a combine." Night air spilled through their open windows from ghost meadows riotous with crickets.

"Where are the stars?" Becca asked. "You're supposed to see millions of stars out in the country."

"It's cloudy. I smell rain." Danielle folded her arms. "I don't want to be driving out here in a downpour."

"*Re-dy-recting*—"

"Shut *up*, you bastard." Danielle choked the wheel at ten and two, lifted her foot from the brake, and the car lurched forward. "This was the last party. There's supposed to be a bonfire. Why don't we see a bonfire?"

"We're screwed," Becca said. "Some cult will murder us and chop us up and spell out a message with our body parts—'CONGRATULATIONS, CLASS OF 2014.'"

"Let's give up." Katie squinted at her wrist where she'd inked the party's address. "Gerber Road? Did we see a Gerber Road?"

"There isn't any Gerber Road," Danielle slowed the car again, this time coasting to the side of the road. "You wrote it wrong."

Katie stuck her pale arm over the seat back. "*You* read it. Should I get a tattoo?"

"I vote for home," Becca said. "We can bake brownies. We have the rest of our lives to meet people."

"Home," Katie repeated.

"Just home?" Danielle asked. "Okay—"

"Then the Peace Corps. Whoa—" Katie rolled half out of her seat as Danielle spun the Toyota into a U-turn. "I spilled my lemonade.

"*Re-dy-recting.*"

"Even Barry wants to go home," Becca said.

Becca was the one who'd thought of the Peace Corps. An English major, she'd decided she needed some gap time and an accomplishment or two for her resume before applying to law school. One snowy January night she'd dreamed she stood in front of a group of blonde girls dressed in folk outfits with fancy stitching. Ukrainians, she knew somehow. Becca had the sense she was telling these children the most important thing in the world. She'd shared her dream with her friends the next morning.

"I'm going to join the Peace Corps."

"Me too," Katie clapped.

"We'll all three save the world," Danielle said. "We'll eat rice and beans and come home skinny."

Becca had patted her belly. "Not me," she said. "I cherish my muffin top."

As it turned out, Katie was the one who'd be situated in the Ukraine, her college Russian deemed sufficient for all Eastern European placements. Danielle's Spanish had earned her a spot in Ecuador. But Becca only knew French. "It's a language for tourists and Canadians," she concluded. "With just English, they'll put me in Africa." Where cute little Slavic girls were in shorter supply than antibiotics and agricultural know-how. "I'll find another way to see the world," she'd said, as her friends filled out applications, interviewed, and celebrated acceptances.

Farmhouse party plans aborted, the three young women lounged in the living room of their flat. Graduation was a week away, and final exams had been taken and passed. Only Katie had work left, a project for her non-major art elective, "The Politics of Regret."

"I need an *idea*—" Katie sank into the living room sofa after smoking a fat joint. The grape wine she'd been gulping from a coffee mug had left her with a purple mustache. "It can be anything. The professor said last year a girl shaved her pubic hair and put it in a baby food jar. She got an A. Help me, guys."

"You want our pubic hair?" Danielle asked. She and Becca, seated cross-legged on the carpet on either side of the half-empty jug of Carlo Rossi, nursed their own mugs.

"It's got to be original. I can't just copycat."

"What would your professor do with a jar full of pubic hair?"

"Knit a tiny sweater," Becca said. "For a mouse."

"For his dick," Katie grumbled. "*He's* a dick. Why do I have to do a project? Come on, guys—be helpful." She twisted onto her stomach and buried her face in the sofa cushion. Her voice was muffled: "I'm not going to graduate, and it'll be your fault, because you've got no imagination." She raised her head. "No Ukraine. No nesting dolls."

"My matryoshkas," Becca sighed, caressing the wine bottle as if it were a glass cat. "You don't deserve them. You stole the Ukraine from me."

"Wait—" Danielle lifted her mug in a salute. "What about *your* dolls—your Barbies?"

"What about them?" Katie's features shrank into a scowl. "I told you you're not allowed to touch them after you made

93

them watch you have sex with Roger. That was sick."

"I washed them in Lysol. And I swear we didn't *use* them."

"They'll never be clean again," Katie struggled onto her back and shut her eyes. "They were humiliated. I should never have brought them up here. They weren't ready for college."

"But now you have to sacrifice them," Danielle said. "So you can graduate. So you can get to Ukrainia."

"Ukraine," Becca said, "not 'Ukrainia.' They're in a shoe box under her bed."

"Nobody's supposed to know that," Katie whispered. "They hate you, too."

"If they catch you smoking pot in Ukrainia, they'll send you to a gulag," Danielle said. She turned to Becca. "Get some markers and scissors. Foil and tape, too. And a knife, the sharp one for bread. I'll get the dolls."

"Oh my God," Katie groaned without opening her eyes.

Two hours later, Katie's graduation had been secured: four modified Barbies and one Ken stood on the coffee table beside their sleeping owner. All but one wore an identifying sash.

"Wake her up," Danielle said. "Katie—wake up!"

"Katie—" Becca whispered. She brushed her friend's hair from her face. "We've finished your art project. You're done."

Katie rolled to her side and blinked at the display with an open mouth. Danielle and Becca exchanged glances that dipped to the scissors, tape, and markers on the floor, rose to the dolls, then settled back on their friend. Danielle cleared her throat. She tapped the shorn head of the first Barbie. "This is 'Iraq War Veteran Barbie.' She had a leg and both arms blown off by an IED. We made her prosthetic hands and feet out of foil. That tiny letter poking out of her shirt pocket is a note from the military psychiatrist documenting that she's also suffering from PTSD."

Barbie number two, a pony-tailed blonde, wore only a T-shirt. She held her head between her hands and leaned forward, staring at her legs: red lines streamed down her thighs and shins. Her feet were red. The sash slung over her shoulder read "Barbie's First Period."

The next Barbie was dressed in slacks, a button-down shirt under a sleeveless sweater, and hiking boots. She wore glasses, and her hair had been cut short and teased into a 'fro. A pair of sashes crossed her torso like bandoleros and she wore glasses. "This one has two names," Becca said. "'Transgender Barbie,' and-*or* 'Transgender Bobby.' You can pick one or use both."

"We should move Ken next to 'Barbie's First Period,'" Danielle said and shifted the dolls. Ken was naked except for the condom rubber-banded over his head and his name-sash. Red dripped from his smooth crotch and ran down his legs. His feet were as red as the Barbie he stood beside. "Ken-struation—" was printed on his sash, "a Hostage Situation."

There was one last Barbie. An experiment, Becca and Danielle had convinced one another during its reconfiguration. Their *pièce de résistance*. A risk—wasn't that what art was all about? The 'Politics of Regret' had to mean something. But Becca couldn't lift her eyes to Katie's, and she nearly snatched the doll from the table.

"This is 'Breast Cancer Barbie,'" Danielle said quickly. "She doesn't have a sash." The doll was bald and naked. The plastic on her chest puckered around twin cavities opened where Becca and Danielle had sliced off her breasts. "We've given her a double mastectomy. And she lost her hair during chemo. But she didn't make it." A black *X* covered each of the doll's eyes. Danielle laid the Barbie in a cotton-lined shoebox. As the two creators sat back on their heels, Becca felt the sash with the doll's first name against her belly flesh—it was crumpled inside the band of her sweat pants where she'd hidden it: "Katie's Dead Mother Barbie."

"Tah-dah—" Danielle swept her hand over the display like a magician.

Becca held her breath as she watched Katie pull herself upright on the sofa, still staring at the final doll. Her lips twitched, but she didn't speak. And though Becca felt Danielle's eyes on her burning cheek, she didn't face her.

Katie rose, tore her gaze from the dead Barbie, and padded down the hall to her bedroom.

The next morning, when Becca woke with a dull ache in her chest that had little to do with a hangover, Katie was gone. She'd taken the dolls and left a note in their place: "*I'm done. Will return to clean out my room and anything you two leave around after graduation. Split my share of the deposit. Thanks for finishing my project.*"

They might have seen her at graduation, arriving late in her black gown and cap to merge into the procession. They might have seen her sideling out of her seat, rows and rows behind theirs, after the speeches and proclamations. Had they seen her glide across the green quad like a windblown slip of charred paper?

⤸

Gap time. Becca remained in town, alone, after graduation, moving into a basement studio in a neighborhood she was afraid to walk in after dark. A starved cat haunted her stairwell, probably deserted by the previous tenant. "I'll get a job and prep for the boards," she promised herself and her parents. "There's an academic atmosphere here—it's a college town." But when sirens wailed down her street after midnight, and another gray dawn exposed the bars in her single window, Becca sometimes felt like her desire to stay hadn't been a choice.

"I thought I was applying for a job at a *creamery*, not a crematorium," Becca lied to her mother after calling to announce that she'd found work. "You know how the city's surrounded by dairyland. I imagined I'd be seeing cows. Free milk. I thought maybe they'd make ice cream right on the premises. Instead they burn bodies. So I switched fire for ice, right? We hold memorial services, too, like a regular funeral home. But we make sure that there aren't any incinerations scheduled when we're holding a memorial service. The smoke, you know? It would be a turn off for the loved ones of the deceased. I've got a lot of responsibilities—I help schedule memorials, and I make copies of death certificates. And I keep track of the bodies sent here from hospitals and adult care facilities and funeral homes. For burning."

97

When Becca's mother, who knew nothing of her daughter's sour last days before graduation, asked if she'd heard from "the girls," Becca realized that her "we" had shifted from her college friends to her crematorium connections.

"Danielle's in Ecuador. I think she had some kind of 'born again' thing. Her letter was full of 'Jesus this' and 'Jesus that.' Katie? Nothing—the Ukraine is a black hole, I guess. But the guys I work with, we're like a little family: Nick, the manager—the one whose wife died and I'm replacing—and Ethan, who does the actual cremating—he puts the ashes in the urns, too. He's divorced and old. Thirties old. It's like these guys have adopted me or something."

Nick's dead wife Rita had been gone two months when Becca was hired at Memory Garden Crematory Services, but her perfume lived on. It visited Becca's reception space nearly every day, wafting from opened drawers and file folders. Nick kept his wife's ashes in a small, bejeweled urn on his desk. He'd rested a plump hand tenderly on the urn's cover during Becca's interview.

"This is my Rita. Not all of her. She was a large woman. We had to have a special casket prepared. Her body is interred down in New Jersey in her family's plot. This urn contains the remains of her heart. Don't worry, I don't expect you to take her place completely. That would be too much pressure."

After three months at the crematorium, the closest Becca came to a date was her Friday lunches with her boss at the Golden Corral.

"Rita and I ate here every Friday," Nick repeated like a blessing over each afternoon's first platter of ribs, shrimp, mashed potatoes and gravy. And Becca surprised herself by digging right in, the mountain of food on her own dish nearly as high as her boss's. But she drew the line at dessert. She kept her back to the gushing chocolate fountain at the pastry and confection table and, instead of a brownie, made sure to spoon an extra dollop of steamed vegetables onto her plate. She watched Nick seem to swell as he ate, his features smoothing out as if they were painted on an expanding balloon, and she wondered if she looked the same to him, and if he liked it.

"We couldn't have children of our own—Rita had too many health issues," Nick shared one Friday. "But we planned to adopt. We were going to go to the Ukraine. The trip was set, and then she passed."

Becca licked mashed potatoes from her lip. "I have a friend in the Ukraine." The chocolate fountain thundered like a waterfall behind her. She raised her voice. "She's in the Peace Corps. I haven't talked to her in a while."

Nick's head bobbed. "They have rules in the Ukraine. Only married, straight couples can adopt. So I lose my wife, and I'm not allowed to have a kid." A tear that might have been a sweat droplet slid down his cheek. Becca's gaze fell to the chicken and rib bones piled on her plate.

On Saturdays and Sundays, Becca purged: a cherishable muffin top was one thing; fat was another. She abandoned exercise in favor of starvation, laxatives, and diet pills, and waggled a finger down her throat when absolutely necessary.

"I'm not bulimic," she insisted to herself. "I'm a friend. I'm accommodating."

Mondays through Thursdays Becca lunched on rice crackers and seltzer with Ethan in his office at the end of the long hallway separating his cremation equipment from the front office and memorial chapel. She sat on a folding chair and picked at flavorless crumbs from the napkin on her lap while he sat at his desk, washing down bites of his sandwich with gulps of coffee. Urns of all kind were stacked on shelves and on the floor. Some of the lidded ones probably contained ashes. Ethan's calendar was posted on the wall over his desk, incineration times highlighted in yellow. Becca watched the muscles in his jaw and throat knot and relax as he chewed and swallowed. When he ran his hand through his curls, she expected the silver tipping them to flake off like ashes. After a season at Memory Garden Crematory Services, Becca only knew one detail about Ethan—he was divorced. But how she knew that, she couldn't recall. Usually, the conversation was up to her. She told Ethan about her college life: books she'd read, professors, parties.

"It seems like a hundred years ago," she said.

One day Becca asked Ethan if he and Nick were close. She'd learned from Nick that the two had worked together at Memory Gardens for nearly a decade.

"I hardly see you together," she said. In fact, she wasn't sure she ever had.

"He's got his wife's heart on his desk," Ethan said, as if that answered Becca's question.

"I know." Before she could ask if he'd noticed the lingering smell of Rita's perfume, Ethan swiveled his chair and faced her straight on. His eyes were black, and something flitted deep within them like bats in a cave.

"Except that it's not her heart," he said.

"Not her heart?"

Ethan cocked his head. "Did you know if you burn up a baby—a dead infant—in a cremator like ours, where it gets to 2100 degrees, sometimes there's nothing left of it? It just disappears. Vaporizes."

Becca blinked. Had he blown something into her eyes? "This happened to you?"

"I read about it. Professional knowledge. I know people it happened to." Ethan said nothing for a ten count. "A heart is smaller than a baby."

"Yes?"

"So—I was afraid I'd incinerate Rita's heart into thin air and have nothing to give Nick. I burned up a book to fill her urn. Two books. I took them from a box my ex-wife still hasn't picked up. She was an English major like you. Now she sells real estate. We got divorced for two reasons: one, she said she'd thought I was funny when she met me, but it turned out I wasn't; the second reason was that I didn't want to have children and she did. I told her that the last page of everybody's story is the same—it ends here at the crematorium. Why bother with kids? If every life came with a set of directions, 'Add fire' would be the last one."

"Hold it—" Becca's head spun from the burst of revelations. "What about Rita's heart? It's not in the urn?"

"*Romeo and Juliet*. And *Anna Karenina*. Books ash right up. They aren't mostly water like people are." Ethan nodded toward the tabletop refrigerator in the corner. "There's only room for one thing in that fridge's freezer, and that's Rita's heart."

"I keep my seltzer there—" Becca stared at the refrigerator as if a glowing heart throbbed through a translucent door.

"You want to see it? It's in a plastic bag."

"No—" Becca stood. She'd lost feeling in her feet and reached past Ethan's elbow to grab a corner of the desk. "Lunchtime's over."

Most evenings, Becca struggled to suppress her work-week hunger, but the night she learned of Rita's frozen heart, she had no appetite. Her own refrigerator threatened her, and instead of the yogurt she'd planned on, she munched Special K from a box. She watched the family with nineteen kids mill about on her TV while she poked at her iPad.

Romeo and Juliet. Anna Karenina. Was there a book to replace *her* heart? If she died, who would choose it? An email message blinked in Becca's inbox, and she caught her breath: it was from Katie, whom she hadn't heard from in half a year. The subject was "*my girls,*" and the first thing Becca saw when she opened it was a photograph of six little girls seated in a semi-circle. Each cradled an identical naked baby doll, except for a heavy girl with braids who balanced hers on her palm as if it were flying. This doll's head was still wrapped in plastic—the dolls must have been fresh donations. Katie's message read, *These are my girls with their new dolls. I got an A. Was it worth it?*

The message and photo had also been sent to Danielle, who Becca knew wouldn't be able to access it in her Ecuadorian village. Any reply would be Becca's responsibility. What was there to say? *Congrats for the A? Cute Kids?* The message was a cue for an apology or at least an explanation. *Dolls.* Becca thought of the Russian nesting dolls, the matryoshka, and typed, *You never know you're at the last doll until you try so hard to open it that you crush it.* She imagined pinching a pea-sized matryoshka into dust, then saw herself stirring the false ashes in Rita's urn. She cleared her reply to Katie—it could wait. They were on different sides of the world now, each committed to a different "we."

"I need the heart," Becca told Ethan the next day. "Tomorrow's Friday, and Nick and I go to the Golden Corral. Knowing what I know, how can I face him across the table?"

"What are you going to do with it?" Ethan asked. "You can't just stick it in the urn."

Becca shrugged. "I'll incinerate it myself and put the ashes where they belong. I know you tried to do the right thing, but last night I couldn't sleep, thinking about it." She'd lain in bed for hours, envisioning empty coffin-cradles and matryoshka dolls shrinking in endless mirrors. She'd seen a giant heart pumping a fountain of chocolate blood. She'd become ravenous, and thought of the men at Memory Garden Cremation Services. Then she'd touched herself, her fingers hidden behind the gentle swell of her empty stomach.

"*I love your muffin top*—" she'd heard Nick sigh in the dark as an ambulance moaned down a distant street.

"*I love your muffin top*—" Ethan's voice had joined in, and Becca had squirmed with the dangerous pleasure she shared with both her men.

"You won't be able to get it hot enough." Ethan dragged

his fingers through his curls.

"I'll figure it out," Becca said.

And a few hours later at the end of the workday Ethan dropped the frozen heart into the shopping bag Becca held open. She glimpsed a red lump for just a second before its weight tugged at her wrists.

"Bring it back if whatever you try doesn't work," Ethan said. "You can't just cook it up like a steak."

"Scat—" Becca whispered at the skeletal cat in her stairwell. She hadn't seen it in months, and it grinned at her with needle teeth when she told it to "Go home." She hoisted the bag with the heart high on her chest as she unlocked her apartment door and slipped inside. She hurried to her freezer and felt a cool puff as she opened it. She withdrew the heart from the bag, worried it might have softened, but it was still stone-hard. Bright red patches showed through the frost covering it. Did the thing that killed Rita still lurk inside? Becca tucked the frozen organ between a carton of ice milk and a bag of Green Giant broccoli florettes.

How would she turn the heart to ashes? The only thing she'd ever burned was toast. She couldn't fry it—that would just cook it, like Ethan had warned. She imagined the odor of a cooking heart—like barbecued ribs? It was Thursday evening, the last of her fasting nights before her Golden Corral Friday with Nick, and she imagined them sitting in their booth, their overflowing plates between them: how innocent he'd been of the deception she was determined to correct. Becca studied her oven's controls. Five-hundred-fifty degrees was its maximum setting, nowhere near the two thousand plus degrees Ethan said the cremator reached. The oven had a self-cleaning function. Didn't that burn the hottest? She'd check the internet.

According to Ethan, an incinerated body came out of the cremator in a compacted chunk. A machine called a cremulator stirred this chunk into ashes and sifted out non-combustibles, metal from repaired joint sockets, for instance, or overlooked jewelry.

"I found a ring once, had it cleaned at a jeweler's, and gave it to my wife," he said. "She put it on, admired it, then asked where it came from. When I hesitated, she took it off and threw it at me. She was right. Keeping cremation leftovers for personal use violates best practice." Ethan's tone had reminded Becca of Nick's when he'd explained why Golden Corral didn't allow doggy bags: "It's 'all-you-can-eat' for one meal, not forever."

Becca sat on her futon, opened her laptop, and puzzled over key phrases to search: "*generating extreme heat*"? "*ashes*"? She paused to check her messages before connecting to Google. Only spam in her inbox, and the message from Katie that had reached her all the way from the Ukraine. She reopened it: there were the little girls with their baby dolls. Wasn't it likely that these children were orphans? Which one might Nick have picked if his wife hadn't died? It would be simple to ask: *Are these orphans?* But Katie's question still hung: *Was it worth it?* That was a question for the life Becca had left behind.

What was Becca searching? *How hot does an oven get when*

it self-cleans? Because she had a heart in her freezer that needed burning. If she didn't take care of it right away, what might happen to it? After a week, after a month, it would get pushed back into the frigid shadows, buried behind bags of ravioli, lost beneath frozen pizzas. But of course she'd get to it eventually, the incineration. Even if the heart wasn't always foremost in her thoughts, it would still be waiting for her, frozen and beatless. If Becca got her act together—*when* she got it together, maybe she'd be free of the men she'd been collected with at Memory Garden Crematory Services. Maybe there'd be law school, marriage, children. But the heart would follow her through a lifetime of freezers, wouldn't it? Whenever Becca came across it in its frost-covered plastic bag, it would remind her that some things change and some things last forever. Until she threw it away.

Obligates

Talia's ten-day round trip to Florida to check on her family's undeveloped New Smyrna Beach property is nearly over. She sails east on the Mass Pike. Wellesley—home—is less than fifty miles away. Unless, as if she's the victim of some adult version of *Chutes and Ladders*, she'll blink away the sun blazing from the cars and trucks streaming around her and find she's still down hundreds of miles of highway and is back in Virginia or North Carolina. Since the very first mile of her round trip, she's been lost—turned inside out—within her own life story, which she envisions as a graphic memoir in black and white.

The dashboard clock says it's nearly eleven—Talia will get to town just in time for the "Book Babies" session for toddlers and their mommies she leads at the public library. Songs and stories, clapping hands and rhymes. "The wheels on the bus," she rehearses, tapping the steering wheel, "go 'round and 'round." Talia's imagined at least a hundred illustrations for her memoir, each picture as vivid as a recurring dream, each as bold as any one of the hundred plus tattoos on her arms and legs she hides on the job under long sleeves and tights. But her Florida trip is almost over, and three thousand miles haven't been enough for her to shape all her pictures into a coherent narrative. Images swirl like birds drunk on rotten berries: to catch them she'd need a stronger mind—or the talent to actually draw something.

Talia glances in the rearview, where her reflection burns through the chaos of day-dreamed pictures. Because she's on her way to work, she's not wearing the jewelry that usually plugs her piercings. In an illustration she's conjured for the cover of her memoir, the tiny holes in her white skin are the width of dimes: one in her cheek; one below her lower lip; one above her right nostril; one through her septum. A version of this picture shows curious children—her Book Babies— poking their fingers into these holes. The chrome mask of a too-close truck grill crowds her mirror, and Talia sucks in a breath. She taps the brake pedal, and the grill lurches closer, then recedes. A red flash—tail lights in front of her—traffic has stopped, and a Connecticut license plate rushes at her. Talia stomps on the brake, grits her teeth, and bucks to a stop a foot short of impact. Her ex loaned her his car for this trip out of guilt after he confessed to cheating on her. She stares at the license plate of the car she almost hit: SI-3460. "SI," as in "Sinclair," her ex. Will everything always remind her of him?

Ahead of her, as far as she can see, traffic is still. The brake pedal squashed under her foot feels like a small animal trying to escape. She's taller than her ex, and she's had to slide the seat back to fit comfortably behind the wheel. Sinclair never bothered to strip the Framingham State University sticker from the back window after buying the vehicle used from a young woman he claims to have charmed into accepting a ridiculously low offer. Rust stains the wheel wells. *Don't judge me by this*, Talia pleads silently to the stalled drivers who are suddenly her neighbors. *This isn't my car.* The chapter of her graphic memoir dealing with Sinclair is titled "The X." She gives him Xs for eyes in all his pictures, like dead bodies in comic strips, even the one that shows him introducing himself to her in a coffee shop. Another picture, labeled "SINK, LIAR," shows her dead-eyed ex chin-deep in steaming shit—in the stink-lines wavering above his head is another image of him, X-eyes bulging as he humps a faceless, dark-haired woman. Talia is a natural blonde.

※

The seven-year-old self Talia pictures in her graphic memoir can draw. She lies flopped on her belly and elbows in the shade of the RV her parents rented for their first-and-only Florida vacation. She carves hearts and angel wings in the cool sand with a small plastic baby doll she holds like a crayon. In her memory Talia hears the murmured pulse of the surf, the jagged cry of gulls, her parents' monosyllabic conversation. The doll is the only toy she's been allowed to bring from home because, "you don't want sand to ruin your good things, do you?" The doll is so smooth nothing adheres to it, but gritty sand clings to Talia's sunscreen-drenched arms. A cluster of beach grass shivers, not ten feet from where she lies. Something that looks like a living rock drags itself through the brush.

Talia has never seen a live tortoise, but knows something about them—she's read the fable where the tortoise beats the hare. She stands up and tip-toes over the sand. The tortoise freezes under her shadow; when Talia stoops, it retracts its head and legs. The shell is its house: old Talia pictures young

Talia imagining a skinny green creature, more like a frog than a turtle, standing inside its home on its hind legs. She picks up the tortoise, which is both heavier and lighter than she expected, and there's the tortoise's beaked snout in the space between the upper and lower halves of its shell. Daring herself, she touches the beak with the tip of her tongue and leaves it there for a five count.

"There," she says to the clammed up tortoise. "I've tamed you. I'm Queen of the Tortoises." Her palms are wet. Tortoises pee? The word "anoint" from church jumps into her head.

"I am your queen," she repeats to the creature she holds to her face like a big sandwich.

Traffic hasn't moved for a quarter of an hour. The margin she left herself to get to the library and her Book Babies is evaporating. She's misplaced her phone charger somewhere on her way back from Florida, and her cell phone is out of power. In her side mirror she sees the door of the truck behind her swing open, and the driver steps down to the pavement. He's got a little dog on a leash—when he sets the pooch down, it tugs him between their vehicles toward the shoulder.

"Hey," she calls out her window, and the trucker stops and leans back, winking against the sun. "Do you know what's wrong?"

He shrugs. "Have you got a phone?"

"Yes," she says, "but it's out of power." She feels her face close up in a frown. She glances up and down the line of cars frozen in the fast lane beside her, drivers stiff as mannequins behind their steering wheels.

"Probably an accident," the trucker says, and follows his dog. Talia pulls her head back in the window and glances at the dashboard clock. Should she picture this delay as a chapter for her graphic memoir? Soon the Wellesley mothers will arrive at the library with their toddlers, but Talia won't be there. How long before they give up and go home? The room they gather in for Book Babies is circular, and its ceiling domed. When the session is in full swing, it's not hard for Talia to imagine that she's hosting a party inside a huge tortoise shell.

❧

Seven-year-old Talia is back on her belly in the RV's shade. She watches the tortoise struggle away from her toward the brush she's plucked it from. It drags the little plastic doll, which she's tied to one of its hind legs with a blade of beach grass.

"Good waterskiing, Barbara," she whispers to the doll. A moment later the tortoise stops and jerks its head and legs into its shell. Talia turns and finds her parents and a stranger looming over her. The frowning stranger wears a uniform and a broad-brimmed hat. Mirrored sunglasses hide his eyes. In Talia's graphic memoir these glasses spread across a two page illustration, one lens per page. Each lens reflects little Talia, prone on the sand, the tortoise and doll in the background. When this image arises before Talia, sometimes she sees faint

*X*s across the lenses behind the reflected figures. Sometimes this seems a brilliant touch and sometimes it doesn't.

The uniformed man stomps past Talia, his shoes black and huge. When he squats beside the tortoise, the stripes on his trousers bend at sharp angles. "You're disturbing the ecosystem of the beach," he says, looking back at Talia and her parents. A badge over his heart glints like his glasses. "This gopher tortoise is trying to reach its burrow. It's protected—it's a keystone species. Its burrow is protected, too." He breaks the beach grass tow rope and tosses the doll in Talia's direction. "Hundreds of species depend on that burrow. Three-hundred-sixty, to be exact. They're called 'obligates'—their whole cycle of life is based on that gopher tortoise's burrow. When you start tying baby dolls to things, you're messing with the natural order of the universe. Is that what you mean to do? Destroy the natural order?"

Talia's graphic memoir is impossible to organize—some of the illustrations don't fit with specific chapters and seem to appear and disappear with a will of their own. Was it her father who told her that several ancient cultures—Native American, Chinese, Indian-Indian—believed that a gigantic tortoise carried the world on its back? She imagines unfolding a picture as big as a highway sign for her Book Babies and their mommies—a tortoise supporting the earth, afloat amidst the stars.

And here is young Talia again, with her eyes squeezed shut in the petting zoo of an animal park. She holds out fistfuls of feed to overeager goats and lambs and disfigured deer. Hairy lips nibble her fingers and rough tongues swab her wrists. Hard muzzles butt her ribs and thighs. Then a sound like a foghorn rises from another part of the park.

"The giant tortoises!" someone shouts. "They're mating!"

Now Talia stands among a crowd outside a chain link fence. Her father's hands grip her shoulders. Inside the pen one huge tortoise leans on another like a toppled armchair. The top tortoise's beaked mouth opens, and it releases a moan so deep Talia feels it in the soles of her feet.

"You know what this is, right, honey?" her father asks, and Talia, even though she's not sure, nods. The crown of her head rubs against her dad's chest while she waits for the tortoise to cry out again.

Traffic is going nowhere. Other drivers have emerged from their cars and trucks. Some shield their eyes and gaze into the distance. Some mince around their vehicles as if the highway is paved with hot tar. Some chat in small groups. By now, word has probably been passed around explaining the cause of the delay, but it no longer matters to Talia—it's too late for Book Babies. She slumps behind the steering wheel and closes her eyes. She leaves the window rolled up to discourage visitors, and, because the air conditioner is shut off, she smells Sinclair. His sweat, his deodorant, his hair gel—and an unidentifiable fungal odor. Talia thinks of sex, sex with Sinclair, slides down further in her seat and peeks out her window. Dare she risk touching herself? Scenes from her memoir rise:

"OBLIGATES," she's labeled the poster board displayed on the middle school cafeteria table. Her project for the science fair lists all three-hundred-sixty species whose survival depends on the keystone gopher tortoise and its burrow. To accompany the list she's drawn a cross section of a typical burrow: a long tunnel angled underground ending in a round bulge where the tortoise resides. Smirking boys pass by her display. "Looks like a big dick," is the snickered whisper that captions this memory.

"OBLIGATES": For Talia's eighteenth birthday, she gets the first of her tattoos. The artist's needle punctures her shoulder—a halo of little stars in the air indicates the pain. The tattoo is of a cave cricket. It's hump-backed like a shrimp; the bend of its long hind legs suggests a woman waiting to fuck—is she the only one who sees this? The cave cricket is an obligate: she has resolved to have one species a month tattooed somewhere on her body. She plans to cover herself with all three-hundred-sixty.

When she meets Sinclair, she is nearly a third of the way there. Sinclair guesses about the obligate tattoos, is it the second or third night they sleep together? They lie side by side on Talia's bed, and he asks about the snakes on her legs.

"The snake around my left ankle is a diamond back rattler; the snake around the right is a gopher snake," she says, and when his fingers tighten over the rattler, it comes to life. Sinclair palms Talia's ass and runs his hand down her hip, her thigh, her shin, then reaches down and cups her heel.

"So," he says, "all these tattoos—if they're all things that live in a gopher tortoise's burrow, that makes you the burrow, right? You're like the what, the physical embodiment of that empty space, is that it?" He falls silent. His hands leave her body. He is so still that when Talia closes her eyes it is possible for her to imagine that she's alone—that he's never been there at all. When he speaks, it feels like a spank that might leave a mark: "'Obligates'—why not?" He squeezes her calf, probably looking at the lizards, toads, and insects tattooed there. "A theme's a theme."

⤜

The destination in New Smyrna Beach Talia returns from is the plot of land her father still refers to as "our toehold in Florida." He bought the half-acre lot the day after the mirror-eyed conservation officer interrupted Talia's play with the gopher tortoise. Her road trip to visit the site is the first time in twenty years anyone in the family has been back.

"Our toehold," her dad repeats when she visits her parents in their assisted living facility and tells them where she is about to go. "It doesn't take much to be a Floridian." Talia pictures her father as a towering giant, his face hidden in a cloud, his toe stuck in a hole in the ground.

⤜

Talia dozes behind the wheel of Sinclair's car in the middle of the Mass Pike, struggling and failing to visualize herself as a tortoise burrow—she can't differentiate between what is solid and what is space. All that appears before her mind's eye is the lip of a burrow: she stands over it with the property

115

manager of the New Smyrna Beach condo community that has risen around her family's undeveloped lot. The manager tells her she's got gopher tortoise problems:

"The fellow that abides here makes his way around the neighborhood," the manager says. "That means the burrow's active. If you want to build, the whole thing's got to be excavated and the tortoise relocated. The process has to be overseen and certified by the department of conservation and wildlife. It'll cost you a few thousand dollars. I can give you contact information if you want to make inquiries."

Talia stares down into the mouth of the burrow, expecting a tortoise to peep out. The skin on her arms and legs tingles, as if all one hundred-plus of her tattooed obligates—snakes, insects, mice, lizards, frogs—are trying to wriggle off her flesh and dive into the hole.

"Did you know," she asks, "that when gopher tortoises lay their eggs, the sex of the hatchlings can be affected by the temperature of the environment?"

"That's a new one on me," the property manager says.

"If it's hot there are more females. Cool means more males."

"Well, what do you know…" The property manager's tone suggests disbelief.

Talia is not interested in developing the property. Her life is in Wellesley. Her parents are too old to uproot themselves from the Northeast. But the burrow—Talia waits in Sinclair's car, parked between beach houses in front of her half acre. The sun sets over the across-the-street neighbor's roof. The sky darkens, but streetlights absorb whatever stars might be emerging. She can't find a moon. It's past midnight—Talia is wondering how much black ink an actual illustration of midnight would require—when she sees the gopher tortoise clawing across the road in front of her, heading toward its home on her land.

❦

Sinclair's car is both shelter and prison—does it deserve an illustration for the graphic memoir? Is this final leg of her trip, where time stands still, an important part of Talia's story? Her right heel burns— a blister's rubbed up from pressing the gas pedal for thousands of miles. Across the tendon above Talia's painful heel is her only non-obligate tattoo: an inch long "Sinclair." She could have it removed, but what if she leaves it and dots the two "i"s in Sinclair with Xs? Or, better yet, what if she dots one "i" with a tattoo of a tick and the other with a sand flea? That would use up two more obligates on her list, and the parasites could suck the blood out of her ex for as long as Talia has flesh.

She looks at the dead cell phone in her fist. The library director will be worried about her, as might some of the mothers she missed today, but the babies won't have noticed. And the graphic memoir? Locked in her head, available only to her mind's eye, isn't her story-in-pictures as dead as the phone? She probably lost the charger when she stopped at the dunes on the Outer Banks of North Carolina on her way back north—where she discovered she couldn't draw:

Talia sits atop one of the white dunes under a sky so blue she regrets her decision to render her memoir in black and white. She glimpses the ocean half a mile away—the dunes are further inland than she'd have guessed. Laughing teenagers surf down them on strips of cardboard. An art pad is open on her lap. A gentle breeze from behind lifts her blonde hair and drapes it over her shoulders and chest. Talia focuses on the blank page. When she points her black marker skyward, saluting the sun, her hair slips off her shoulder, exposing a dozen inked creatures huddled there.

She takes a deep breath and outlines a female figure. She draws a hole in the torso, then shows one of the figure's hands clutching something torn from within—or maybe catching something that's burst out on its own. Then she caps the marker with trembling fingers, closes the pad, stands, and takes several deep breaths before gliding down the dune with strides so long she feels as if she's bounding off the moon.

In the parking lot of the state park, neither dunes nor ocean visible, Talia clears the trash of the road from the car— food wrappers, coffee cups, water bottles— before looking at her picture. When she finally opens the pad, she blushes so hard her empty piercings sting. Her belly aches—this child's scrawl couldn't be hers—couldn't be her. It's proportioned like a gingerbread man. Only the sheaf of hair distinguishes it as female. That black scribble in the middle, the supposed opening to Talia's core, looks like an attempt to cross out the whole picture. And the thing from inside that the figure holds? Just a naked, shell-less turtle, as ugly as an abortion.

Finally, traffic on the Mass Pike begins to move. Drivers

rush back to their vehicles, engines roar to life, exhaust spurts from tailpipes. Talia starts Sinclair's car and inches forward with traffic, her foot tapping back and forth between the brake and gas pedals. The two lanes merge, and the truck in her mirror is eclipsed by an SUV. Ahead, state troopers wave orange cones and direct the single line of cars from the highway to the shoulder. Talia's palms sweat, and she turns up the air conditioner so high her forehead aches as if she's gulped down a Slushy. Is that Sinclair's odor wafting again from the upholstery? When she gets back to Wellesley, she'll drive straight to the library, where she'll explain her lateness to the director. She will call her parents to let them know she's back in town. "The property is fine," she'll say after she reminds them where she's been. Then she'll send a message to Sinclair thanking him for the use of his car and informing him that he can pick it up in the library parking lot. Or maybe she'll wait to send that message until after she's had a chance to rest. She'll leave the car in the library lot for the weekend at least. Maybe for another full week. Sinclair doesn't need to know she's back. If he needs the car, too bad. Let him walk or take a bus.

The creeping line of traffic carries Talia along the shoulder. Police cruisers, ambulances, fire trucks, and tow trucks, their lights flashing in discordant rhythms, block the highway lanes. They look as if they're circled up to repel an attack. Talia knows that soon she'll pass the kind of wreckage that will mark the history of lives she'll never know; she sets her jaw and resolves to keep her eyes forward. In the distance, yellow-vested men direct traffic from the shoulder back to the double lanes of the turnpike, and vehicles speed off like released fish, leaving anonymous tragedy behind them.

But here is a trooper approaching Talia. He holds one hand up and points to the side of the road, an instruction he's given no one else. Mirrored glasses hide his eyes, and Talia shivers—suddenly the air conditioner is intolerably cold, but she's afraid to make a sudden move to shut it off. Gravel crunches under her tires as Talia pulls beyond the shoulder and stops. She blinks hard. Does the officer bending toward her window think she's fluttering her lashes flirtatiously? Does he mistake her wince for a smile? Her gaze slips from his glasses—she's afraid she might see Xs—and pauses on the inspection sticker in the corner of Sinclair's windshield. The sticker has been there for all three thousand miles of her trip, but she's never noticed it. Something's not right: a registration sticker should show a future year, not a past. Has Sinclair really let her drive the width of the country and back in a car with a registration that expired long before they'd even met?

The sleeves of her sweater hide her tattoos, but Talia feels her obligates shuddering all over her arms and legs as if they sense a threat to their home. If Talia disappears, if she turns to air, all hundred of them will scatter from her empty clothes. She holds her breath, waiting for the trooper to tell her what to do next. He'll demand documents. Will he ask her to leave the vehicle? Will he insist on searching Sinclair's trunk? Talia's heart pounds. She hasn't opened the trunk since leaving the family lot in New Smyrna Beach, where, under a moonless, midnight sky, she slammed it shut on the gopher tortoise she couldn't allow to possess her property.

Demi-Christmas

While Dahlia assesses her reflection in the mirrored doors of her closet, smiling with professional approval at her smart figure—she is a casting agent with a full client list—the cellphone on her dresser hums. She watches herself answer; she looks every bit the modern working mother in spite of the failed womb her tailored suit covers. It's Dr. Morrison, the fertility specialist who has laid the groundwork for the surrogate birth that will make Dahlia a single mom in a week. Delivery will be induced on June twenty-fifth.

"Dahlia? We have a situation—"

Dahlia can barely hear Dr. Morrison's voice, and she maximizes the volume with a thumb jab. "What's that?" she asks crisply. Dahlia's business success depends upon her reputation as a no-nonsense negotiator and problem-solver, and she wears the persona as if it were a superhero's outfit. Her role-playing has allowed her to conquer a shyness that was nearly crippling in her childhood: she routinely handles reluctant performers, abusive directors, and parsimonious producers. She has never left a request for a seemingly non-existent character type unfilled. Because each day is a performance for her, Dahlia believes she has an insight into the psyches of actors that other casting agents lack. "Tough, but sensitive," is the tag-line she's give herself.

Dr. Morrison's concerned tone hasn't been lost on Dahlia—but she's learned that potential problems often

121

shrink away in the face of optimism. "Wait, let me guess—" she says before the doctor can speak. "Henry's come early!" Dahlia knows the sex of her imminent child. His nursery has been ready for a month. Her heart flutters. She looks at her watch to confirm the date—it's the eighteenth of June. "But it's okay—I'm ready. No appointments I can't postpone. It's just—I'd gotten used to the idea of June twenty-fifth—the 'Demi-Christmas' thing."

"This isn't about Demi-Christmas, Dahlia. It's the surrogate. She's missing.""Clarify, please." Dahlia sees her mirrored figure sagging to the bed and resists, standing erect, the hand on her waist seeming to lift her. She is a disciple of body language—posture can persuade where words fail. But what exactly is she standing up to? By choice, Dahlia has never met the woman who has been carrying her child. Doctor Morrison had made all arrangements in cooperation with an agency specializing in surrogacy. "Experienced, healthy, and health-conscious," he'd said about the woman he'd selected. "A true friend of women in your situation." Dahlia has already paid half of the $50,000 Henry will cost. A dietary regimen was prescribed and guarantees made regarding exercise and ambience.

"She missed yesterday's appointment. She didn't pick up or return the message from our office. I called her myself from home last night, but was taken directly to voice mail. Same thing this morning. I went to her apartment—you know I've worked with her before—I *know* her. I convinced the superintendent that this was a possible medical emergency— she's obviously *very* pregnant—and he unlocked her door.

There was no sign of her. Just a pile of circulars under the mail slot. Expired milk in the refrigerator. Bananas gone black in the fruit bowl."

Dahlia's reflected lips form a red-lipsticked O. Her eyes retain the surprised look they never lose after the flesh-tightening that has made late-thirties seem less improbable an age. She turns away from the mirror and sits, careful to keep her spine straight. When she'd told Dr. Morrison she didn't want to meet the surrogate, he thought it "unusual, but not unprecedented." Dahlia had thought that if she never laid eyes on the woman, she could imagine that her baby was being carried by a version of herself—a perfect twin with an unobstructed birth canal. Meeting the surrogate would have placed an unnecessary body between herself and her child. Had she miscalculated? Without Dahlia's face looming before her, mightn't the surrogate mistakenly believe the thing growing inside her, sharing her blood, was her own? Didn't possession trump a scrapbook of sonograms?

"Couldn't she be visiting someone?"

"But she's never missed an appointment—not in three pregnancies. I tried all the emergency contacts we have on file. None are real—she made them up."

"Made them up?"

"They're cartoon characters. 'Uncle Snoopy.' 'Oscar Groucherino.' They have fake phone numbers and email addresses. We've never had anything like this happen before. I couldn't find an address book in her apartment."

"What about the police?"

"It's too early—she's not officially a missing person yet.

And I believe they have to be notified by next of kin"

"This is crazy—she has my baby. And I'm *his* next of kin."

Clicks interrupt Dr. Morrison's silence. Someone is trying to contact Dahlia. For a moment she's sure it's the surrogate, maybe with apologies, maybe with demands. But the number is Dahlia's office, and she ignores it. "Dr. Morrison—the implant was—*is*—mine. I've paid half—"

"Mm. The money's one thing. Who the baby belongs to is a legal issue . . . it's technically a contract dispute. Listen— there's probably an excellent explanation. Unless she's already given birth, nothing's less invisible than a woman about to give birth. Let's not panic. I'll start calling hospitals."

Could it be, Dahlia wonders, that she's already a mother? Wouldn't she *feel* it? "Maybe she's left the country—" Dahlia pictures her twin, her perfect self, hurrying through airport security—it isn't clear if she's pregnant or smuggling something under her coat.

"I doubt it. If she's had your baby, it'll need a passport."

❧

Dahlia calls her office back and cancels her appointments, then sinks into her pillow. She kicks off her heels and props her phone on her belly, wondering who to call. Her attorney? A private detective to search for her missing child? Neither seems the right place to begin. She has to wait. She needs to separate herself from the surrogate. The bearer of her child is *not* her twin, not the better self she's been imagining. Who is she, then? Dahlia envisions a slim woman, her features smoothed over like a mannequin's, waltzing with a shopping bag—a white paper bag with an indistinct logo from an upscale department store. The dancer whirls—Dahlia waits for a newborn to lift its head from the bag and blink with astonishment at the spinning world. But the daydream fades when the phone on Dahlia's belly buzzes.

It's not Dr. Morrison's number. It's Kirkland's. Dahlia won't answer. Right now she'd find her friend's sympathy unbearable. He'd sigh tragically at her news, a therapeutic sigh, the kind he'd share with his sigh-therapist at his next session. Kirkland's inability to hide his feelings is one of the reasons Dahlia rejected the offer of his sperm. He's too much of a child himself to share the responsibility of parenthood, and he could never be trusted to remain the silent partner she demanded. "I may be gay, but I've got macho sperm," he'd sulked after Dahlia's rejection. Kirkland is short, balding, and thick-thighed. Creative, but dour and easily offended.

An absentee father, an ex-husband, and a dozen lovers have disappointed Dahlia. "Male-o-factors," she'd punned to herself when browsing the online catalogue suggested by Dr. Morrison. *Find the characteristics you prefer,* the catalogue invited. *Search for race, ethnic descent, hair and eye color, height and weight, education.* Picturing an ideal child, *not* the perfect mate, Dahlia had settled on the sperm of a blond, blue-eyed, water-polo playing medical student who listed "Shakespeare appreciation" as a hobby and requested anonymity. Only for a moment had she worried that the donor was too young for her. Then she remembered it wasn't a date. Though Dr. Morrison has reminded her "there are no guarantees— genetics can be finicky," Dahlia is certain her baby will be gorgeous and deep-souled—she takes her confidence as proof that her mother's intuition still works in spite of her internal imperfection.

◈

After Dr. Morrison had informed Dahlia that a zygote had been successfully implanted in the surrogate and that her baby would arrive at the end of June, she and Kirkland celebrated the sperm and egg's "marriage" with a champagne toast.

"The perfect pregnancy," according to Kirkland, "allows for the mother's intoxication without the danger of fetal alcohol syndrome." Demi-Christmas had been her friend's idea: "My birthday's the week after Christmas. It's always an afterthought. Second-rate presents—leftover junk that didn't fit in the stocking. Wrapping paper with Santa Clauses, as if it's my fault I was born so close to Jesus. June twenty-fifth is the perfect birthday—exactly halfway around the calendar from Christmas—*Demi-Christmas*!"

Months later, when Dr. Morrison offered induction as an option for delivery because "control will help personalize your birthing experience," June twenty-fifth proved a viable due-date, and Dahlia had shared Kirkland's suggestion.

"*Demi-Christmas*?" the doctor had smiled. "Why not? Unless nature overrules us first."

◈

But Dahlia's baby has been stolen. Everything is in flux. The double dose of Xanax she's swallowed has left her drowsy, and the warning on the bottle, "DO NOT TAKE IF PREGNANT OR PLANNING TO BECOME PREGNANT," blurs. The phone hums on her stomach like a mother buzzing into the belly of her giggling infant. The vibration tickles through Dahlia to her spine. It's Kirkland, still trying, his friendship relentless. He probably has more questions about Henry's nursery: he's already taken dozens of photos and measured the room, the crib, the pictures and posters, the bookcases and toy chest. All for an installation he's planning: he's constructing life-sized thematic Barbies "that interface with the trials and tribulations of the wider world." So far he's completed one diorama: Osama bin Barbie, the terrorist stretched out and bullet-ridden under a hawk-eyed, machine gun-toting Barbie Obama. "The installation will be kind of a freaky *Madame Tussaud's!*" Kirkland had gushed. He needs the dimensions of Henry's nursery so he can rebuild it in miniature and insert it into a pregnant, glass-stomached Brangelina Barbie. "Like the cows they used to fix up with glass stomachs in agricultural colleges so students could watch them digest. In Brangelina Barbie's womb-nursery there'll be dozens of tiny babies of all races and creeds, cooing and toddling. And only you and I will know it's Henry's room. Consider Brangelina Barbie your baby shower gift."

Dahlia's lips are numb, and she imagines that she's chosen to speak to Kirkland, that he's taken the news of her lost baby with surprising calm, that he's resolved to re-envision his latest project, abandoning the big Barbies. Instead, the entire installation will be about the nursery. *Black Nursery* is

127

what he'll call it, and instead of Henry's room being tiny, "It'll be huge—I'll fill an airplane hangar—a football stadium. The room will be reproduced in perfect proportion, but swollen to a size that matches the misery of a mother who's lost a child—and as dark as the other side of the moon!"

And Dahlia is staggering through the Black Nursery, the fibers of its carpet knee high and as thick as the rushes beside a midnight river; its ceiling is starless; an inaccessible crib towers over her. Too high to see, but so vast she feels its colossal weight, swings a mobile the size of a solar system. She sinks into the carpet, crushed into a dream-memory: a slumber party—Sherri Aspinall has locked herself in the unlit bathroom. Sherri is the only one of the tween girls brave enough to tempt the "Blue Baby" urban legend. Dahlia and the others huddle on pillows and beanbag chairs and hold their breath. They stare at the bathroom door. Dahlia covers her eyes with moist palms. In her chest throb the words of the incantation she knows Sherri recites—"Blue Baby, Blue Baby"—thirteen times. Sherri will rock her arms as if she holds a newborn and stare into a mirror she can't see in the dark. According to the legend, she'll soon feel something in her arms; it will grow heavier and heavier and begin to claw wildly, until, after the thirteenth rock, a hideous woman will appear in the mirror, shrieking, "Give me my baby!" Unless Sherri throws the invisible baby into the toilet and flushes it, the mother-in-the-mirror will kill her!

Dahlia's eyes pop open, and she squints against the brightness of her vaulted bedroom ceiling. She remembers: a toilet flushes, and the waiting girls gasp; Sherri Aspinall bursts from the bathroom with frantic eyes, tiny scratches across her throat like the tracks of birds. Her screeching friends swarm over her but avoid each other's glances—if any share a nod or smirk, the thrilling terror will be spoiled.

But Dahlia is confused. Hasn't she had the wrong dream— this should have been the dream of the thieving surrogate. *Dahlia* should be the witch in the mirror—*she's* the woman with the empty arms. Her throat is sore, as if she's been shouting: *Give me back my baby!*

A week has passed. It's the night of Demi-Christmas, and the surrogate has not been located. Dahlia's attorney has arranged for a private investigator. Documents are being examined; precedents are being sought. What kinds of guilt, her attorney has asked, does she most want rectified? Financial? Ethical? Dahlia has told him she only wants baby Henry, who may or may not have been born. The date of the scheduled induction has lingered on the calendar like a canceled party.

Dahlia is working: she sits in a theatre evaluating actors for an important client, a renowned director. The play she's watching, *Dinghy*, is an adaptation of a J. D. Salinger short story; it features members of the author's famous Glass family, primarily a young mother and her hypersensitive pre-school son. Playing the mother is a former starlet notorious for her trips to rehab. Dahlia had expected little from her, but her performance has been touching, even memorable. Where had this childless woman—this *actress* legendary for her bad behavior—learned to play a mother? Is nurturing taught in rehab?

Dahlia watches the young woman squat and smile bravely into the eyes of her pretend son. The world threatens to overwhelm him, and, afraid she's losing the child to his fears, she tousles his blond curls. Could it be that mothering is nothing but pretense? Dahlia winces at the thought, but it confirms a feeling that has been rising in her for the last week.

This performance will resurrect the career of the actress playing at motherhood, Dahlia is certain, but her client won't be interested. He needs little boys, dozens of them, for yet another remake of *Lord of the Flies*. Unfortunately, the youngest star of *Dinghy* is disappointingly unexceptional, a small-featured, dyed-blond dandelion fluff of a clichéd nothing: the worst kind of an imitation of a child. His actress-mother might as well have been hugging a doll, whispering playful gibberish into the ear of a stuffed monkey—setting cookies and milk before a child whose existence would have been better represented in pantomime. But this production gives him legitimacy; Dahlia will call his agent in the morning.

The first act ends. Applause falls like tin confetti as the curtain drops on a bright kitchen with the mother frozen behind a mixing bowl, her son at her feet stacking boxes of instant pudding. Dahlia's professional responsibilities have distracted her from her personal woes. Her agency is short of satisfactory boys, and she sighs, but whether for herself or her business she isn't sure. The sigh reminds her of Kirkland's therapy. She's yet to tell her friend of the missing surrogate, texting only that she was "too busy with preparations to talk." He's sure to have been lost in his Barbie world. But he won't have forgotten that it's June twenty-fifth—he'll expect a baby. She won't be able to put him off much longer.

Dahlia stops clapping and studies her French manicure as the houselights rise. Kirkland had created Demi-Christmas; she knows it's not fair, but she blames him for the failed baby project. Henry *who*? Hadn't Kirkland picked that name, too? She thinks of Dr. Morrison. Maybe the next time she sees the fertility specialist will be in court.

The intermission will be brief—five minutes. Dahlia scans faces in the audience and recognizes no one, which is unusual. The seats on either side of her are empty, paid for by her agency for clients. If things hadn't been so complicated, she might have asked Kirkland along. She smiles at the cloud-haired woman two seats over who squints in her direction. But the woman is gazing past her at someone else. No one who looks at Dahlia would guess that she's supposed to be having a baby this very evening. She turns on her cellphone to check her messages just as the houselights wink to signal the beginning of Act II. The slivers of darkness remind her of the Black Nursery—something else to blame on Kirkland, though she knows the giant room came from her own dream. She holds her breath, waiting for the shadow of the huge mobile, praying that that it won't come—if the curtain rises first, she tells herself, she'll be safe. Why had there ever been a baby in the first place?

Her phone glows: a new text message. From Dr. Morrison: *We have your baby! Bellevue Maternity Hospital. Neo-natal ICU.*

Congrats. Come now.

❦

Somehow Dahlia has negotiated the hospital's fluorescent maze, the glare of polished tile, glass, and steel. As she dons a white gown and mask, she remembers the satin swish of the wedding dress she'd slipped into a decade past. She tugs her fingers into latex gloves. A gleaming door opens with a whoosh, and she recognizes, after a moment, the masked face of Dr. Morrison. His eyes are moist—he's either smiling or in pain.

"Here," he says, and waves her forward. Nurses gather behind him. Something cold fills Dahlia's torso. The doctor stands aside, and the nurses part. There's nothing between Dahlia and a plexiglass incubator. Wire tendrils descend from it.

"But it's empty," she begins, before she sees, laid out on a white cloth, the broken, eye-less doll—so pink it's red, so red it's blue. No, only blue. Dahlia chuckles in horror. Dr. Morrison takes her arm above the elbow and guides her forward, but she resists. A nurse leans toward a monitor on which a red light blinks and touches something.

"No," Dahlia says through her mask. She lifts a hand as if she's swatting through a rack of sale blouses she knows she'd never buy. "No!" She turns to the doctor and narrows her eyes. "Where did you find the mother? Where is she? How do I know this is mine? What's your proof?"

Dr. Morrison's eyes shrink. Dahlia is sure there is a wet-nostriled snout beneath his mask. He shakes his head. Dahlia shakes hers.

"Dahlia," the doctor pleads, then more firmly, "Dahlia—this is your baby!"

She chuckles again. Her gaze skips across the half-covered faces of the nurses. She won't look at the incubator. Where are the men, she suddenly needs to know. Where had they been when they'd planned this? She'd had a husband once, whose face she can't remember, and a father who's been dead for years. Somewhere is a young blond man equally responsible for the shriveled thing encased in glass. How easily she'd been abandoned—why had she been the only one dragged from the theatre?

"No!" Dahlia wrings the doctor's hand from her arm. "*Where's the mother?*" There has to be a woman, freshly purged, lying nearby, and Dahlia needs to find her. She backs through the steel door into a white hallway, which she hurries down. She passes several rooms with closed doors and stops before one marked "WOMEN." The knob is cold through her latex glove, as is the lock she turns once she's inside. Dahlia glimpses a sink, a toilet, and her own white-swathed reflection before she finds the switch and darkens the room. She pulls off her mask, and the air is cool on her face and in her lungs, comforting until the odor of ammonium stings her eyes. Dahlia knows she's staring at a mirror, but sees nothing. Maybe on the mirror's other side, through the wall, the awful baby's true mother lies. She laces her fingers together at her waist—through the gloves they feel like cold sausages.

Dahlia sets herself in motion. "Blue Baby," she says, swinging her arms. "Blue Baby . . ." On which rock-a-bye will she begin to feel the weight? "Blue Baby . . ." She shifts her blind gaze for a moment, guessing where the toilet must be. "Blue Baby . . ." She mustn't fear the face in the mirror when it rises before her. "Blue Baby . . ." When the witch demands her child, Dahlia will yell, *"Take it!"*—eager to surrender her terrible mistake.

Blue Madeline's Version

Eric pulls up short of his driveway. It's eleven a.m. on what had begun as a work day, and his house doesn't look right. He's seen it catching the mid-morning sun on weekends, but this is different. Everything else on the block of modest homes seems switched off—no cars or hum of mowers, no kids on bikes. He doesn't see a squirrel or a sparrow—and if he had seen a bird overhead, frozen in mid-flight as in a museum diorama, it wouldn't have surprised him. But Eric's Cape Cod glows: the bricks seem kiln fresh, the red door and shutters blaze. The hedges swell with vibrant green. His home seems lit from within, like a poorly timed holiday display.

Three hours earlier, he'd left for the office, passing his jogging neighbor, Larry Feldstein, the bachelor retiree. "DMJ," Eric called—Dead Man Jogging. Twelve times around the block for Larry, like clockwork since his triple bypass five years ago. "DMW," Larry responded, pointing at Eric. Dead Man Working. They share this exchange most mornings. DMW no longer, Eric hopes Larry hasn't noticed his early return.

At 9:30, Eric had been called into the third-floor conference room and sacked. *We recognize your contribution*—the director of human resources said, smirking, as if the firing was a preliminary reading for an absurd play. Eric had never heard her voice until that moment. Kurt, his boss, didn't lift his

135

eyes from a document that could have been a script. *But you haven't met the agreed upon goals set at your last performance review.* Performance review? Eric couldn't recall such a meeting. At the water cooler a few months earlier Kurt had asked about Eric's family, nodded, and encouraged him to *get those numbers up.* That had been a performance review? *Up* was a goal? He'd had thirty minutes to clean out his desk, then was paraded by security past his former colleagues.

Now Eric stands on the stoop of his empty home—Celia is at a three-day button convention in Buffalo. Nothing is familiar. He fumbles for his keys before finding them in the hand grasping his briefcase. He might as well have left that behind. All he'd shoveled into it was a staple remover, a box of ball point pens, and the photograph of Celia and his children, David and Eva, taken a dozen years ago on a Lake George beach. He's thinking of that white beach and the deep blue water behind, the green Adirondacks humped in the distance when he stumbles over a package on the welcome mat.

Returning home to a package is a first. Celia would usually have claimed a delivery by the afternoon, and nothing ever came on weekends. Is this something from work? *Recognition for his contribution.* A gold watch? Or something, he can't imagine what, acknowledging that a mistake had been made—*please accept this token of apology and return to work tomorrow morning.*

The package is the size of half a shoebox and weighs almost nothing—no gold watch. Eric's name isn't on the label: "Training Facility, 232 Van Curler Road." His address is 232 Verona. The police training facility is two blocks south.

There'd been a mix up once before. On a Saturday afternoon, an officer had stepped out of his cruiser and presented Eric, who was wondering if he was about to be cited for an unmuffled lawnmower, with what turned out to be a box of copper buttons addressed to Celia. Never before, however, has something intended for the police been left at their door.

The return address on this package is for Atlantic Chemicals in Union, New Jersey. Clamping the box under his arm and sweeping the street with a wary glance, Eric unlocks his front door and steps in, calling, "Hello!" out of habit. A man should accept his dismissal stoically. He wouldn't interrupt Celia's pleasure trip with his bad news—she'd leave her convention to offer her unnecessary support. He can afford to retire, if they're frugal. There'll be severance pay, then unemployment, and before long his pension and Social Security. They're mortgage free, and the kids are responsible for their own graduate school loans.

No one will expect him to complain; he's gruff, not much of a talker. He'd run out of things to say to his children years ago, and, unlike Celia, who bemoans their absence, he can celebrate memories without a *corpus delecti*. Children move on; it's the way of the world, and silence needn't imply the washing of hands.

And Celia lives blissfully in her world of antique buttons. "Imagine the hearts that beat behind these bits of bone and horn and metal," she mused once, stirring a cookie tin filled with her favorites. Eric woodworks, a pastime both physical and practical. It looks to the future. His wish for more time to pursue his hobby has been granted.

The couple has faced life placidly for years. Only once had Celia's mask loosened: ten years past, when a beloved younger cousin died tragically of an aneurism. No father in the picture, her orphaned five year old had only her grandmother, Celia's aunt, who, Celia fretted, was "nearly deranged, possibly an alcoholic. If we offer, she'll let us have Madeline. We've got the guestroom."

Romantic fantasies about buttons were one thing. Raising a stranger probably damaged by both nature *and* nurture was something else entirely. Eric and Celia had the one boy and one girl of the perfect family. A new, unplanned child would have subverted the mathematics. No noble gestures, he'd declared. The fire in Celia's eyes flickered and died. "Impulse buying has messy consequences," he concluded. His wife whispered her final accusation: "You are a hollow man." They never spoke directly of the little girl again, though somehow Eric knew the grandmother had proven unsuitable, and the child had ended up in foster care.

From the folding chair beside his basement work table, Eric contemplates the mis-delivered package. If the police come looking, he'll deny knowledge of it. He cuts the packing tape and opens the flaps. Nestled in shredded green paper is an ampoule of golden liquid. When he plucks it out and holds it up to the fluorescent light, a yellow streak runs down his wrist, as if the ampoule is leaking color. An invoice lists a single item: "Cadaver scent." Neither the price nor directions are included, though a bold-faced statement cautions, "Simulated cadaver smells are available only to certified training facilities."

Eric grimaces—on this of all days to have the smell of death delivered to his home. Artificial, yes, but death nevertheless. He's seen "cadaver dogs" featured on TV—German shepherds digging through the smoldering ruins of the Twin Towers or the rubble left by an earthquake in a South American city. He's seen them bounding through marshes on taut leashes, their nasal receptors stimulated by the smell of decaying human meat. What draws a dog so powerfully to a scent, Eric wonders. Does instinct feel like an emotion? He'd never have guessed these animals were trained in his own neighborhood.

Eric sets the ampoule on his work table, where it stands like a golden bullet. There are laboratories, he's read, that concoct artificial scents and flavors: luncheon meats, French fries, and even the essence of death. When had they known they'd perfected "cadaver"? Maybe a caged dog drooled. The ampoule glows with cloudless purity. Would the essence be considered artificial if it had been distilled from a dead heart?

"Uncle Irk—" Because the voice is feather light, it doesn't shock Eric. He turns to find a young woman—a girl?—sitting midway up the open basement steps. She's thin, her arms and legs sprawling from her black tank top and cut-off shorts, every inch of her visible flesh a silvery blue. Her face is lost in the shadows, but when she pushes back dark bangs, her eyes gleam. "That's what I would have called you, when you lectured me about, I don't know, not doing my homework, or spending too much time on the phone, or not helping Aunt Celia with the dishes. I'd have pretended to be miffed, but it would have been playful. 'Uncle Irk.' It probably wouldn't have stuck. Maybe I would have left it at 'Eric' and 'Celia.'" She pauses, as if counting breaths. "Surprise! I'm Madeline!"

No surprise. Given the unsettled state of his thoughts after the morning's firing, it's no wonder he'd forgotten to lock the front door. If not the police looking for their cadaver scent, why not this girl? He's been thinking about her, hasn't he? "Of course," he says. It's Celia who would have been shocked. She would have cried with joy to see her cousin's child. But the idea of hosting is exhausting; he gestures toward the floors above them.

"The guest room is the second door on your right after the kitchen. The bathroom is the room before that. Towels in the bathroom closet, and take anything you want from the refrigerator. Have a glass of milk."

"Un-hunh." Madeline's voice tickles his ears. "What's that you've got there? Is that a pee-sample? You don't need one for work anymore, right? You would have threatened me with one, and we would have had a fight about it, but you'd have believed that I was clean, I think."

Eric picks up the ampoule. An air bubble shifts through it. "It's scent," he says, "for training dogs—it smells like cadavers. So they can rescue dead bodies."

Silence. Across the basement the hot water heater ticks. If he closes his eyes, he might be alone, the stairs unoccupied. A giggle: "You don't 'rescue' dead bodies. I mean, it's a little late for a rescue once you're a body, isn't it?"

"Not 'rescue.' I meant 'recover.' Sorry—tough day." Eric suddenly sees himself as his coworkers must have, trailing the security guard past their cubicles. Had he really held his briefcase like a lunch tray?

"And what are you going to do with it?"

"I don't know. It was delivered by accident."

"Are you sure it was an accident?"

"It had the wrong address. It was supposed to go to the place where they train the dogs."

"Mmm—" A thoughtful pause. "Maybe it got there. Maybe one of the dogs brought it over. He thought you needed it. Did you check the box it came in for teeth marks? Saliva?" The girl shifts on the steps, crosses her legs, and there's a shimmer like bubbles released underwater.

"Maybe." Conversation and concentration are impossible to maintain. He feels the weight of his house on his shoulders.

"So—what are you going to *do* with it?"

"Tomorrow," he murmurs as his eyes close. "I'll think of something tomorrow."

"Okay if I look at it?" the blue girl might have asked.

⁓

It's morning, and Eric sits at his kitchen table with a mug of coffee he doesn't recall brewing. "Late for work," he mutters, then remembers, as if stepping into a cold rain, that there isn't any work. Routines will change. Time will unfold differently. He can read the paper now instead of waiting for the evening. It had been his daily custom to pull it from the box at the end of his driveway and toss it toward the front door for Celia, giving himself a mental fist pump if it reached the stoop. If Larry was jogging by, Eric would wave: *"DMJ!"* *"DMW!"*

But what if Larry passes by this morning when Eric—who still wears a sweatshirt and flannel pajama bottoms—is fetching the paper? He leaves his coffee and hurries to the front door, where he squints through the small, chin-high window. His eyes rove the street and adjacent lawns, alert for movement—if not Larry, maybe a dog, a trotting German shepherd with a lolling tongue. He remembers the package, the cadaver scent, and Madeline.

How odd, he thinks. On his way back to the kitchen, he checks the guestroom. The door is shut. He peers into the hall bathroom, and there's a rumpled towel on the rack. The faucet drips, and he tightens it. His reflection in the medicine cabinet mirror startles him: his cheeks are raw red, frosted with silver stubble; brown stains pollute the whites of his eyes. His lower lip sags to a frown at the thin hair pasted over his crown. There's a new toothbrush in the holder, wet.

On his way back to the kitchen, he pauses outside the guestroom door, but hears nothing. He's about to sit back down to his coffee when he notices the blink of the answering machine. It's a message from Celia he's somehow missed: "Hello, Eric. Everything's fine, the convention is fine, I'm fine. Lots of networking and trading. I've got a bid in for a Czech unicorn turquoise. And Eric, unless there's a problem, I won't be coming home Sunday. Some of us are going to Toronto. There's an exhibition there, too. International buttons. Three more days. So carry on without me—I'll call again soon."

᳅

Eric is in the basement, where he's spent most of the day, forgoing lunch. He's been measuring and sawing long white pine boards for a built-in storage bench for his work area. He doesn't remember when he bought the wood, but the pine smell reminds him of the camping trips the family had taken in the Adirondacks. Now and then he catches a golden wink from his work table—the cadaver scent—and he listens for footsteps overhead. Taking a break from sawing, he picks up the ampoule, shakes it, and watches the froth of bubbles fizz out until the liquid is again clear and golden. It's only half full. Is this all there was?

"I'd have shared a tent with Eva when we camped." Blue Madeline has returned to the shadowy basement steps. "David would have shoved toads and newts under the flaps, and we girls would have screamed and held each other's hands, even though we weren't really scared. Eva's how much older than me, Eric?"

"I don't know—how old are you?"

"Fifteen."

"Then ten. Ten years older." Eric has been staring at the white pine so long his focus won't adjust; the figure on the steps wavers like a blue flame.

"So she would have been like I am now. We would have gotten David back, though—maybe we'd have stolen his shorts from the shower building. Swimming in the lake would have been good enough for the rest of us, but David always wanted a shower. Celia would have said he was 'preening for the ladies.'"

"He was older—"

"—And used to drink beer with the boys down at the boathouse when he thought everybody was asleep. But Eva and I would have sneaked down and watched from behind the trees. The boys would be swimming without their suits. I would have thought their bare bottoms were as white as the moon, and I'd giggle—and the boys would have pulled their shorts on and called us out—mostly for Eva, she was so pretty. And we'd have toasted marshmallows at a campfire while the boys drank more beer and Eva tried some. When we all got back to our campsite just before dawn, we'd hear you snoring, and it would have made you seem harmless. Oh—I took care of things for you."

Harmless? "Took care of things?" Before Madeline's last words, Eric had retreated with her to the Adirondacks—crisp air and sunshine, campfires and boggy soil, mildew waft of camping equipment used once a year. The kids—just his boy and girl, younger than Madeline's version, slick and wet, slipping through black inner tubes into the blue lake. And Celia, in cuffed jeans over her swimsuit, her face unavailable to his memory—as featureless as one of her copper buttons.

While he's listened, Eric has framed his bench and measured the seven-foot planks he'll use for its top. He'll fix it to the wall perpendicular to his work table. The top will be hinged for storage. Why had she said "harmless"?

"You took care of what?" he asks again.

Madeline's voice floats like a gull in an empty sky. "You'd

have said, 'This isn't real camping—showers and RVs and paved roads.'" When the girl imitates his voice, Eric feels the weight of each word in his throat. "What I took care of is that lady from your office—the one who had the pig-faced grin when she fired you. Did you know she just finished putting in a pool?"

"I didn't, no."

"Um-hmm. Hadn't filled it yet. I guess they were waiting for it to set. But imagine all the work . . ."

"Work?"

"To dig it up. Underneath it, when they're looking for the body."

Eric wipes sweat from his brow with his wrist. The girl shimmers like a leaping fish. She drops her hand from her smile, and her teeth shine.

"You'd have gotten me braces when you saw the big space between my front teeth. I imagine the police are still at that lady's. A little of that cadaver stuff down the pool drain, and a call to the police—not from here, don't worry. An 'anonymous tip.' You know that kidnapped baby they've been looking for? From Pittsfield? Missing a few months? Imagine if someone told them it was buried under that pool. They'd have to dig the whole thing up, just to check it out, wouldn't they? Especially when a cadaver dog sniffed out something down that brand new drain. It would sure make a mess for that lady. Lots of questions, and, well, she won't be using that new pool for a while after they chop out the whole bottom. Can't you just see it? It only took a few drops of that scent."

Eric looked over at the ampoule. It was half empty.

"That'll be a headline story," Madeline says. She sighs. "I'd have been so close to Eva. Would she have been in college when I had my first period? She'd have been a comfort. Maybe she would have been home on vacation. Celia would have given me 'the talk,' though. Is this embarrassing you, Eric? Girl talk?"

He doesn't answer. He's envisioning a swarm of police invading the backyard of a suburban mini-mansion, scrambling over the manicured lawn and draping the coiffed shrubberies and ornamental trees with yellow tape. Shovel and pick ax wielding workers attack a swimming pool. Chunks of aquamarine concrete and fresh red dirt pile up, and police officers surround a woman who clasps her pink robe to her throat—the human resources director. All stare at a gaping hole at the bottom of the destroyed pool. A police dog strains against a leash, barking into that void, where a hip-deep officer sifts blindly with gloved hands.

"Do you think I could have convinced you to get a puppy after Eva left?" Madeline asks. "A dog would have filled a pretty big gap. What're you making there? That's quite a box."

"It's a storage bench," Eric says.

❧

The next morning already? Eric, half-hidden by a drape, stands at the living room window, staring at the street. If he chances a dash to the mailbox, he'll find the morning paper, flush with the details of the "Search for Lost Baby under Suburban Pool." But if Larry Feldstein jogs by, Eric will have to explain about his lost job. Curiously, papers are piled under the box, as if someone thought he'd want souvenir copies. But if anybody knew, then wouldn't the police? Madeline suggested that a cadaver dog might have brought the package to his stoop. Maybe a German shepherd would trot up his driveway right now. And here's Larry—*DMJ*! His neighbor stops at the pile of papers, glances at Eric's house, then kicks the extra copies onto the curb. He keeps jogging.

The guestroom door is shut. Eric doesn't check the bathroom. Confusing messages flood the kitchen answering machine. Eric listens twice, then a third time. First is David— it's been two years since he's heard his son's voice, though Celia keeps in contact: "Dad, we should talk. I'll try again."

Next is Eva; he doesn't understand her message at all: "Sorry we missed you, Mom and Dad. Stephanie wants to show you where her tooth fell out. I think she's hoping her grandpa is the Tooth Fairy. It'd be nice if she were right. Ryan says, 'Go Yankees,' Dad. I forgot—Mom is away, isn't she? Okay, we'll talk soon."

Stephanie and Ryan? Who are they? The names are familiar, but placing them is like thumbing through a book written with a foreign alphabet. There are two more messages from Celia: "Toronto was great. Buttons galore. But now the gang is heading to Ohio for Button Week, if you can believe it, and I figure I've only got this one chance, so off I go. Defrost something for yourself, there's plenty in the freezer." His wife's second message, the last on the machine: "Don't ever let anyone disparage Cleveland. We had loads of fun, although I have to admit, I haven't much use for that rock music hall of fame. But the word's out about a private exhibit just outside of Denver. My friend Dierdre knows somebody who knows somebody, and we think we'll be able to get a peek. This could be the experience of a lifetime! I'll let you know how it works out."

Certain he's missed something, Eric is about to listen to the messages for a fourth time when the doorbell rings, and he freezes. The doorbell rings again. He isn't dressed for company—he still wears the sweatshirt and pajama bottoms. And for how long has he been barefoot? He could step on something on the basement floor if he's not careful. The doorbell a third time. Eric hunches and shuffles down the hall to the living room's second archway, where he might be able to glimpse a visitor. There's an elbow—yellow reflective fabric—Larry's running suit. Both men hold still for nearly a minute. When Larry finally leaves, Eric exhales and drifts away.

❦

That evening, Eric is sanding the pine bench when Madeline arrives.

"I'd have been a Girl Scout, like Eva," she says from her usual perch on the steps. "Our projects never involved woodworking and race cars and things you made for a while when David was in the Cub Scouts. It was the Pinewood Derby car that made him hate you, wasn't it? When he wanted to glue Eva's Barbie to the top, and you hit him? I think it was Ballerina Barbie—she had a pink tutu."

There's a flap of torn skin on Eric's knuckle, oozing blood—has he sanded through his flesh while lost in thought?

148

But when he looks closer, there's nothing there. Then he sees himself reaching toward young David. Blood drips from the boy's nose onto his lip; the boy flinches from his father's hand. His eyes shine with defiant tears.

"Just a slap—he moved into it—he wouldn't stop whining about the doll. Like a broken record. A doll on a race car? We'd made such a beautiful car, and he wanted to ruin it."

"That was the end of projects, wasn't it? Did Celia even know? But you did sell Girl Scout cookies for Eva at your office. She was afraid to go door to door. You would have done that for me, right? But if I was still selling cookies, how would you get them to your office for my customers?"

Mention of doors reminds Eric of Larry at his. His neighbor will be back.

"That Mr. Feldstein must have run a million miles by now," Madeline says, dipping into Eric's thoughts. "Do you remember how Eva and David switched rooms because Eva thought Mr. Feldstein stared into her window? 'Like I'm supposed to wave,' she said. It was nice the way David always tried to protect her. Wasn't that why she stopped selling cookies in the neighborhood? Didn't Mr. Feldstein invite her in and 'try something'? You said she had quite an imagination. I'm glad my room doesn't face the street. Celia said you had to go over to Mr. Feldstein's right away and get to the bottom of it. You said you didn't know what to say. Your solution was to sell her cookies at work. Eva cried, and David switched bedrooms with her. Hey—how do you want to use up your cadaver scent?"

Eric squints at the ampoule. Not much is left. His throat

is scratchy—sawdust clings to his lashes and covered his forearms. "You girls were always safe," he croaks.

"Of course," Madeline says. "You know what we could do? We could find some real killers, and we could use your fake scent to lead the police to them. Maybe make a trail from the perp to the hidden body. There are crimes everywhere, right? And bodies. You could be like Robin Hood, and I could be your sidekick. Robin Hood had a sidekick, right?

"He had Merry Men."

"I thought he had a sidekick in a red outfit and mask that matched his green one. A kid. Both of them had bows and arrows—"

"That's The Green Arrow and Speedy. From a comic book I read when I was a boy."

"Un-hunh. Well, David would have read it to me. You saved your old comic books—that's your legacy. With Eva I would have read *Archie*. The paper would have been musty and flaky. Do you think I'm more like Betty or Veronica?"

"Veronica," Eric says without thinking.

"Probably. She's a little bitchy, right? Eva's more like Betty—a girl next door. Hey, you know, wouldn't it be something if Mr. Feldstein was ringing your doorbell before because there was something wrong with him? Didn't he have a heart transplant or something?"

"A triple bypass."

"Wow—that sounds worse than a transplant. Maybe he came over because he was having chest pains and didn't want to keel over alone in his house where nobody would find him. What if you'd let him in, and he'd sat down at the kitchen table, and you'd brought him a glass of water, but he slumped over and died right there—at the kitchen table."

Eric pictures Larry, who'd never been in his house, lifting a glass of water toward worm-colored lips, then dropping it, the glass shattering on the table. The jogger's eyes roll back, and he slips to the floor like shifting freight and lies spread-eagled. Does Eric dare call 911? Won't the police find the mis-delivered scent? When Eric looks up from his fallen neighbor, he sees the blinking answering machine. He steps over Larry to play them back.

David: "Dad?"

Eva: "Dad?"

Celia: "The Pacific Ocean is beautiful, Eric—we should have made that cross country trip with the kids. I have no idea what the time difference is here in Honolulu, but I guess you're asleep. The buttons are spectacular—coral and shell, like nothing I've ever seen."

"I think they'll look for Larry at his place first, when somebody figures out he's missing," Madeline says. "Too bad about him. It's a question whether he really deserved what he got."

Somehow, the girl and Eric have switched places, and he's on the shaded steps. Madeline scintillates under the fluorescent light, poised over his pine bench with his hammer in her hand. She's so bright, so silvery blue, it hurts as much to look at her as it does the white boards of his project. What evening is it?

"Eventually, they'll start poking around the neighborhood, and before long, they'll be here. A dog will catch his scent. Or maybe the dogs will catch *your* scent—oh, but wasn't yours *theirs* in the first place? It's hard to keep track." Blue Madeline pauses. Eric, wincing, sees that she points his hammer at the work table. "But all of your scent is gone!" From the stairs, Eric can't make out the ampoule. "Now how are we going to be Robin Hood and Speedy?" She slides a pine plank into place, sets a nail down, and the hammer drops. The sound echoes from the concrete walls and floor. She sets another nail. How thin she is. Translucently thin. She pounds the second nail.

The lights dim, but Madeline is impossible to watch. Eric wants to tell her to hinge the bench top, not nail it. If it's nailed, who will find whatever's inside? But his tongue is thick, and she's working so diligently he doesn't dare stop her.

"But your scent was artificial, right? Now we've got the real thing, right here in storage. We'll figure out a way to use it sooner or later—you know, for leading police to the bodies criminals have hidden." Her words are hard to decipher. She might be holding nails in the corner of her mouth. But it sounds like she's slipping into a different language. She keeps pounding away, and each concussion hurts Eric's ears. He wraps his arms around his head, but the sound grows louder. He's smothered himself in total darkness.

"You know—" the voice penetrates from above, the pounding now more like knuckles on a wooden door—only every few words are audible because of the knocking, "—it would have been . . . to have grown up . . . family. . . Spectacular!"

Snow Angels *sans Merci*

My sister-in-law's got me trapped in my bedroom. Her soundless presence in the living room below competes with the silence of the snow I assume has been falling for hours. And Blanche's sleeping like a stone on the sofabed. She's been visiting for a month and shows no sign of leaving.

My wife lies beside me. I gaze at her with love, but I pity both of us. Who should have such a sister? Not Estelle— look what Blanche does to me! I sit on the bed's edge and stare at my moon pale feet. To see them I lean to the side. I think of myself as round like a planet, not fat. Solid. It's a matter of opinion. The fact that Blanche lurks downstairs whets my appetite for everything she keeps me from—my recliner, my entertainment center, my well-stocked kitchen. When I tell my wife how confined I feel, she scoffs.

"You're joking," she says, her dark eyes twinkling. "How could you be afraid of sweet old Blanche?" Estelle is eleven years younger than her sister.

The first morning after Blanche's arrival I descended the stairs dressed for work, hungry for sweet rolls and coffee. I tip-toed past the sofa bed, where my sister-in-law lay hidden in a tangle of sheets. When my eyes adjusted to the half-light, I saw Blanche's wild mass of hair inches from my thigh. One false step and I'd have explaining to do. I backed away and bumped into my recliner, pawing the blouse Blanche had flung there. I groped the stiff fabric of the bra twisted within it, panicked, and puffed back upstairs. I vowed never again to pass Blanche while she slept.

So I've been sitting at the edge of my bed mornings, an inflated version of Rodin's thinker. I stare at a Brueghel print above the dresser—villagers skating on a pond. Each morning I expect to see one skater less. I search for a hole in the ice that a heavy fellow might have dropped through. One morning will I see a web of cracks, and the next find the ice broken into tiny floes like white cornflakes in ink? I have been hungry ever since Blanche's invasion.

Frost clouds the glass, but through a clear strip I see flakes dancing like sperm. It's Saturday morning, no work, but I don't have the freedom of my house. I lay my hand on Estelle's side. "How about breakfast?" I ask, afraid she'll tease me again about her sister.

Blanche's marriage ended a year after Estelle and I wed. I remember two things about Don, her ex. One is that he was brilliant. She'd met him while both were graduate students at MIT. Her field was atmospheric sciences. Don supposedly invented nanotechnology or discovered a theoretical entity lurking within black holes or formulated a multi-digit "constant" like those on charts referenced in high school physics classes. The second thing I recall about Don is that Blanche divorced him "because he wasn't smart enough." They had no children. A footnote on Don's brilliance: we played Trivial Pursuit once, the four of us. Before we were married, Estelle brought me to Boston to meet the couple, and the game followed an unsatisfying vegetarian stir fry. Don had the first turn. He answered everything right. Whatever the question, whatever the category, Don responded as if he'd written the cards. No one else got a turn as he marched his piece indifferently around the board. I think he mistook the activity for a conversation. The details of Blanche and Don's courtship are beyond imagining.

Blanche has kept an apartment in Cambridge since she and Don split up. Her share of the profits from his patented "processes" has left her financially independent, and she chooses not to work. She travels. Estelle receives postcards monthly from exotic locales—European spas, Asian capitals, unheard of Pacific atolls. Blanche's cards mention only the weather. A note from Algiers backing a picture of blue-green water and blindingly white buildings, reads, "Unseasonably cold; temperatures in the low 60s during the day, 30s at night. Humidity imperceptible. Love, Blanche."

I met my wife when I hired her as an office temp at my insurance company. It was a busy summer for thunderstorm damage, and Estelle was waiting for September and her first teaching job. I didn't ask her out until her last day. During the month of August, I struggled to maintain my professional distance in the face of Estelle's charms. I locked myself in my office, safe from the bright smiles she offered while pecking away at her computer. I trembled in her company, grumbling instructions with downcast eyes. I brought a second shirt to the office because the first was sweat-soaked by noon.

Five minutes before she would have walked out of my life forever, Estelle accepted my muttered dinner invitation. She told me over dessert that she'd thought I hated her, and, as I invented a company policy forbidding dating, a tear of relief welled up in my eye, spilled down my cheek, and slipped into the crease between my chins.

I cower behind Estelle as we negotiate the living room on our way to breakfast, but Blanche's gaze pins me against the wall like a weather map. She sits cross-legged in her flannel nightgown. Her hair swirls in a black cloud; white streaks flash around her head like smothered lightening. She calls the style "natural." Blanche's face always surprises me. Though it's precisely my wife's, it's capable of expressions unimaginable on Estelle.

"You two are down late," Blanche says. "Nothing I wouldn't approve of, eh, Rich-head?"

Estelle giggles like a middle-schooler. "He asked you not to call him that."

Blanche's been calling me "Rich-head" ever since I asked her not to call me Dick. I told her Dick made no sense because I didn't have a "D" in my name. Now I'm "Rich-head" at least once a day, and I hear "Dick" no matter what she says.

I clear my throat. "It snowed," I say. "It's still snowing."

"Un-hunh," Blanche grunts, feigning disinterest in the weather with professional ennui. "What's for breakfast? Plenty, right?" She eyes my stomach, which I pat protectively. It's rumbling. Her grin twists, as if to remind me that she's not Estelle.

Estelle pulls aside the curtain. "Oh—" she gasps, "Look

at the snow!"

We gaze together at the tumbling flakes—so many, too many. We look through their veil at the deepening snow, our neighborhood transformed. I draw Estelle close.

"What a waste, hey?" Blanche calls, and I jerk away from my wife. "What's the point if it's not going to get you off from work, right? What's to stare at, Saint Richard? You're not going to melt it away. That's at least an hour's work in near blizzard conditions." She looks again at my belly. "Make it two hours."

So now I'm a saint. "Not enough wind for a blizzard," I mutter. Blanche, of course, knows this better than I do. Estelle has slipped away and crawls onto the sofa bed beside her sister, who takes hold of her wrists in mock compassion.

"Tell me all about it," Blanche coos. "Is big, bad husband treating you cruelly?" She pats her baby sister's tamer hair, streakless, but as black as her own. Alone at the window, I look at the snow. It's overtaken the bottom step of the porch and half the next. Cars are buried. Trees and fence posts have sunk. Furrows from foolhardy motorists are filling in, as are the walks of the neighbors who have shoveled once already. And if I wait until the storm ends, it will be too deep for me.

"No reason to think this will stop before midnight—maybe not before morning," Blanche says. "Good thing we're set for supplies. Wheee! Snowbound!" She and Estelle bounce on their knees on the sofa bed, hair and breasts flouncing.

"We'll keep the coffee hot and make muffins," Estelle offers, lashes fluttering, "if you decide you want to shovel now, you know, so you won't have to do it all at once tomorrow."

"Twenty-four to thirty inches, then clearing; temperatures dropping into the lower teens, maybe single digits. With the anticipated high winds, near white out—" Blanche stops. She smirks at me with my wife's lips, parodies Estelle's lid-flutter. "Of course, we don't really believe in windchill. If it's cold, it's cold, right? But you'd better not put it off."

So the sisters want me outside. I turn dejectedly to the hall closet for my shoveling clothes.

"If you are going out now, would you make us a snow angel?" The request strikes my back like a snowball. I'm breathless. Which sister asked? I focus on the closet and raise my hand in acknowledgement. "A nice round one!" one of them adds as I zip my parka over my firm gut.

I've cleared the porch, and I'm nearly done with the sidewalk. I pile the snow in heaps that mark my progress. Too much effort for too little reward. Even ditch diggers have a permanent ditch when they're done. One good thaw and the lawn and cars and trees will be as bare as the sidewalk I'm laboring to clear. Nobody shovels the forests or the beaches, but they'll be snowless in a matter of months. It's a trick of time, I decide. I invent an objective as I dig and throw: maybe I'll uncover a genie's lamp or pry off the lid of Pandora's box. In what movie did scientists defrost a frozen alien in the Arctic?

The sisters sit inside, drinking my coffee, eating my muffins. I picture them plotting my demise— ("Shall we poison him? Cut his throat in the night? Or should we just lock him out. Or just let him shovel out there—his heart can't possibly take much more!") Their laughter surely spins into the thread of blue smoke rising from the chimney.

I pause, shivering. The wind penetrates my layers and chills my damp T-shirt. Down the street parked cars squat like buried bison. I've always pitied bison—so powerful, but such easy prey. My car will be entombed in our back alley garage until the city plows it out, probably tomorrow.

Last night, anticipating the storm, the sisters returned from the supermarket with bags of snack food. Blanche stood tiptoe to shelve a package of Oreos, and my gaze accidentally slid down the curve of her back.

"Don't expect to do any driving for a couple of days," she said, as if she felt my eyes. Arms circled my waist from behind, my wife's. Her fingertips couldn't quite touch. She laid her cheek on my back.

"We bought you that sweet coffee you like," she said. "The hazelnut cream."

"Exotic tastes," Blanche mocked.

Since it's Saturday, it shouldn't bother me that my car is trapped, but what would I do in a crisis? Ten feet of shoveling will end the job. With the resolve of a tunneling convict, I throw myself into the task.

People think I'm my wife's age, but I'm really as old as her sister. Chubbiness smoothes the lines from my face. Maybe I've got youthful mannerisms.

What would have happened if I had met Blanche before

Estelle, let's say in college. I couldn't have competed with the brilliance of someone like Don. What social context would we have shared? Blanche would have been in classes that I can't imagine myself sitting through, classes I walked by, peeked in the windows of—blackboards covered with numbers, disconnected letters, and symbols—and always a skeletal professor, with his back to his attentive students, scribbling, scribbling, scribbling. I see my wife's face among the students, but of course it's Blanche. Then I am with her, Blanche, my cheek nestled in the cloud of her exploding hair, the soft flannel of her nightgown between her breasts and my chest, her bare thigh lifting, sliding higher, climbing over my thick legs and broad hips, her perfume as dizzying as fermenting wine…and on our bed upstairs Estelle, dew fresh, lies like the petals of a flower, a gossamer breath from waking. I hesitate, naked, in Blanche's embrace.

I've stopped again. Spinning flakes absorb my breath. Through them I see the wildly waving figures of Estelle and Blanche. They press their identical faces against the window, transform into grotesque creatures, then pull away and become themselves. They trace hourglass figures in the air, and their hands flutter like wings where the shoulders would be. Then Blanche and my wife flap their arms with such energy that Blanche's nightgown lifts to her hips. Estelle leans upon her sister's back, her teeth bared with inaudible laughter. They want their snow angel.

They're begging me to frolic. I flap my arms, shovel in hand, to let them know I've got the idea, then shrug and point at the snow I haven't cleared. But they've left the window, probably gone back to the kitchen for more coffee and muffins. I'm ravenous. I keep flapping because the motion loosens my back and shoulders and warms me up. My arms are so hammish the angel idea is absurd. I need a temperate climate, an azure sea, like in one of Blanche's postcards, where I can bob weightlessly while native boys with glistening dark skin float me trays of food and exotic drinks.

If I peer like Superman through the walls of my house will I see the sisters in the kitchen, cheeks like chipmunks, eyes moist with choking laughter? Blanche puts down a steaming mug and a muffin and draws a circle, adding wings. She hooks a thumb toward me through the invisible wall. I'm the round snow angel. Estelle gags on her muffin. Is this what I mean to these women?

They're back at the window, hands and arms flapping. I could give them the moment's harmless play they crave, but I'm freezing and starving and my job isn't finished. If I refuse, will Blanche leave? Exactly how long is she intending to stay? I could clear the last stretch and be done. Muffins, French toast, sausages beckon. Salivating, I shrug off their muffled rapping. Let them make their own angels!

My shovel rips into the snow, but I strike something. It gives slightly, like a bundle of rags. I pull, but the shovel sticks fast. I try again, leaning back with all my weight. I risk toppling onto the sidewalk, already disappearing under fresh inches, if the shovel jerks free. But it doesn't budge. It feels as if something's holding it, answering each of my tugs with a yank of its own. I strain mightily, my eyes squeezing white into black. Stars swirl as I gasp and pull even harder. Gaining a bit, I peek, and the shovel is torn away! I see two hands the size of a baby doll's drag it under the snow.

I stand paralyzed, my hand over my heart, but I feel nothing but the vacuum of terror. The snow where the shovel has disappeared shifts and crumbles, and I bleat and churn toward my house, my legs dream heavy. I stagger and fall forward, arms flailing, and I glimpse the house and the sisters at the window.

I'm face down in the snow. Flakes settle on my neck. I'll leave a crater if I'm removed, a deep scar in the shape of a fat angel. Something the size of a cat steps on my back and treads with careful paws. I play possum, while the hair at my nape is picked at. I see stars again from holding my breath. Whatever is on me is patient. It drapes itself over my shoulders like a fur collar. It whimpers, and I respond with a moan.

Then I hear my name, echoing across a mountain range. The weight on my neck pins my head in the snow. Strong adult hands pull at me, lift and slap snow from my belly and legs. Slender figures murmur encouragement, guide me up the porch steps and into the bright sudden warmth where darkness melts over me.

I wake to Estelle's smile. "You're okay," she says. "Blanche says your heart is fine. You had a panic attack from over exerting. You hyperventilated."

But I'm not in my own bed—no Brueghel on the wall— only an uncurtained window, alarmingly white. I'm on

Blanche's sofa bed. "You've got to lose a little weight, Saint Richard," my wife's sister says, and she sits beside me. I feel her hip. "That hole you left hasn't even filled in yet." A piercing whistle startles me.

"That's your hot water," Estelle says. Her eyes sparkle. "Blanche says tea would be best. I'll bet you're starving. Could you eat a muffin? I'll bring you a blueberry muffin."

"We've got to warm you up," Blanche says. She shifts closer. I let my eyes close. "Like sled dogs around a tired hunter." A hand settles on my belly, as if to tame my hunger.

"Shhh," my wife whispers in the kitchen. "Shh, now." Is she talking to me? I haven't said a word. It sounds like she's calming a pet.

"Shh," Blanche hushes. I feel her nails through the blanket. "Don't get excited. Everything's perfect."

Smooth

She expected the tattoo parlor to smell like seared flesh and hot tar, but it doesn't. It smells like hand sanitizer, and a little like nail polish remover—probably the ink. It doesn't look like anything now because she's got her eyes closed. Not everyone does lids. Almost nobody does lids. Laser, of *Laser's Tattoos and Piercings* does lids, but Jenna had to take two buses to get here. And she knew the minute she stepped onto the first bus outside her gated community that she'd forgotten her smart phone: no calls, no texts, no tweets. She might as well have forgotten one of her senses. But since it's never, ever happened before, leaving her phone behind is a kind of message, isn't it? Laser says nothing when Jenna says she's eighteen.

"Stars of David," she says. "One on each eyelid." Twenty-five dollars per lid. Duct tape covers rips in the arms of the chair she's settled into, as if customers had been tearing at them. "Won't you hit my eyeballs? I heard that you slide a spoon under." She shivers, imagining the spoon she plunged into her breakfast grapefruit cupping her naked eyeball, its handle pressed into her cheek, her lid stretched spoon-shaped.

"No spoon. I'm careful," Laser says. He's squat, but a big squat, like a giant dwarf. He's neckless, and his head is square. Before she shut her eyes, he was fiddling with his inking tool, checking its sharpness on stiff paper. The apparatus works

164

with a foot pedal, like her grandmother's sewing machine.

"Yeah," she says, "because you don't want me leaking out my viscous fluids." She imagines her cheeks wet with something like egg whites, like thick, sticky tears. "I wish I could watch."

"Should I tape 'em down? Hard to do that and tattoo 'em."

"You don't have to. What will it feel like?"

"Weird," he says. "You'll love it. Stars of David."

"Yeah. Yes," she says, and holds her breath. Laser hasn't got a single tattoo, has he? Cool. It makes him more of an artist somehow. Does he notice her lack of eyelashes? That she has no eyebrows? Can he guess that her pubes are shaved? That under her hot pink wig her head is as smooth as a beach ball? Could he guess that she's devoted to the spunk and spirit of Annabelle Hadley?

"I'm starting," Laser says.

"Okay."

"See you later," someone, a man, calls. Jenna doesn't remember anyone else having been in the parlor when she got there, and she nearly peeks. Whoever it is must have been in the back—there's a door, isn't there?

"Later," Laser says. The front entrance jangles when it opens and shuts.

There's a hum, and Jenna pats her thigh, but there's no phone. Then her lid is alive with the crawling feet of bees. On YouTube she'd seen a man's face dripping with a live-bee mask. Through the tickling she feels the push and nip of Laser's tool: the first star is being formed. Intersecting triangles will make a Star of David for each wink, double stars when she blinks. Annabelle Hadley is Jewish and probably had a bat mitzvah. Jenna's Jewish, too; her parents aren't religious, but she's been to the bar and bat mitzvah's of relatives. She imagines Annabelle Hadley's sweet voice filling the sanctuary as Annabelle chants her Torah portion. Those lucky enough to have been there must have died listening, but been reborn as something better—flowers or butterflies. Or stars. Annabelle has made two record albums, but her lovely voice drowns in guitars and synthesizers.

"Hummm—" Jenna buzzes along with the tattooing.

"Hurts?" The pressure of the tool's point lifts, and the bee dance stops.

"Un-unh."

"Then shush. Shush unless it hurts."

"I thought you'd use a spoon."

"No spoon," Laser repeats. The hum resumes. Annabelle Hadley is smooth. Slick as a seal. *Alopecia universalis*. No hair at all—that's the "universalis" part—perfect, because it's total. Annabelle's total baldness is a one in 100,000 shot, which is a sign of her blessedness. The wigs no one knows she wears are made of natural hair, grown by young women hired to grow it for her. Annabelle pays them with money from her Scaredy-Cat clothing empire and whatever she's saved from the movies she used to make. They live in a special house, these girls, but nobody knows where it is. Growing their hair long for Annabelle is their sole occupation. They're like priestesses. Once their hair is shorn, they never allow it to grow again; they shave themselves totally smooth, out of devotion to their employer. Then they move to upper floors in the special house, which is in a gated community, Jenna believes, much like hers. Jenna wishes she could give up her hair for Annabelle's wigs, but she can't. Jenna has alopecia, too.

But Jenna's alopecia isn't perfect like Annabelle's. Jenna's is "totalis," a funny word for "partial." Jenna's hair is patchy, and her mother shaved her head and fitted her with her first wig before she was five. That first wig was like a golden helmet, the wig of an aging Broadway diva, or a grandmother. Now Jenna chooses her own wigs, shocking pink and purple, and shaves herself smooth.

It's Annabelle Hadley's alopecia, not her problems with drugs and alcohol, that has kept her out of movies since she turned twenty. She'd grown tired of hiding it. Her addictions are a front. Her disease is probably the most closely guarded secret in Hollywood. Jenna might be the only one who knows. Hairlessness changes the way you see the world. You learn about hiding and intuiting.

Fifteen is paradise! Fifteen and smooth, and she'll have stars and stars and stars every time she blinks. Jenna has an idea for a tattoo of a pair of baby lips about to take her nipple. Unlike the voluptuous Annabelle Hadley, she's flat-chested. Jenna's mother and her Nana are also small-breasted women. But though a tattoo of a pair of baby lips about to take a nipple is a beautiful idea, how do you *do* it? Could you tattoo the indentation in the breast made by the baby's cheek? The tiny lips would be hovering in the air. How do you tattoo the air?

"Unh—"

"Sorry."

Jenna's eye tears—not from pain, but for Annabelle and her secret suffering.

i am the little girl of svidrigaylov's dream

This was the first tweet she read of Annabelle's, before Jenna understood. She'd loved Annabelle in *Super Siblings*, the first movie she'd ever seen, and had worshipped the young star in her last hit, *Cool Girlz*. But what was this tweeted "svidrigaylov's dream"? Jenna Google-searched, and found:

> 1. Svidrigaylov: a Russian noble in Dostoevsky's novel *Crime and Punishment*. Svidrigaylov's moral decay is illustrated by his dream of rescuing an impoverished little girl who transforms into a prostitute before his eyes.
>
> 2. *Svidrigaylov's Dream*: a film begun by director Raymond Walchuk (see *Son of Kong, Teddy*); production was terminated when Walchuk was accused of making "inappropriate sexual innuendoes" to ten-year-old costar Annabelle Hadley (see *Journals of a Princess*, *Super Siblings*, *Cool Girlz*, "Celebrity Rehab," Scaredy Cat Enterprises.) The subsequent scandal, settled out of court, effectively ended Walchuk's career and launched Hadley's.

"First one's done. Need a break?"

"Un-unh." Jenna smells blood now, faint, through the odors of sanitizer and ink.

"Okay. Keep 'em closed." Tickles and nips on her second lid—Jenna again reaches for the phone she forgot.

i am the little girl of svidrigaylov's dream

That tweet, the beginning of history, is seared like a beautiful scar onto Jenna's brain. Accompanying the movie reference Jenna found a photograph of Annabelle Hadley at ten dressed and made up as the dream prostitute. The brassy wig Annabelle wore was identical to Jenna's childhood wig! (That wig had frightened her classmates. Why else had they avoided her?) The young Annabelle's Scaredy-Cat green eyes, her lids, lashes, lips, cheeks and brows, all painted provocatively, had mesmerized Jenna. Poor Annabelle! Had she been bald already? Or had the trauma of playing a prostitute at ten, of suffering the director's inappropriate advances, shocked her system into rejecting her hair? Jenna has studied Annabelle's subsequent films; she has poured over celebrity shot after celebrity shot. Everything is a wig! Jenna knows: swathed in borrowed hair, Annabelle Hadley mourns her stolen childhood.

Late afternoon is the prickliest time for Jenna, and sitting in Laser's warm chair is nearly unbearable—so many hours after she'd risen at five a.m. to complete her first shaving. Before bed she'll shave again, every square inch of skin, polish herself with creams, and luxuriate in the coolness of her sheets. And each morning, dark, bristly islands will have re-surfaced.

There would be new tweets from Annabelle if Jenna

hadn't forgotten her phone. The messages are a disguise, nonsense about "clubbin" and "parteez," each tweet like a Band-Aid strip covering a wound. Jenna peels away the Band-Aids and translates the tweets into feelings: Annabelle needs something to nurture. A baby would make up for the childhood she's lost.

"You pluck out your eyelashes?"

Jenna doesn't answer.

"Because some people can't grow them." Laser's monotone doesn't harmonize with the buzz tracking across her lid. "Some people don't have hair anywhere," he says. Jenna tenses. There's something beneath Laser's words. She'd told him she was eighteen and would have forged a document to prove it. Does he suspect something about her or Annabelle? A wave rises and falls inside and a blush warms her cheeks. This morning she'd drawn her brows to match the arches over the green eyes of Annabelle's Scaredy-Cat logo. (The tops were for tweens, and Jenna wouldn't dare wear them. But seeing Annabelle's eyes branding the chests of little girls never fails to steal her breath.) Did boys hurry home to their locked bedrooms after school, dreaming of her and Annabelle's eyebrows?

"Your parents going to like 'em? They know you're here?" Laser asks while he works. "They going to like you starry-eyed?"

"They'll be surprised. What's not to love?" Her mother rolls her eyes at Jenna's pink and purple wigs, as if to say, "I was young once." Her father never seems to notice them. The stars will be a declaration. The stars are a way to see and be seen, and with them she'll rise to the heavens with Annabelle Hadley.

Before Annabelle, Jenna pulled clumps of hair from her Barbies and hid the dolls. After intuiting Annabelle's perfect alopecia, she resurrected them, pulled out the rest of their hair, and moved the bald Barbies into her box of treasures. She could ask Laser: *Do you do invisible tattoos?*

Jenna feels a cool blot on the first tattooed lid. There's a whiff of disinfectant.

"That's a pad," Laser says. "To stop the bleeding. Almost done. Ready?"

"Un-hunh."

Jenna can't remember the interior of the tattoo parlor. Did the walls display strange shapes, symbols, and creatures? Elaborately lettered slogans meant to last a lifetime? She's forgotten the shop's exterior, too, and its address. It would have been in her smart phone. There'd been bus rides through deteriorating neighborhoods. She might as well be deep in a forest, inside the witch's house with Hansel and Gretel, the house made of candy and cookies; she'd left nothing to mark her trail home. She sees footprints on midnight pavement shining under ultra-violet streetlamps. Above, countless six-pointed stars twinkle in a deep purple sky. She squirms, and the buzz, tickle, and nip stop. "Whoa!"

"Sorry." If she asked, would Laser tattoo a drop of milk, two drops, leaking from her nipple onto her breast—like milky tears? How much would that cost? But the drops of milk might look like blood. A moist weight compresses her second lid.

"Okay," Laser says. "Just sit for a couple of minutes."

"Done?"

"Done."

"I want to see."

"Wait."

Laser's voice is very close and far away at the same time. She smells smoke. He's smoking while they wait. She wouldn't smoke, but she's not against it. Annabelle Hadley smokes.

"Do you know Annabelle Hadley?" she asks. "You know who she is, right?"

"The rehab slut?" Jenna's whole body frowns, but then there's a glow like the illuminated footprints she'd envisioned outside the parlor. She sees beneath Laser's words: *She's beautiful*, he means! What does he look like—no tattoos? a face like a bull's?

"You're not really eighteen."

"Next month. Sorry I lied." Fifteen must be the legal age of something.

"You live a long way from here, right? You needed directions when you called." Smoke wafts into Jenna's face. Her eyelids sting under the pads. "You need a ride?"

"I guess. Can I see what I look like?"

"In a second. You live in the hills, right?"

"Way out. In a gated community. In a cul de sac." She knows so little about her own neighborhood. Gated. And not half a mile from hers, another gated community. Maybe Annabelle Hadley's girls, the ones who supply her hair, live there. Or maybe they live on Jenna's block, safe behind her neighborhood's gate.

"I'll drive you. Let's get these off."

The pressure on her lids lifts, like tiny birds taking flight. Jenna squints. Laser has turned off the work light. The parlor swims in shadows. She exercises her lids as if they're the drying wings of a new butterfly.

"Here." Laser hands her a mirror. Why had she thought he wasn't tattooed? The backs of his hands, his thick arms, even his neck are nearly black with arabesques, figures, and obscure lettering. But his face is square and flat, as if it had been squashed into a large glass cube. A gold ring pierces his septum and hangs over his upper lip. The hair he's pulled back into a ponytail is threaded with silver. His eyes are small and black, and his teeth are very white, even though he smokes.

"Crazy wig," he says as Jenna stares at her new self. At first she can't see the change—the light is dim, and her lids retract like a baby doll's. She closes one eye, and there it is! A beautiful star, etched in thin lines of ink and blood. She switches eyes—the second star is as beautiful as the first. She flutters her lashless lids, and, the stars twinkle—perfect under Annabelle Hadley's Scaredy-Cat brows. She giggles, and bats her stars at Laser, who nods and flashes his teeth. He looks at her closely, admiring his work. He examines her so thoroughly, she feels him inside of her.

"I'm an artist," he says.

Jenna remembers the bills folded in the pocket where her phone should be and tugs them out. "Thanks," she says, and holds the money toward Laser, half-expecting him to refuse it. But he doesn't; the bills disappear into his tattooed hand.

He steps back and takes in all of her.

"Nice eyes. Crazy wig. It's gonna be dark. I'll take you home now."

"Okay. Thanks." Jenna stands for the first time in an hour. Figuring out the bus would have been a drag, though she could have showed off her stars. Her legs are weak. Laser takes her arm; his fingers test the firmness of her tricep. His touch is as gentle as the pressure of his tattooing tool had been on her eyes—she feels like one of those fancy Easter eggs.

"Annabelle Hadley," he snorts. "Loser."

Jenna is charmed by what she knows lies beneath his words.

"Wait," Laser says. His face is inches from hers. His attention is on her stars. "You're still bleeding. Got to put the pads back on." Jenna has an urge to wipe the oil glistening on his flat nose with a sterile towelette.

She waits, gripping the frame of the door she's been led to, as Laser dabs at each of her eyes. It stings. She smells antibiotic cream and tobacco on the fingers that swab her lids and lay fresh gauze over them. Tape adheres to her forehead and cheeks. She worries—silly, she knows, after tattooing—about the instant of pain when the tape is stripped. And won't her Annabelle Hadley eyebrows be marred?

"I've got to lock up. Don't want to get robbed," Laser says, and leaves her, sightless, at the door that surely leads through a back room to an alley where his car, maybe a pickup truck, awaits. She hears the grating and clanging of metal—Laser is dragging the steel barriers across his shop front. The parlor feels empty and frigid. If she could see, her breath would be visible. She remembers there'd been someone in the shop when she'd arrived, someone who left after she closed her eyes. Just a voice. Maybe it was somebody clean, the tattoo-less figure she'd confused with Laser. It's nice to think of Laser having a friend.

He's back. Jenna anticipates his touch; his cigarette breath warms her face. She hears a deep sigh. If this were a fairy tale, Laser would be devoted to her service. She might be a distressed damsel—she'd lost the royal infant the queen had placed in her care! Together, she and her protector must find a child to replace the missing baby. They could look in one of the gated communities, where there are plenty of children. Jenna sees herself elevating a fresh, cooing, squirming infant before Queen Annabelle Hadley. Even if Annabelle guesses the child isn't her own, nobody will mind. Behind Jenna, Laser would be kneeling with his square head bowed.

"Ready?" Laser asks, as if he knows what Jenna is imagining and has the story by heart. She paws the air for him. What will he say when she reveals her smoothness?

Fiji Mermaid

Fiji smiled and nodded, but rolled her eyes behind her dark glasses at her dinner date's joke. "'Trusting Cripples,'" he'd called the service that had matched them. The actual name was "Trusting Couples, Inc.," and the agency specialized in bringing together those with minor, non-disfiguring or dangerous physical, emotional, or psychological challenges. Fiji had profiled herself as an "achromat"—someone not only acutely sensitive to light, but also completely colorblind. "My spectrum covers all the shades of gray between black and white," she'd noted.

"This corner dark enough for you?" Dem, her date asked. Dem, short for Demetrius. "They called me 'Demmy' when I was a kid," he'd said after they'd settled at their table. *Dem . . . Demmy*, Fiji thought—he sounded like one of her many "speech impediment" dates—through "Trusting Couples" she'd met and slept with stutterers, lispers ("th-" and "slushy"), and "Elmer Fudders." Dem's speech was fine, but his profile for "Trusting Couples" listed two flaws: a "compromised heart" and a "distinctive and private pattern of birthmarks."

Because "Trusting Couples" clients tended to be insecure perfectionists who both over-estimated and over-compensated for their often undetectable defects, they were, on the surface, almost always more attractive and accomplished than the "unmarried" general public. The agency protected its members from outsiders seeking to prey on their good looks, healthy bank accounts, and vulnerability by requiring that all "conditions" be documented. Fiji, for her part, had sat through an eye exam, shrugging away as an optometrist pointed around a color wheel.

Except for her cumbersome dark glasses, Fiji knew that she and Dem were both magazine-ad beautiful: slim, toned, and cleft-chinned. His hair was a mass of fair curls, while hers cascaded to her shoulders with the sheen of black satin. They were a couple that turned the heads of the less imperfect.

"You're my first 'colorblind,'" Dem smiled. His teeth were white and even.

"I think I'm the only achromat in the system," Fiji said. "I've had 'bad hearts' before." She chose not to mention the "distinctive and private" birthmarks.

"'Achromat,'" her date nodded. "When I first saw that on your profile I read it as 'acro-*bat*.' I couldn't figure out how that was a condition. I thought maybe you needed to hang upside down, like a bat. 'Acro-bat'—that's a double pun, right? Now I can't get 'gymnast' out of my head when I look at you. All I see is flexibility. Like *Cirque de Soleil*."

An achromat from birth. This was the identity Fiji had slipped into years earlier like a second skin—the lie that had gained her access to the handsome, needy "Trusting Couples" men to whom she was now addicted.

Like most lies, Fiji's had its roots in a truth: her discovery in college that she was red-green colorblind. One night, while flipping through her roommate's physiology textbook, she'd stopped at what she thought were pictures of abstract paintings. Each was composed of colorful bubbles: they were Ishihara tests for colorblindness. Fiji saw nothing in the bubbles when she should have seen digits, like her roommate, who spit out numbers as she flipped the pages: "74, 19, 41— you don't see them?"

Fiji had been dismayed to learn that there was something wrong with the stunning green eyes her mother had told her would "break boys' hearts." "Mine did," Mom had said, not long before she died. She'd lain in her hospital bed, her head on a thin pillow, and fluttered purple lids as if ashes had been blown into her special eyes. Pink lines threaded their whites, and their irises were the color of dying grass.

Those faded eyes haunted Fiji—and so did the invisible Ishihara digits. What else might be lurking in the pretty bubbles that she couldn't see? The night she'd discovered her deficiency, she'd stared at the test pictures until she was bleary-eyed. Nothing. And then, as her eyes were about to shut from exhaustion—an epiphany: *Colors were a prison!*

Hadn't she heard something like that about words? That naming an abstraction—an idea, a feeling, a passion— confined it? A named feeling was like a bird shot in mid-flight: it might drop within reach, but the price of accessibility was death. Fiji's red-green limitation was a gift: Ishihara tests would forever remain oceans of infinite possibility.

Relieved and energized, Fiji kept turning pages. Each bubble-field, void of numbers, thrilled her now—she imagined herself swimming through a Macdonald's Playland pit full of bright plastic balls. And she bumped into a miracle! *ACHROMATOPSIA.* The condition leaped out from the very first paragraph following the Ishihara tests. *Complete colorblindness!* In the wink of an eye, Fiji envisioned her future—and it was colorless. Could there be a more original and unfettered way to see?

Because the rest of the world was color-drunk, it had taken Fiji years to transform herself into a practicing achromat. She'd needed to think colorlessly, and had removed pigments from her environment where she could: her dark glasses cloaked the world in shadows; she decorated her apartment in black and white, and eliminated colors from her wardrobe; she adjusted the filters on her television and computer monitors so their screens mimicked an achromat's world.

When Fiji's employers accommodated her demand for a darkened environment by allowing her to work at home, she found herself marooned on her very own achromatopsic island— the "original and unfettered" lifestyle of her own invention. But often, late at night, she'd remove her dark glasses and gaze at her green eyes in the bathroom mirror. *Eyes to break boys' hearts,* her mother had called them. Then she'd lie in bed, feeling her eyes glow like emeralds behind her closed lids, and she'd touch herself, while reds and blues and yellows streamed around and through her.

❧

By the second bottle of wine, both Fiji and Dem had become confessional.

179

"I have a cat named Yin," Fiji said. "I named her Yin-Yang at first because she's black and white—unless they lied to me at the animal shelter. But really, she's only got one little white spot around one eye. Mostly, she's black. She's just a Yin."

Their conversation shifted easily from topic to topic. Each knew the other's job from their "Trusting Couples" profiles: Dem worked in "computer services"; Fiji, fluent in Russian, translated foreign correspondence for a pharmaceutical company. Dem brought up the subject of "lying."

"So, most of us 'Trusting Couples' members started out as liars, don't you think, before we got honest enough to confess our flaws? I could hide what I didn't like about myself in my made-up stories. I used to tell people I was a sitcom baby—I'd pick an old TV show from twenty years ago—*Family Matters* or *Who's the Boss?* or something, and I'd say to a date, 'remember the episode when there was a scene with a neighbor's baby? Well, that was me!' How could they check?" Fiji caught the sparkle of Dem's eyes through her dark glasses an instant before he closed them to take a swallow of wine. He put his glass down, and looked up, grinning.

"What about you? I'll bet your closet's full of old lies. How about your name—'Fiji'?" One sweat-darkened curl was pasted to Dem's forehead. "That's an island-name, not a person-name. You're hiding something, right?"

Fiji, slightly drunk, searched for the beat of Dem's "compromised" heart in his flushed cheeks. She ran her fingers through her hair, snagged a nail, and waved her hand to free it. She adjusted her glasses, tapping the lenses, confident in their opacity, and pointed the finger with the bad nail at her date, who held up his hands.

"Don't shoot, Masked Man!" he laughed.

"Fi-ji—" she purred. She made a V with her fingers. "Actually, there're two lies. My given name is Sarah. I used to tell people in my Russian classes in college that I was adopted from mother-Russia when I was a baby. That's lie number one. Then I told them that I was so sad when my adoptive mother died the year before I graduated, I changed my name—here's how it went: 'Sarah' sounds like 'sorrow', which means the same thing as 'grief,' which, if you say it backwards—because I swore to myself I'd be the opposite of sad—it comes out something like 'Fiji.' That's lie number two."

"Whoa—" Dem scribbled with his finger on the tablecloth. "'Fiji' isn't anything like 'grief' backwards!"

"Enough like. Not exactly. Besides—it's a lie, as I said—it's lie number two."

"So you're not a Russian orphan."

"No, but my mother did die before I graduated."

"I'm sorry."

"It's okay. I never knew my father—I've learned to depend on myself. So, for all intents and purposes, now I *am* an orphan who *speaks* Russian, at least."

"And what about 'Fiji'?"

Fiji paused. Knowing how much to share with a "Trusting Couples" date was always an issue.

"I made 'Fiji' up for myself when I moved to the city to work," she said. "I named myself after the island. I've never been to a tropical island, but I like the idea of them. The ocean, sunsets, blooming flowers—they're a challenge to the way I see things. I've covered my walls with black and white pictures of Pacific islands. They give my imagination a workout, just like when I read about colors in books—I have to figure out how to visualize them. How's my *red*-gray different from my *blue*-gray and *yellow*-gray, and so on. And poetry? 'My love is like a red, red rose?' What's *red*? My spectrum is white-gray-black. That's *my* rainbow. My imagination doesn't work like yours or anybody else who's got colors. We can't see the world the same way."

"Why are your island pictures in black and white? Wouldn't they look that way to you anyway?"

Fiji nibbled her lip. "A color-free world can be a beautiful place," she said, ignoring the questions. "That's the way an achromat learns to think." She felt Dem's eyes on her face as if they were fingers. Of course he couldn't breach her glasses. It would be up to her when and where to reveal the secret of her beautiful green eyes. Surely he knew it was bad first-date form to probe a "Trusting Couple" match on the nature of an imperfection. She would never ask about his heart trouble or his "distinctive" birthmarks. It was enough that these left him insecure enough to seek empathy in a "Trusting Couples" partner.

❧

"Trusting Couples, Inc." had been a godsend. Fiji's need for sex—and for the taste of color she'd come to associate with it—now dominated her life. Her matches, she knew, expected her to squint like a mole when she removed her glasses, or ogle them with bug-eyes she got from straining to see colors. They needed her flaw to match their lisps or left-ear-deafness, their gluten allergies or eczema-flaked elbows. But the moment Fiji shed her glasses, not long after she'd joined her dates in bed, and they measured their inadequacies against her startling eyes, they were lost. Fiji used them up and tossed them away. So far, there had been no second dates.

Then, each morning after her night's partner scurried out of her apartment, freshly humiliated by his twitching, scratching, or stuttering, Fiji would leave her bed and visit the roll-top desk in her walk-in closet. Black Yin would curl on her lap or bat at the hem of her robe while she withdrew her treasures from hidden drawers and cubbies: a purple, teardrop-shaped Christmas ornament; a square of wrapping paper as blue as the sky she never allowed herself to see; a postcard of Van Gogh's "Sunflower"; a kaleidoscope—its shifting splendor stole her breath.

Having indulged her thirst for color, Fiji next flipped through a thin pad she called her "miracle book"— her collection of Ishihara tests. Colored bubbles swam across every page, but revealed nothing—a sobering pleasure. After sex, after her "color fix," there was nothing to expect but the "original and unfettered" reality she had created for herself. Fiji would replace her treasures, don her glasses, and re-enter her achromatopsic world.

❧

"I thought maybe you took your name from the Fiji

Mermaid," Dem said, eyes bright. "That would make sense, don't you think?"

"What's the 'Fiji Mermaid'?" Fiji pictured Disney's Ariel—did *she* have green eyes? She couldn't remember.

"P.T. Barnum exhibited it at his circus sideshow. Along with the midgets and pinheads and the bearded lady. He'd stitched the head and body of a little mummified monkey to the tail of a fish, and claimed it was a real mermaid. I've seen pictures of the nasty little thing! The head is shriveled, and it's got deep, empty eye sockets—"

"Stop!" Fiji waved her hand, frowning with disgust. What she was imagining had to be even worse than the real mermaid. "You think I'd name myself after something from a freakshow?"

Dem shrugged, not quite apologetically. "I thought, since we were talking about lying, and, since the Fiji Mermaid was a hoax . . ." He paused. "I'm sorry," he half-smiled—he *was* handsome, Fiji couldn't help note, above average even for a "Trusting Couples" match. "I guess it doesn't make any sense. Fiji Mermaid." He shook his head. "Maybe I'm just talking about myself."

"Let's change the subject," Fiji suggested. "What else did *you* lie about besides being a sitcom baby?"

⤌

Fiji definitely had too much to drink. On the cab ride back to her apartment, she found herself dizzied by Dem's stale cologne and the onions on his breath as he leaned against her, pointing through her window at everything that glowed in the city night. Clearly tipsy himself, he was trying to teach Fiji what "color" was, in spite of "Trusting Couples" decorum.

"What's that?" he asked about the traffic light they waited at.

"Red," Fiji said. "But that's easy—we're stopped, and I know red is on top."

"Okay—what about those lights around the window of that restaurant—*Le Bon Appetit*—the little ones that look like candles—the blue ones—oops!"

"Blue!" Fiji giggled. Dem would want to kiss her soon. What imperfections qualified him for "Trusting Couples" again? Heart trouble—and strange, "private" birthmarks? Fiji pictured an army of black ants circling a bloated penis. She belched, tasting stale wine and salmon, excused herself, and pressed her cheek against the cool glass beside her.

Dem peered out the rear window. "What color's the Empire State Building?" Fiji craned her neck for a look and let her head fall on his shoulder. The skyscraper's red-lit top burned through her dark glasses.

"Also blue," she sighed.

"Correct! Amazing—*who* doesn't see her colors—or are you just a lucky guesser?"

So Dem was toying with her—let him. When she got him in bed, when he saw her eyes, he'd see who was toying with whom. Fiji played along. "I *sense* the colors," she said. They passed a *Saks Fifth Avenue* window display—headless mannequins posed in a violet haze. "That display window's lit in yellow," she declared.

"Ennnh!" Dem buzzed. "Nope! It's green. Green as

envy—a dangerous, dangerous color!"

"Yellowish-green, maybe?" Fiji feigned innocence—Dem was such a fool!

"Nope—as green as the White House lawn on Easter Sunday." Suddenly, his gaze dropped to Fiji. Could he see himself in her glasses, or was the cab too dark? "What am I doing?" he asked. "Listen—I'm sorry."

"You mean the window *was* yellow?"

"No, it was green. But I shouldn't be making fun. It's against the rules. It's not nice." Dem snuggled closer to her and lifted an arm over her shoulder. "Forgive me, little acrobat?"

"Achro-*mat*," Fiji corrected. Her head had cleared—she was alert and turned on. If Dem wanted to kiss her, she was ready.

✌

They kissed in the cab and in the elevator on the way up to Fiji's apartment. At her door, Dem pressed into her back while she dug in her bag for her key. Inside, she touched a wall switch, and a lamp in the corner of the living room flared weakly, like a dying ember.

"I keep it dark. Sorry." A shadow darted from behind the sofa and ran down the hall. "Yin!" Fiji called. "That's my little Yin."

"But you said you were 'Yang-less,' right?" Dem looked around the room, and Fiji followed the whites of his eyes.

"Yep," she said. "Yin's enough. I wonder if being Yang-less affects my balance. Something to drink?"

Dem touched her shoulder and she pivoted to him, lifting a hand to his cheek. He glared down at her—he was definitely trying to penetrate her glasses. Of course he wondered what secrets they hid. He declined the drink offer.

"Here's one of my islands," Fiji said, gesturing at a framed photograph of a palm tree on a beach.

"I remember about them—all of your pictures are black and white."

Safe at home, Fiji found an explanation: "They give my visitors a glimpse of my world."

߷

While Dem waited for her on the bed, Fiji stepped into her bathroom, where she removed her blouse, skirt, and underwear and tugged on a thigh-length kimono. She looked in the mirror, tossed her hair, and, for the first time in hours, lifted off her glasses. Her eyes winced from the brightness after being hidden all day. But look how they expanded like fresh butterfly wings! Aroused by the twin stabs of green, Fiji licked her lips. How would Dem handle the revelation? Like all the others, of course. But when she replaced her glasses, the sudden darkness stalled her. She steadied herself and caught her shadowed reflection. She shivered. *Fiji Mermaid*, the blank eyes in the mirror proclaimed: *Liar.* She shut the bathroom light. No mirror. No reflection. *Not a lie,* Fiji corrected—*a choice.*

Dem lay naked, half-propped against a pillow. Fiji measured him from the doorway with a long look. She dimmed the track lights above her headboard—just a bit— because he would expect her to. They'd help highlight her eyes when the time came. She mounted the bed and crept toward him on all fours, as her cat Yin might have done. She kissed him. Was he still trying to see through her glasses? *Wait*, she thought, *not yet, Big Fish.* She pushed herself back and kissed his hairless chest. *Heart trouble.* Would there be a scar? Nothing but wisps of hair. She licked one of his nipples, then the other, and his chest rose and fell with his sigh. *And the birthmarks?* She lowered herself further, looking up at him with a pouty smile.

"Mm-hmm," he murmured, grinning. "'Trusting Couples.'"

"*Trysting* couples," Fiji said. "Shh." Her face hovered over his waist. *Trysting cripple*, she thought, *you're mine!*

And there were Dem's birthmarks, spread from hip to hip, a constellation of them above and below the cock stiffening in her hand. Hundreds of black dots swarmed across his torso, separating it from his legs like an embroidered belt. Fiji blinked—her dark lenses obscured what might have been a pattern—the marks were like nothing she'd ever seen. She'd study them quickly when she freed her eyes.

But her glasses stayed on. "Kiss!" Dem commanded, and Fiji dipped to the marks like a thirsty doe. She kissed. His skin tasted like a spice she couldn't place, and her eyes closed. She saw the colors of her secret treasures, and she felt them, too—Van Gogh's sunflower yellow, the ornament's purple, the wrapping paper's blue—it was as if she were tumbling inside her kaleidoscope. A shadow flitted—Fiji gasped, remembering her intent. Lips still on flesh, she fumbled at her face.

"No—" the voice above her growled, and she froze. "Leave them on!" Fiji steadied the glasses and peeked upward, but couldn't see past the frames. "Keep them on!" Dem repeated. And she complied, because there seemed no other choice. His hand—had Fiji known it was so huge?—gripped her skull, and she was sure he felt the colors exploding in her head. Had her tongue smeared one of the marks? She couldn't tell. She might have tasted ink.

❧

Fiji, spent, sore in unaccustomed places, woke to painful sunlight. Hours earlier, in the gray pre-dawn, she'd been aware of Dem's body close to hers. But now the sun—it had been years since she'd lifted her bedroom shades. Blood tingled in her cheeks as she recalled the evening's progress—had Dem really POV-ed her with his smartphone? She pawed her night table for her dark glasses, but couldn't find them. Then she realized she was alone.

"Dem?" She sat up and repeated his name. She rose, snatched the kimono from the floor, and yanked it on. She padded on bare feet into the living room—the shades were lifted there, too, and blades of light glanced from the pictures on the walls. Across the bright room Fiji made out Yin, a humped silhouette on the back of the sofa. "Dem?" she called again, but the bathroom and kitchen were empty.

Her limbs like lead, her head as empty as a papier-mache globe, Fiji slouched back to her bedroom, where she jerked down the shades and sank onto her bed. The night's sex wafted from her sheets. Her glasses had to be somewhere in

189

the tangles—soon she'd pat them out. After a few moments, her gaze wandered to her closet—and she groaned. Her desk was open, its top rolled back. Colors spilled across it—her treasures had been exposed! With a cry she scrambled from her bed and rushed to them.

Her purple teardrop ornament, the sunflower postcard, the sky blue wrapping paper, the kaleidoscope—all had been removed from their cubbyholes and left on the desk's writing surface. And there were her dark glasses, set before the eyepiece of the kaleidoscope, as if they were peering into it. And her pad of Ishihara tests—a business card stuck from it, which Fiji withdrew. "Demetrius Witkowski," it read, "Quality Control Investigator, Trusting Couples, Inc." The telephone number was underlined.

Fiji opened the tablet and snorted. Numbers! 29...58...84. She flipped and flipped—digits rose from each test like hungry fish: 86...19...4...! By the last page she'd solved the miracle—the numbers had been drawn in with a highlighter. She clutched the collection to her chest, took a deep breath, then held it out at arm's length as if she were looking in a hand mirror. Dare she trust the digits? Couldn't Dem have written them over random bubbles, like some kind of cruel graffiti? Lying, like he did with the colors during the cab ride.

Fiji re-examined the card: "Quality Control Investigator." So she'd been the subject of an investigation—but hadn't *her* trust been violated? Maybe she *had* humiliated her "Trusting Couples" matches with her misrepresented eyes, but Dem's birthmarks were obviously faked, and without a doubt he had a perfectly healthy heart. Still, why had he underlined his phone number? Fiji turned the card over and found two words she'd missed, printed in green: *FIJI MERMAID*. That hideous, stitched-together hoax! What had Dem meant? Had he written that as an indictment? A signature? Yet it felt like . . . a Valentine.

"Dem!" Fiji whimpered, "Demmy..." If she called his number, what did she stand to lose?

Lactophilia

Dahlia attended the exhibit, "The Scandalous Family," because her artist friend had contributed an installation celebrating her surrogate pregnancy. As she stood with Kirkland before his work, the casting agent peeked at her cell phone—though the due date was a week away, Dahlia's doctor had hinted that the young woman contracted to bear her child had appeared "suspiciously ripe" at her last examination; Dahlia might become a mother at any moment.

Half of Kirkland's installation was a black and white film displayed on a gallery wall: a pair of silhouettes set on railroad tracks in a desert. The first shadow figure crouched on all fours like a dog. The second figure—long-legged and spike heeled, Barbie-breasted and obviously pregnant—towered over the first and brandished a whip. Chains cuffed both figures to the rails.

The scene was projected from the headlamp of a perambulator-sized locomotive standing on steel tracks that ran across the gallery's hardwood floor and joined the rails in the film. A small cradle hung from the locomotive's headlamp, and in it a baby doll, hooded in black and swaddled in a leather diaper, rocked. The silhouettes on the tracks ignored the locomotive bearing down on them. Occasionally, the pregnant dominatrix dipped forward, threatening her partner with her whip, breasts, and belly.

Dahlia's white wine warmed in its plastic cup, while

Kirkland warned patrons passing between the locomotive and the projection to "Mind the tracks."

"I can't make up my mind," he said. "Am I part of the installation? I could punch tickets like a conductor."

Kirkland called his piece "Madonna of the Whip." He'd fussed mildly when Dahlia had chosen the sperm of an anonymous donor over his for the *in vitro* fertilization of her eggs, but he'd understood. "Who would play genetic Russian Roulette with a fully loaded gun?" he'd sighed, acknowledging his physical deficiencies. And Dahlia had scoured the donor-catalogue, eventually settling on the sperm of a blond, blue-eyed, rugby-playing, Shakespeare-loving medical student. The life she was casting didn't call for a father with paternity rights.

Kirkland admired his work before turning to Dahlia. "The drama of the American family," he said. "Look in the mirror." But Dahlia didn't see herself in the installation. Yes, a baby bore down on her immediate future, but the dominatrix couldn't be her—she wasn't pregnant with anything. And who was being whipped? Dahlia sneaked another look at her phone. No messages.

"Careful—" Kirkland touched the upper arm of a young woman wearing glasses who stumbled over the tracks, then held out his palm. "Ticket, please."

The woman paused to take in the artist, Dahlia, and the installation. Her shadow blotted the figures on the wall into a Rorschach until Kirkland moved her out of the locomotive's beam. After frowning at the silhouettes, she stabbed a finger across the gallery. "Those are mine."

"Lovely," Kirkland said, squinting. Dahlia followed her friend's gaze, imitating his wince as if narrowed lids were the secret to understanding art, and saw a set of four paintings. All featured flesh-pink, brown-nippled globes. Dozens of pink melons were arrayed in a leafy field in one. Nippled balls dangled amid tinsel and lights from a Christmas tree in another. In a third the pink balls lined a subway bench like plump, nude commuters. In the last and largest, a fleshy globe had been stretched flat into a map of the world, the oceans a darker pink than the land. The world map's nipple rose like a huge chocolate kiss in the center of North America's Continental Divide.

Kirkland nodded. "'Motherhood.' Same as mine. But not as subtle."

The young woman shook her head so hard her glasses shifted and her large breasts swung. Two spots darkened the white fabric of her T-shirt. Were these spots—they looked damp—part of the exhibit?

"Subtlety is dead and buried," she said. "We've cycled back to sincerity." She caught Dahlia staring at her shirt. "I'm padless, today. Did you know most primates can lactate without pregnancy? Also lemurs and dwarf mongooses."

⁊

Later, Dahlia and Kirkwood took their new acquaintance, Lizzie, for coffee. After a trip to the restroom, Lizzie opened her backpack and showed Dahlia a plastic breast pump and a Tupperware container of freshly expressed milk.

"I donate to the milk bank," she said, sipping her latte.

Lizzie explained that she'd just ended a long relationship. "When things started, it was all about sex. All about my breasts, mostly—he'd have squeezed, licked, and sucked for twenty-four hours a day, if he hadn't had to go to work. And I'd have let him. But then they swelled. My nipples enlarged. One night, he drew milk, and it shocked the hell out of us. He smacked his lips and wanted to nurse. I cried. I had to be pregnant, right? But tests said no. According to the doctors, I have super excitable hormones. Pretty unusual, but not unheard of. For a while—for just a very little while— my boyfriend and I both got into it. Lactophilia. It's a fetish thing—there are chat rooms. People have 'adult nursing relationships.' But I got sick of it—I'd wake up in the middle of the night short of breath from the weight of his head on my chest and the sound of him slurping. He wanted to get married. But who wants to marry a giant infant? He'd have fought our babies for his fix. Anyway, I cut him off, weaned him cold turkey, and now he's gone."

Lizzie paused and stretched, pushing her chest with the half-dollar stains toward Dahlia. "I haven't let myself dry up," she said. "It's not sexual anymore, but I *like* lactating."

"It's a mothering instinct," Kirkland said.

"Maybe. But I'm not longing for a baby. What I feel is a kind of overwhelming *generosity*. That's why I donate. It's too bad milk banks don't pay, like the blood places used to. I can't make my rent by myself."

"So you need a way to keep yourself in brushes and paint . . ." Kirkland turned to Dahlia. "She's ripe and ready, kiddo," he said, then leaned back and considered the two women. "I think you two are a lot closer to believing in God than you were when you woke up this morning."

"Who doesn't believe in God?" Lizzie asked.

Kirkland's eyelids dropped. "Those who prefer fairy tales."

Dahlia may not have understood art, but casting was her business, and Kirkland had identified a match that seemed pre-ordained. A deal was struck: Lizzie accepted a position as Dahlia's fulltime nanny and wet nurse. The following week, Robbie was born and surrendered by the surrogate. New momma Dahlia brought her son home to his wardrobe of colorful onesies, his designer nursery, and his endless supply of mother's milk.

∞

At eleven a.m., Brahms' Lullaby lit Dahlia's cell phone, as it had every day for three months since she'd returned to work after Robbie's birth. It would be Lizzie, with a report on the baby's morning. Dahlia always picked up, unless occupied with a casting obligation—a meeting with a producer, a director, a hopeful performer, or a stage mother. Her niche agency represented three groups, exclusively: Asians, who'd been hot lately; "working mother" types, for which Dahlia saw herself as the prototype—she'd wink at her slim, business-suited reflection in boutique windows and mirrored restaurant lobbies; and, finally, children with "a special difference." When Lizzie called, Dahlia was sorting through portfolios from this last group in preparation for a lunch meeting with a new producer.

She let the melody play through a second time and studied

the picture the phone displayed: fuzz-headed Robbie in his red pj's, a milky bubble on his lips, snuggling in Lizzie's white arms. But Dahlia didn't pick up—lately she'd been re-thinking the eleven o'clock arrangement. Routine sapped the joy out of things, potentially. And restraint could teach valuable lessons. Better that she be less regular in doling out her affection.

The ringtone cut out after the third *Lul-la-byyyy*, and the final note hung over Dahlia's desk. She bowed back to the pile of portfolios culled from her list of "different" child clients: brave, beautiful little boys and girls in wheelchairs, on crutches, or angelically bald-headed, each indispensible in his or her own way for background scenes in commercials demanding diversity. Even these youngsters had their ambitious stage mothers.

Dahlia's assistant buzzed in word of a surprise arrival— Shawn Anderson, the new client she was scheduled to meet for lunch to present her shortlist of "specials." Before she knew it, the squat stranger had pushed into her office, dropped into a chair, and humped it up to Dahlia's desk. He ignored her offered hand.

"Can't do lunch," Shawn Anderson said. His leather jacket cloaked his right shoulder—purple fingertips emerged from the ace bandage wrapping his slung arm. "Racquetball. I just got out of the emergency room. I've got to see an osteopath— my shoulder's probably dislocated." The portfolios scattered across Dahlia's desk caught his eye, and he tilted his head for a better view. "I need one of your babies." Then he saw Dahlia's phone, frowned, and hunched forward. "There," he said, jabbing at the picture of Robbie. "That one's perfect."

It shouldn't have taken Dahlia as long as it did to explain that the baby on her phone wasn't available, wasn't a "child of difference," was, in fact, Dahlia's own "perfectly healthy, perfectly normal, non-show business little boy." She shivered a little—was it pride?—as she held the phone under Shawn Anderson's chin and scrolled through picture after picture.

"Here's Robbie nursing," Dahlia said. "That's not me, that's Lizzie. She's Robbie's wet nurse. That's him in his crib. He's looking at his mobile. I think he's smiling. Here he is on Lizzie's lap. She's reading to him. It's a book about rainbows or something. But see—there's nothing the matter with him. He's perfectly normal. Better than normal—he's a darling. I think he's cute enough to cast as a 'non-different'—if this was that kind of agency and I was that kind of mother. For diaper ads and baby food commercials."

Shawn Anderson's snort startled Dahlia. He sat back. "Whatever you say. You're the expert. So what else do you have?"

Dahlia pulled the portfolio of a lovely five-year-old girl with platinum curls, porcelain skin, and rosebud lips. The child's photos emphasized her thick glasses and hearing aid. "She's got experience," Dahlia said, and listed the child's sitcom and commercial appearances.

"Not exactly what I had in mind." Shawn Anderson grimaced—his aching shoulder? "I want a *baby*. I've got little girls."

Dahlia shook her head. "Infants of the kind you're looking for are hard to find."

"But you don't get what I'm envisioning. It's supposed to be an extended family. It's for *life insurance*. I need a baby of a certain kind, I don't know, hooked up to something, maybe in a special stroller; the others—sisters, brothers, parents, grandparents group around him—then the camera shows them from above, and we see that the baby is the bull's eye of a gigantic target." Shawn Anderson bit his lower lip. He needed a shave and his hair was a mess. "A little deaf girl," he sighed. "Well, if that's all you've got—" He tapped the blonde child's glossy. "Let's try this one."

Dahlia called the girl's mother, muffling the woman's exclamations with her hand as she passed the phone to Shawn Anderson. He confirmed the offer, clarified a few details, and ended the connection.

"Sorry about lunch," he said. "Another time." He stared at the picture of Robbie glowing in his palm.

"Good luck with your shoulder." Dahlia reached for her phone, which Shawn Anderson surrendered. He stood awkwardly

"They'll probably do an MRI. Wet nurse? That's really a thing?"

"Good fortune threw her in my path. She also happens to be a talented artist." This time Shawn Anderson took the hand Dahlia extended—she tugged it away when he seemed about to kiss it. His focus slipped back to the phone Dahlia had placed on the desk.

"He looks cold," Shawn Anderson said.

❧

Dahlia sat at her desk, dabbing yogurt between lips she barely parted. She peeked at the phone picture of Robbie. What had Shawn Anderson seen? Her baby looked cold, he'd said. *Cold?* Was Robbie noticeably uncomfortable? Or had Shawn Anderson meant the baby looked cold to the *touch?* Was *Lizzie* cold from holding him in her arms? Did Robbie chill his wet nurse's breasts?

What *did* Robbie feel like? Dahlia strained to remember the touch of her lips on her son's forehead when Lizzie offered him for a "night-night" kiss before carrying him off to her bed. She resolved to take the baby's temperature. After the gym and a quick bite downtown with Kirkland, she'd go home and paste the external thermometer she was sure was in the medicine cabinet across Robbie's forehead. 98.6 was the target. Possibly Kirkland had noticed something about her baby boy. If the conversation turned that way, she might ask.

But at Pilates, Dahlia couldn't concentrate on her core. On all fours, as she mimicked the bends and stretches of her instructor, she thought of the shadow couple chained to the tracks in Kirkland's installation. Then her brow contracted, and she felt her features meld somehow with Shawn Anderson's. With a shared face they frowned at the little picture of Robbie on her phone. Dahlia jerked her head with a snap that hurt her neck. She concentrated on her reflection in the mirror behind the instructor. *The core, the core*, she thought, coordinating her twists and stretches with the poses of the dozen other slender figures in her class. For a shocking moment she saw her body laden with the breasts she'd had surgically reduced long ago, when she was still a teen. Dahlia had insisted, and her mother had given permission. She'd so wanted to dance professionally. But at her new arts school she'd faced a stark truth—the career for which she'd reshaped herself demanded talents she'd never have.

Dahlia blinked sweat from her eyes and, relieved, found herself again as sleek as her Pilates-mates. But her abdomen felt slack. And hollow. She dug her fingers into the mat and focused on her knuckles as she stiffened into a plank. Shawn Anderson's fingertips had been swollen like purple vegetable tubers. Once, when she was very little, Dahlia had ridden a city bus with her grandmother. The fumes had nauseated her, and Nana had smoothed back her hair and told her to "focus on something." The dark-skinned man sitting across the aisle from her cupped a hand with shriveled fingers against his chest as if he held a dying bird. Dahlia stared, and when Nana noticed, she'd leaned over, her large bosom warm and stale-smelling against her granddaughter's cheek.

"Thank you for your service," Nana had said to the man, who ignored the senseless remark.

At dinner, Dahlia began the story of Shawn Anderson.

"He wanted a baby with a difference for an insurance commercial—"

"Your 'babies with differences.'" Kirkland made a face.

201

"And you say you don't get art. You're as creative as God. You can make a fake person out of anyone."

Dahlia swallowed her tasteless Merlot, waiting for Kirkland's banter to run its course. She had a headache. So Kirkland thought her creative. What about the miracle of her fertilized eggs? Twelve, an even dozen, eleven of them frozen "in case the first implant fails." And it had failed. Dahlia pictured a white-coated lab technician retrieving an egg carton from a freezer. From that icy nest he picked Robbie.

A rattle of cubes, and startled Dahlia upset the glass the busboy was filling. Water and ice collected in her lap, while Kirkwood and the busboy pushed at the spill with napkins. A minute later, Dahlia stood in a locked restroom stall, rubbing the damp spot on her skirt with a paper towel. Then she was in her car, driving home, having excused herself on account of her aching head.

Dahlia had shrieked so loud her ears still rang and her teeth ached even after she'd collapsed on her sofa. Lizzie hung like a ghost in the hallway door, clutching frantic Robbie to her side.

"I thought—" Dahlia gasped. But she couldn't say what she'd thought—it was too horrible: she'd stepped into her house, into her living room, and called for Lizzie, who'd materialized suddenly in the half-lit hall, her T-shirt and arms blood-soaked, her hair clotted—and the baby, smeared with red, splayed in her arms.

Sacrifice—the idea had struck Dahlia like a fist to her sternum. Her arms flailed against imagined knives as she fell back—Helter Skelter! Was Lizzie a victim or a perpetrator? Were curses scrawled on the walls with her baby's blood? Who was calling her name?

"Dahlia—*Dahlia!* No! We were just painting. Robbie and I were *painting.*" Lizzie patted her drenched chest, lifted her bloody hair from her forehead. "You were supposed to be at dinner with Kirkland. We were just starting to clean up. I'm so sorry—this must look—" Was Lizzie half-smiling her apology? Naked Robbie, quieting, burrowed between her breasts, then pulled back, his face a red mask. Lizzie's glasses were speckled with paint that Dahlia had mistaken for gore. Lizzie *was* smiling, her teeth white and sharp.

"You okay now? Okay? We were, like, *finger*-painting. Except I was using Robbie." Lizzie coughed a chuckle. "Like he's a big stamp pad. 'Baby Parts,' I call it. Red finger paint on brown paper—I've got it rolled out on the bathroom floor. Don't worry—everything's washable and non-toxic. We'd have cleaned it all up before you got here if you hadn't been early." Lizzie jostled the paint-smeared baby, who reached for her chin. "Isn't that right, little man? Really, Dahlia, I'm *so* sorry. Can I get you something from the kitchen? Water? A glass of wine? I want to keep off the carpet in case we drip."

Dahlia hoisted herself into a slouch. Not wine. "No, thank you. Sorry," she wheezed, still trying to catch her breath. "It's been a difficult day—casting a horror film," she lied. "—My imagination got the best of me." She waved a limp hand. "I want to help with the bath. Give me a minute."

"You change, and I'll feed Robbie first. It'll sooth him." Lizzie and the baby disappeared into the kitchen. Dahlia heard a chair scrape across the tiles. She pictured the wet nurse lifting her shirt. Had the paint soaked through to the skin? Would she wash her nipples so her milk wouldn't mix with the blood—the paint?

"It's all non-toxic, right?" Dahlia called.

A ten count passed before Lizzie answered. She kept her voice low. "Um-hmm. Oh—I almost forgot—you had a visitor. A Mr. Anderson? I thought he was the cable guy. He said he was in the neighborhood, and I should tell you he'd thought it over, and he decided against the arrangement you made today. He said to tell you he wanted to go back to his original idea. You'd know what he was talking about, he said."

"Oh—yes." Shawn Anderson in her house? Dahlia peered, round-eyed, into the room's dark corners—empty.

"He was kind of weird. He made me nervous, the way he wouldn't leave. He asked to hold Robbie. Called him 'My special little man.'" Lizzie's words were muffled, like moths fluttering in a jar. "I told him Robbie didn't like to be held by strange men. One of his arms was in a sling. It looked dirty. Stained. He said you knew how to get in touch with him, and he left."

᠁

In her bedroom, Dahlia stripped in a methodical burlesque, observing her movements in the mirror as if she were gathering evidence. Should she place blouse, pants, jacket, and underthings in labeled plastic bags? They appeared clean, but you could never be certain. If she'd embraced the child, she definitely would have ruined her outfit. She tugged on a sweatshirt and sweatpants. The tub was filling in the bathroom: Lizzie hummed an old song over the gushing water—Beatles or Rolling Stones?

Why hadn't Shawn Anderson left his message at her office? *Special little man?* Lizzie shouldn't have opened the door. What if it had been that ex-boyfriend, the lactophiliac, crazy for a fix of mother's milk? And if Shawn Anderson returned, asking for Robbie? Dahlia abandoned the plan to take her son's temperature—how would she explain it?

"I'm putting him in—hurry up, Dahlia," Lizzie called. Sitting on the edge of her bed, Dahlia shivered. She pulled up a sleeve. Goose bumps covered her arm. "Hey—" she heard, "I should call my painting 'Rubber Baby Buggy Bumpers.' You'll see it when you come in. Hurry up."

Dahlia slipped her hands up under her sweatshirt and cupped her breasts, but she couldn't feel them. Which was numb—her flesh or her fingers? Her ribs she found. She started to count them and thought about the egg carton with her zygotes. Ten left. They must be so cold!

"Dahlia?" Lizzie must have been on her knees, bent over the tub, the infant naked and slippery in one hand while she scrubbed off the red paint with a washcloth. Rosy swirls must be blooming in the bathwater. Splashes. "We're shampooing now!" Was that a giggle? Her son's first laugh?

What were little boys made of? Half of Robbie came from a medical student—lover of Shakespeare—blond, blue-eyed rugby player. Did that man also have a horrible hand like the stranger Nana had thanked for his service? Like Shawn Anderson? Dahlia couldn't remember her own father's hands—either the sight or touch of them. The half-closed casket had hidden them.

Dahlia had Lizzie. Had it really only been three months? Three months made just one season. It seemed much longer.

"I don't know you," Dahlia murmured toward the bathroom.

"What? Do you want to towel him off? This is murder on my back—"

"You're not even my friend," Dahlia whispered. There was so much more to come—nursery school, grade school, high school, college. Friends. Lovers. Her boy was too small for any of it. Shouldn't he have been bigger by now? Was that what Shawn Anderson had noticed? Dahlia jolted upright, her hands pressed against her cheeks, her mouth a dark oval. She should have seen it herself: Robbie was tiny! He wasn't growing larger, he was shrinking. Now, in the warm bathwater, he'd be melting in Lizzie's hands. He'd lose something with every bath—first his little arms would disappear, then his legs—he'd become a torso with a featureless head, a lozenge, with Lizzie wiping and wiping at him as he shrank away.

"Dahlia—" Lizzie called, "at least help me get him into his pj's. He can start in bed with you, if you like. You can cuddle. I'll take him back in a while, 'cause he's sure to get hungry."

Dahlia shuddered, but her features relaxed. Her mouth closed. If Shawn Anderson wanted her baby for his commercial, why not? Now both of them knew what Robbie was. And Dahlia could assume the role for which she was best prepared—she'd represent her own child. If she rescued her baby from the tub now, while there was still something left of him, she could give him the most valuable thing she had to offer—a career.

"Wait," she said. Her tightening chest forced the words from her mouth, "I'm coming."

X

I

The man who finds her stands with the moon over his shoulder, his slim silhouette a hole in the desert night-sky; he's darker than the greater darkness surrounding them because he blocks the stars.

"Why are you in my yard?" he asks. "Can I help you?" He crouches as he speaks, still two-dimensional. Her bald head is cold, her throat dry.

"Sick," she says, which is a kind of truth. "Cancer," she whispers, which is a lie to explain her baldness. "Attacked," she says, a second lie, this to explain the dried blood on her thighs that streaks to her bare feet.

A pair of hands emerges from the silhouette and slides under her. Only after she's hoisted—as easily as if she's the husk of something—does she feel the shape of the rocks she's been lying on. She's swung away from the moon, wants to see it, but hasn't the strength to turn her head.

She wakes swathed in cool sheets on a bed in a lit room. Poster-sized artwork covers stucco walls. Her abdomen aches. She touches herself, peers under the sheets that are so white they seem fluorescent. Crusts of blood edge her wounds, but the blood has been washed off. Red spots startle her—just the polish on her toenails; she's not hemorrhaging. But when she hears a male voice, pain wracks her. The speaker stands in the door-less entry to the room. He is tan, with hair like straw. The voice and thin body match those of her rescuer. He won't allow his gaze to shift from her eyes. His are blue.

"I washed and cleaned your wounds. You stopped bleeding. I haven't called an ambulance or notified the authorities. Do you want me to?"

She remembers—before she'd become too dizzy with pain and exhaustion to think straight, she'd created the beginning of a story: she was sick, the narrative went—cancer; she'd been on her way to Mexico City on the promise of an alternative treatment when she'd gotten lost on a side road, and her car broke down; a gang of young men in a beat-up car stopped to help; though she was suspicious, the day was so hot and the road so empty that she had no choice but to accept. What rescuer, seeing the blood, wouldn't believe that she'd been assaulted? Who wouldn't marvel at the will to survive demonstrated by her courageous escape? And she *had* run—that much was true—but she'd lost consciousness before coming up with a reason why the police should not be summoned.

The man in the doorway purses his lips—he isn't young—age spots mark his hairline, and his leathery face is deeply creased. His beard is so white it makes his teeth look stained.

"You've been on television. We're less than a hundred miles over the border, and I get American TV. They know who you are. The child you gave birth to is healthy. A boy. Did you know that? Did you see? Before you ran? If you're hungry, I've got soup, Mindy—your name is Mindy something, right?"

"Water, please," Mindy whispers, admitting nothing. Screaming has left her painfully hoarse.

"Beside you." The man nods to the glass on a night table, and when Mindy reaches for it, her ribs ache and her thighs cramp. What's the right play here? Should she hide her pain or exaggerate it? But when she tries to lift the water, her palm stings, and she sets the cup back down with a short cry. She looks at the heel of her hand, the heels of both hands—tiny puncture wounds—her nails had done that when she clenched her fists? She picks up the glass in her finger tips and drinks. The water sears her throat like cool fire.

"You said 'Cancer,'" the man says. His voice echoes—the floor is tiled, the ceiling high with track lights to illuminate the pictures. Mindy reaches for her bald head. How much does this man know? Does he know there's no chemo, that she's hairless because of alopecia? Does he know that she's not perfectly smooth? Patches surface: one on her thigh, another under her arm, and an inch wide strip that runs front to back on her head like an off-center bird's crest. *Almost* perfect—being absolutely hairless would be divine, but her patches are an insult. Shaving herself smooth has been a lifelong chore. Her fingers ease over her scalp until—bristles. When she groans, her empty uterus spasms.

"The reporter on the news said, 'Look for a young woman in a yellow raincoat. It might be blood-stained. She could be wearing a wig, because she doesn't grow hair.' Did you lose the wig?" The man shakes his head and lowers his voice. "Cancer is something you shouldn't fake," he says, as if that

210

pretense is the worst of her crimes.

Mindy feels her nostrils dilate. An instinct tells her to escape, but she knows her body wouldn't obey if she were to try to run. Where would she go? Her eyes glide around the room, over the pictures—searching for an exit. Large windows, three on the wall to her left, one on the wall in front of her, are set above the pictures, too high to reach and black because it's night. To her right is a small bathroom— she sees a shower stall, a sink, and toilet— no window or door. The only way into or out of the room is through the doorway that frames her host.

"Don't call anyone," she says. "I just need rest. Where am I?"

"You're where you fled to. No one expected you to run. You confused the border patrol. They underestimated your strength. But they found your bag and ID, Mindy, and your gun. They're looking for the man whose vehicle got you to the border. They know he was your doctor. They assume he was your accomplice. He must not be a very brave man to leave you alone."

He's dead, Mindy remembers. *I kidnapped him back home—to drive, and in case I started labor early—and I shot him in an arroyo when we got close to the border. No one will ever find him.* But she'd miscalculated her needs—her first contraction came just moments after she pulled the trigger—the gunshot had been so loud she had nothing in her experience to compare it to. She thought she could still make it over the border to her Mexican connections. And they did find her, too late, somehow recognizing her yellow raincoat as she dodged through traffic. When they swept her into their black-windowed car, she was empty-armed and exhausted.

"Where is the baby?" they'd demanded as she gasped and bled over a creamy leather seat. The man in back with her offered her his handkerchief. She thought they'd shoot her, but instead they drove and drove, on shrinking, rutted roads, until the red sun dropped behind scorched hills, and they pushed her out of the car.

"Call us when you got something, *puta*," she heard, before the car spun off, spitting pebbles.

"Hungry," she says. When her host—captor?—cleaned her, he'd have wiped away her drawn-on eyebrows. What had he thought as he erased her rakish expression? What else had he noticed? Certainly the drops of mother's milk tattooed beneath her nipple that some of her lovers mistook for tears. And the whole world now knows she's smooth. Did her bristly patches confuse him? She would rather shave than eat, but she won't ask for a razor—he might think her desperate and dangerous. Where are the mirrors? None even over the bathroom sink. Just pictures, everywhere.

"Soup," the man says, "but—" Before he can finish, something bursts between his legs, streaks across the floor, and leaps onto Mindy's bed—a speckled, piglet-sized dog with radar-dish ears and blazing eyes. Its sudden weight rocks her and wakes her pain.

"*Mee-go!*" Mindy hears as she covers her face and lifts her knees, her last sight a lolling tongue between grinning jaws. The snorting creature digs with eager paws at the sheet between her legs and tries to tug it away, and Mindy screams as if she's giving birth again.

II

"I find that I'm a different person in different rooms of my house," Claude says without looking up from the wooden tablet he cuts into with one of his knives. Every morning he brings a tablet, a portable work table, a folding chair, and a leather case of carving tools into Mindy's sunlit bedroom. While he works, Mindy often gazes up at the windows, waiting for a bird, an airplane, even a cloud to pass. When something does float by—or when it rains, and the glass seems to melt—Mindy's heart beats faster, as if she's about to learn a secret. Then the windows return to rectangles of skim milk blue or white or gray. At night they're always black. Beneath the windows the pictures—prints made from woodblocks, she's been informed—are bright with colors, but Mindy focuses on the figures in them only when Claude points them out.

This morning she's staring at the carving tool in Claude's hand. When he lifts it, her eyes trace its path as if it's a magic wand. The blade reminds her that she hasn't shaved her excess hair for over thirty days—since she woke up in this room. She's marked the passing of time by notching the bedpost with her thumbnail. Claude pares her nails, but not too short to make her marks. Migo curls against Mindy's thighs, his snout against his hindquarters, as if he's one of those snakes that swallow themselves.

"I only have this room, so that's all I am," Mindy says. She has no idea how many rooms are in this house.

"But you had a life back in the States. You lived somewhere. Who were you then? Always the same, no matter which room?" Claude peers up from his work, his forehead grooved like his tablet. *Each woodblock I cut is for a different color of a print*, he's told her. *After all are inked and printed onto the paper, the picture is complete.* She imagines that Claude is cutting her face and figure into his tablets, and when he inks the print, she'll be able to see herself. But what he's actually fashioning are poster-sized versions of the small woodblock prints produced by Yoshitoshi, a nineteenth-century Japanese master of woodblock prints. Claude's "expansions" hang on Mindy's walls. *You'd be surprised what they sell for*, Claude said. *Only the most foolish tourists mistake them for originals. But they are original, in a sense. It's like making a movie out of a book—a different version of the same thing, just bigger. I contribute size.*

Rooms? Who was she in the tiny custom's booth where she disgorged someone else's child? There was space only for herself and the sweating official between her legs. A roll of unfurling paper towels flew over her, struck one of the windows filled with faces and white and blue uniforms. Pain—a Milky Way of exploding stars—then a wail, and then the blinding sunlight, confused shouts, and car horns.

History: the night before the customs booth, a room at the Blue Daisy Motel with fat Doctor Morrison—Doc Mo. He spent the night chained to the drainpipe under the sink in the bathroom he'd never have guessed would be *his* final room. Who was Mindy as she dry-shaved her bristling head-strip—for the last time—on the Blue Daisy's sagging mattress? She'd been someone who thought that the seventy-five thousand dollars awaiting her in Mexico was three times better than the fee she'd contracted for in the States.

III

Migo is blind and deaf, Claude has said, which Mindy never would have guessed. "He knows you by your scent." Mindy runs her hand along the dog's rash of spots. His blind eyes glow white—sometimes she strains to see herself in them.

"His name is 'Amigo,' but without the 'a,'" Mindy says as she watches Claude cut into a fresh woodblock with a thin blade. Purple ink from a print run stains his fingers. "Does that mean he is or isn't a friend?"

Claude's glance lasts a blink. It's morning, and Mindy spoons oatmeal sweetened with brown sugar from the bowl on her breakfast tray. Claude prints a few hundred copies of each of his enlargements. The prints he hangs in Mindy's bedroom are first runs, their colors especially vibrant.

"Friend," Claude mutters, as if it's an idea he hasn't considered. Mindy still doesn't know if she's a guest or a prisoner. Since Claude has established no restrictions, if she asks for nothing, then nothing is denied. This is freedom. She's brought three meals a day, and the bathroom is stocked with shampoo, soap, toothpaste, fresh towels, and the terrycloth robes that are her only clothing. Before Mindy settled in, she wondered if anyone else lived in the house—maybe it's honey-combed with dozens of chambers just like hers, like a hive. But Claude couldn't care for so many guests and still spend most of his day in her room, working. She's free to explore, as far as she knows, and free to inquire, but the curiosity that might prove her freedom a false idea has shriveled. She's quit counting days—there's no more room for fresh grooves on her bedposts and headboard, and no point in deepening old ones.

IV

Mindy recognizes two universes—her room and her body. Bored with the windows, she now studies the prints that surround her and leaves her bed to study them. Claude has told her that the Asian men and women featured in the prints represent figures from Chinese and Japanese history, literature, and legend. Today, while Claude works, she lingers before a new print, hoping that Claude will explain it.

"That's Wu Gang," he says, putting down his knife. "Because he abused the practice of Taoist magic, he's doomed to chop down the golden-blossomed cassia trees which give the moon its brightness—every time he cuts down a tree, a new one grows in its place. The print shows Wu Gang resting over his ax. The moon hangs over him, his perpetual burden."

"That's like the myth of what's-his-name," Mindy says,

"the guy who pushed the rock up the hill, and it kept rolling down."

"Sisyphus," Claude says. "Same idea."

Later, alone, Mindy returns to the print of Wu Gang and the moon made of golden flowers. It's the magician's ax, not the blossoms, that attracts her. With a blade like his, she could shave off the lengthening hair on her head and the patches on her thigh and under her arm. And if she polished the ax, it could serve as a mirror. She runs her hand over her naked scalp until her fingertips bump against her lop-sided crest. Mindy remembers seeing horses with braided manes, and winds a finger around a lock of crest-hair, thinking of ribbons. It's a wonder that Claude never mentions her unusual feature, or the two other fuzzy places that mar her smoothness. His only involvement with her appearance is the trimming of her nails.

When Claude slices off Mindy's nails with one of his cutting tools, he works delicately and quickly with the same intense concentration he gives to his woodblocks. Mindy holds out each hand like the brides she's seen in wedding ceremonies on TV shows—palm down, fingers spread, in anticipation of the ring. When he's finished with her nails, Claude shifts back to his work table, while Mindy eats, examines the prints on her wall, or showers.

Mindy often sings while she showers: she runs a bar of soap over her smooth flesh and kinked patches as if she's shaving and hears in her own voice the sing-song rhythm her mother used when she scraped away her little girl's unsightly bristles—*Sooo-smooth, sooo-smooth*. Or Mindy mimics hip-hop performers and sways her hips and slaps her wet ass—*mothah-fuckah* this and *mothah-fucka* that—memories and tunes that are rootless and carry only sound. Mindy's crest-hair has grown long enough to shampoo, and massaging it to a soapy froth delights her. *Mine*, she thinks, as she squeezes her fists through the foam, *all mine*.

Often, after showering, when she returns to her bed in a clean, white terrycloth robe, Mindy discovers that Claude has hung new prints. This morning, as she lies back on her pillow, water leaking from her crest down her neck, she notices two.

"Prostitutes," Claude says with a swipe of his tool in the direction of the prints. "Yoshitoshi called the first 'Moon of the Pleasure Garden' and the second 'Streetwalker at Night.'"

Mindy listens to the titles and tugs her robe to cover her cleavage. Migo, already comfortable against her hip, lifts his head and stares toward her like a blind sphinx. Her first day in this room, the dog had crawled onto her legs, stretched himself along her sore abdomen, and tucked his muzzle under her ripe breasts. *He wants my milk*, she remembers thinking. Then, as now, she'd thought of the tattooed droplets and clamped her arms over her chest.

"Migo is ugly," she says.

"Migo is a beautiful and perfectly bred truth," Claude says, returning a blade to the tool case and selecting another.

"His head comes to a point, like a sharpened pencil. And his spots look like some kind of filthy disease."

"Both result from generations of street-breeding—the pointy head so he can stick it in tight spaces for trash to eat, the spots for camouflage in trash heaps."

"He has fishy breath. How did he get here?" It's the new prints that vex her, not the dog, Mindy knows.

"I found him in my yard with a broken leg. Probably hit by a car. A street dog like him isn't likely to wander this far away from a populated area, so he's something of a mystery."

"Was he blind when you found him?"

"No, but his vision was probably failing, which may be why he got hit. And drivers here often aim for small animals."

"They hit things on purpose?"

"Dogs, armadillos, tortoises, anything that isn't likely to damage their vehicle. Not much regard for life."

Claude finishes for the afternoon, leaving Mindy alone until dinnertime. The sky in the high windows is the washed out blue of the streetwalker's scarf in one of the new prints. The depiction of this prostitute includes a verse in Japanese, which Claude had translated for Mindy: "Like reflections in the rice paddies—the faces of streetwalkers in the darkness are exposed by the autumn moonlight." This woman in the print is of the lowest class of prostitutes, and she carries her rolled straw mat along a riverbank. For what purpose will she next roll out the mat, Mindy wonders—to sleep or to ply her trade? Mindy turns from the white-faced streetwalker to the elaborately robed courtesan—lucky enough to reside in "pleasure quarters." This woman's face is hidden as she watches cherry blossoms sift from tall trees like moonlit snow. An attending child watches the falling blossoms with her mistress.

What's to become of this little girl? She's sure to follow her mistress's trade, but will she inherit the "pleasure quarters" or will she be dismissed to the streets with a rolled mat? Mindy presses her hand against her stomach, anticipating a pain that doesn't come.

V

"Can you bring me ribbon?" Mindy asks Claude. It's the first request she's made since she's occupied the room. If she pulls the hair from her crest over her ear, it reaches her jaw. The hair is honey-colored, much lighter than the patches in her armpit and on her thigh. At night she lies on her back and tickles her nose with strands of it. She hopes Claude will bring a pair of sheers made of polished metal with the ribbon—she imagines admiring herself in the blades after she's decorated her crest. A fragment of a nursery rhyme floats to Mindy like a moth: about Johnny who went to a fair, and, in trade for a kiss, "He promised to buy me a bunch of blue ribbons, to tie up my bonny brown hair." Mindy blushes at the sudden idea that Claude might think of kissing her. She peeks at his crimped face as he works. He's so old. Is he frowning because he's mulling her request for a ribbon? In what ways does she inhabit his thoughts? The eyes of many men she's known have run over her like thirsty fingers after they've learned of her smoothness. To kiss Claude—Mindy watches him bite his lower lip with his stained teeth while he works, and her mouth clogs as if she's stuffed it with the yolks of hardboiled eggs.

220

"What color ribbon?" Claude asks, flashing his eyes.

"Blue." Mindy clears her mouth with her tongue and blinks from Claude's face to the sky in her windows. She gasps—bisecting the view from the middle window on the long wall to the left of her bed is a thinly branched tree.

"There's a tree!" she exclaims, shrugging herself up on her elbows, turning back and forth from the tree to Claude. Her flesh goosebumps—her underarm and thigh tingle under their growths.

"That's Migo's tree. I planted it last night. It's a Mexican Sycamore."

"Migo's?" Mindy's excitement contracts into a knot deep in her chest. It's been days since she's seen the dog. "Where's Migo?" she whispers.

"Migo's dead," Claude says. Does his gaze slip from her eyes to her crest? "He didn't wake up the other morning. I mixed his ashes in with the roots when I planted the tree last night." An arched eyebrow: "You had feelings for him?"

Mindy sinks back into her pillow and stares at the tree— its trunk and branches remind her of a fish skeleton hanging from the lip of a trashcan. She remembers the feel of Migo's mottled coat under her hand, his weight against her side. Claude had said Migo was "beautiful."

"I got used to him," Mindy murmurs. "He was familiar."

A groove between Claude's eyes deepens. "He was a killer. Did you know that? Before I took him in, my house was full of life. I had a parrot and a cat. And another dog— an old husky. The parrot talked. '*Buenos noces*,' he could say, and '*hermosa luna*': 'good-night,' and 'beautiful moon.' One day Migo brought me the parrot's body—he jumped on the couch next to me with it in his jaws as if he was carrying a rolled newspaper—and dropped it on my lap. The perch was too high for him to reach. I don't know how he lured Rodrigo down. The cat, which I admit I never liked much, I found murdered in the yard. And Migo tortured my old friend the husky for months, biting him on his back and belly and ears when I wasn't around. I'd find Mukluk bleeding. I tried to separate them, but the husky whined to be with his tormenter—Mukluk understood that murdering was part of Migo's nature, part of his perfect breeding, and he longed for the company, even if it was killing him. Eventually, his big heart burst. So, for a long time— until you came—it was just Migo and me."

Mindy shivers and pulls her sheet up to her neck. She runs a palm over her bare scalp, finds her crest, and pets it. Claude nods toward the window with the tree, the creases on his face lengthening with his smile.

"Keep your eyes on those leaves," he says. "See if they don't grow bloody teeth."

VI

For the first time since she gave birth, Mindy dreams: She is behind the wheel of Doc Mo's SUV—she's moved from the passenger seat after forcing him out of the vehicle. She winces against a blistering sun at the fat doctor, who lumbers past cacti, stones, and tumbleweeds toward a parched gully.

Look for the wounded animal I saw, she's insisted. *It's your job to take care of the injured.* Her swollen belly presses against the wheel—driving will be difficult, but the border isn't far. The baby inside her kicks through her flesh, sounding the horn, and the doctor looks back over his shoulder. He can't see the pistol—it feels like a toy in Mindy's palm. *Further—* she waves with her free hand—*the animal I saw was limping further away. Do your duty.* She's never shot at anything but a target. Should she aim at his head or his body? Mindy's dream-perspective shifts: now she sees herself from outside the SUV—is that really her in the curly black wig and yellow raincoat? And that belly! It seems so long ago. The doctor turns his back to her and throws back his shoulders—a puny act of defiance—or maybe resignation. Mindy watches herself calculate—is she sure she won't need him? The phone on the passenger seat buzzes like a snake's rattle, and she's looking at a close up of the gun's muzzle. She feels her finger jerk the trigger—and a silent explosion engulfs her in black.

Mindy's eyes spring open. She's safe in her room. It's morning. Migo's tree, its branches now thick with leaves, blots out most of the ashy sky in the middle window. Lately, Claude has been replacing the prints on her walls while she sleeps instead of when she showers, and she glances about for any changes. She half-expects to see a Yoshitoshi print he described the previous afternoon, though he'd told her its lack of color would make it unprofitable to reproduce:

"In the print the ghost of a maid rises from the well she's haunting. She committed suicide because she broke a dish, part of an extremely valuable table setting. The ghost counts to nine, over and over again."

"She killed herself because of a broken dish?"

"Why not? It was her duty to maintain a complete set. But people needed the well she haunted. How do you think her ghost was exorcised?"

Mindy had tried to picture the obsessively counting ghost, but instead saw her mother—emerging from a fog, waving the pink Lady Schick razor she'd used to shave Mindy clean. "Oh," Mindy sobbed. Claude's head had snapped up from his work, and she found herself staring at him.

"'A broken dish,'" she repeated. "Oh—your hand—"

"Ah—" And Claude had lowered his gaze—he'd sliced open his index finger. Blood ran along it and dripped onto his woodblock. He'd grinned wryly before wrapping his finger in a white handkerchief—a red stain bloomed. He'd gathered his things—awkwardly, because of his wound— and left without a word.

VII

Mindy's dream and the memory of Claude's blood spreading on the handkerchief have left her restless. Now he's late with her breakfast. Should she take her shower before eating? She reaches for her crest. It's festooned with blue ribbons that dangle past her shoulders. Each shower soaks the ribbons, which stiffen after drying and rustle like wind-blown branches when Mindy tosses her long crest-hair.

She looks at Migo's tree, as she does a hundred times a day, and remembers the feel of the dog's body against hers. She shakes her head a second time, glimpsing fluttering bits of blue. Claude had brought her the roll of blue ribbon, but not the shears with mirroring blades she'd hoped for— he'd sliced the ribbon into pieces himself with one of his knives. As Mindy cranes her neck, enjoying the weight of her hair, she discovers two new prints, side by side over her headboard. Hung while she dreamed. Turning, she looks up at them from her knees.

The first print depicts a nobleman squatting on a mat. In a nearby dish of water he sees the reflection of a female demon about to attack him from behind, and his hand tightens around the hilt of his sword. Mindy sucks in a breath—the puddles on the floor of her shower—had she ever tried to see herself in them? She hops off her bed, sheds her robe, and hurries to her bathroom. But when she steps into the shower and turns the faucets, nothing happens. She twists until her palms hurt, but no water. She tries the sink—again, nothing. And the toilet, which might, if she'd ever thought of looking, have provided the most reflective surface of all, is dry. Mindy licks her lips. Her mouth and tongue are pasty. Where is Claude? Disappointed, thirsty, and hungry, she returns to her bed. Glancing once again at the "demon in the water dish," she heaves a sigh, slumps onto her side, and frowns up at the second print. Its central figure is a lovely young woman.

This woman contemplates a broken wooden bucket lying at her feet. Like many of the prints on Mindy's walls, this one features a Japanese inscription. Examining the calligraphy, Mindy feels her lips move, as if she's uttering a prayer, and a translation emerges: "The bottom of the bucket has fallen out—the moon has no home in the water." *But I don't understand Japanese*, she thinks, bewildered. *What can this mean?* And she hears herself whisper an answer: "No reflections."

Mindy's face drops onto her pillow. Lying on her stomach, she scratches the itchy patch on her thigh, then picks at the hair under her arm and sniffs her fingers. She worries that her crest is really nothing more than a lop-sided Mohawk. Its dry ribbons irritate her neck. She imagines quenching her thirst from the nobleman's water-dish, in spite of the demon in it.

VIII

She waits. Darkness comes, then light, then darkness again. Maybe it's the same day with rare dark clouds, maybe many days pass. When it's light, the leaves on Migo's tree glisten, sharp and dangerous. From her bed she calls, or thinks she might call, Claude, but she doesn't hear her voice or feel it in her throat. "I'm hungry—" she whimpers with closed eyes, as if she's a baby. It's hard to fill her lungs. When she lifts her lids the pictures on the walls spin around her like a color wheel. The wheel slows and stops. Directly across from her, right where it's always been, is the print of Daruma, the founder of Zen Buddhism. Daruma sits in his red robe, his legs folded under him. *It took Daruma nine years of meditation to reach enlightenment,* Claude has told her. *So much time that he lost the use of his legs. But you can buy little round figures of him. 'Dharma dolls,' they're called. You can get them anywhere, even in the shops that sell my prints. The little red dolls are self-righting—tip one over, it pops back up. They symbolize optimism.*

Mindy tries to hold the image of the meditating holy man. Red spheres swirl like tiny planets around her head—no, not planets—dharma dolls. Mindy hugs herself and draws her knees to her breasts, curling around an emptiness that's the size and shape of one of those dolls.

An acrid odor burns her sinuses. Is that her? Her eyes would tear if they weren't so dry. No water to drink or wash with or see herself in. She reaches for her crest, her arm as weightless as papier-mâché. The ribbons, stuck in clumps of waxy hair, crumble at her touch. Has Claude been allowing her ugliness to ferment? She thought he was protecting and nurturing her, but maybe he's been trying to protect the rest of the world. From her. Had he been saving the world from Migo, too? At the expense of his other pets?

Mindy pictures Doc Mo collapsing in the arroyo, *feels* the volume of the gunshot that started her labor. How long would it have taken the doctor's fat body to decompose in the desert heat? Bacteria first, insects next, crawling inside his clothes, then winged and four-footed carrion eaters—like the Mad Hatter's tea party, Mindy imagines. But now she sees herself perched on the dinner table, and the guests surrounding her are the legendary figures of Claude's Yoshitoshi prints—warriors and poets, buddhas and courtesans, demons and ghosts. Circling the table is the mad young woman from a print Mindy had forgotten—the woman wanders the streets at midnight, her letter to a dead lover unspooling all the way to a silver moon.

Who would be looking for Mindy? Authorities couldn't be bothered—the parents of the baby she failed to steal are twenty-five thousand dollars better off. Her Mexican associates have surely found another willing thief. Would she recognize the child she bore? He's no kin to her, though her blood fed him. She winces at meditating Dharma. How long until her legs become useless? She lifts herself to her hands and knees in the center of her mattress. Her robe hangs open, and her breasts dangle like forgotten fruit, the tattooed drops of milk crawling like ants from her nipple. The strip of stucco between her headboard and the prints is daubed with red—Claude's blood? She looks at the doorway he left through, and it seems as impenetrable as the prints covering her walls.

IX

The doorway—Mindy's hand a lily on its dark frame. The wall outside it is close enough to touch. She feels the weight of the stone tiles under her feet. She closes her eyes and tries to remember the exhilaration of her rush to freedom after giving birth—too numb for pain, the blinding sun thrown at her from the metal and glass of a thousand cars, the baby she'd hoped to barter left behind.

To her left—the hallway ends abruptly. To the right—she

blinks, startled: on an easel stands a print, more colorful than any in her room—yellow, green, blue, red, purple, orange—a print like this would have required a dozen woodblocks. She leans on the doorframe, one foot hovering over the threshold. The print is less than ten feet away, its colors swirl, and Mindy understands—it isn't a print at all, it's a *mirror*. The mirror is angled so it reflects not her, but something incredibly beautiful—a garden?—at the end of a connecting corridor. A few paces, and she'll see herself, then run to paradise. But she hesitates—at the base of the easel there's a little red globe—a dharma doll. Stuck in its head like a pick in a 'fro is a gleaming blade. An invitation to shave? Mindy grabs her crest, and ribbon-dust falls into her eyes. There's a mark on the dharma doll's belly.

"*X*," Mindy reads. *X, like the eyes of the dead in comic strips?* Not a Japanese character, but still a message. Her heart hammers harder and faster until the beats don't separate. She sees Claude, the blood leaking from his hand like a silk rose from a magician's sleeve, his last question left hanging . . . about the ghost of the maid who broke the dish and endlessly counted to nine. *How was she exorcised?*

Mindy comprehends: "Not *X*," she cries. "Ten!" And as she hears her own voice, like ripping paper, the colors in the mirror whirl into a blinding, saturating brilliance that fills her core. Her limbs dissolve, and she is absorbed by her completion.

Annabelle's Children

From up here on the ceiling, I see three scalps beneath me. Their owners are having a meeting. The fluorescent lights illuminate one head that's shaved and gleaming with an indentation in the center that looks like a sunken grave, one with a hairline receding to dark curls, and a third with a comb-over that fails to cover skin the color and texture of butterscotch pudding. This head and the head with curls belong to men I knew

when I was alive.

I've been dead for days and days, and this is the first time I've recognized anyone, so I don't know if my presence in this room is by coincidence or design. "Dead" for me has been a completely passive experience. Every morning I wake up attached to something that's living—something different each day, no repeats, at least not so far. Yesterday I was with a goldendoodle, the day before a Starbucks barista. Today, it's this spider on the ceiling. I've got no will of my own, no physical essence. Where my host goes, I go. And though I share my partner's space, I'm neither seen nor felt. So far I've had no appetites at all. I recognize emotions, but I don't seem to feel them. I have extraordinary patience—have you ever spent a day connected to a clam?

This morning the men down at the conference table are talking about me and the eggs harvested from my ovaries before I lost my battle with acute myelogenous leukemia.

Carl, the one with the curls, was to have been my husband. The comb-over guy is P.P. Frederico, the filmmaker who gave me my big break after my last stint in rehab, years before my death. The shaved scalp belongs to a stranger. The three are discussing an idea for a reality TV show—*Annabelle's Children*, one of them called it.

"You say you've got full legal rights to Annabelle's eggs?" shaved head asks.

Carl clears his throat. "Zygotes," he says, "not eggs. Annabelle and I were told that fertilized eggs would survive the freezing better. I supplied the sperm. The zygotes are legally mine."

Carl's right. My eggs were harvested because aggressive chemotherapy and radiation were going to sterilize me. His sperm fertilized the salvaged eggs *in vitro*, and the zygotes were frozen so we could have our own biological children when I recovered. Which I didn't.

Light reflects off the stranger's polished head. He must be a network executive. His fingers drum the table. "I don't know. Isn't the point of this show that each couple—each husband of the couple—will fertilize one of Annabelle's eggs himself? The way I understood it is you have the competitive stuff first—the sports and the trivia contests and whatever—singing, if you want—with the usual up-close-and-personals, followed by the audience vote. Then the winning dads fertilize the eggs, which get implanted in their wives."

"We plan at least one show on the science of it all," P.P. says. "Doctors, test tubes, petri dishes. Footage of sperm penetrating eggs. We stagger the implantations so we get about eight weeks' worth of births at the end of the season. Twelve couples is the target."

"Hunh," the network guy grunts. "But Annabelle is the attraction. People want to be connected to *her*! No offense, but what's the appeal of kids that are half Carl's?"

"Didn't you read the market research we sent?" P.P. asks. "Focus groups couldn't differentiate between "egg" and "zygote." We just de-emphasize Carl. We lose him in the scientific mumbo-jumbo, as far as the TV audience is concerned. For potential competitor-parents—ninety-five percent of those questioned deemed the father's biological involvement 'unimportant.' This *is* about Annabelle and nothing else, Larry."

"If we include episodes on the impact of environment on child development, it'll be better scientifically if all the kids had the same biological mother and father," Carl offers quietly.

"But," P.P. says, "what we're selling is Annabelle and her children."

Carl's head has flushed pink, but he's silent. Is he angry? It seems this bargaining with my eggs would have disturbed me once. Was it Carl or P.P. who cooked up this reality show idea? They'd collaborated on the cartoon-horror remake of *The Island of Doctor Moreau* that resurrected the career I'd done my best to trash. The animated *Moreau* flopped, but the voice I gave to the wretched dog-man M'ling found empathetic ears among the lonely and miserable, and my performance drew raves. With P.P. to vouch for my rejuvenated work ethic, offers poured in. Broadway called, and I won a Tony playing a young mother. Then serious films—more mothers. Even illness couldn't keep me down—when work became impossible, I became a role model, a leading advocate for cancer research. Those *Thrive* awareness anklets, the magenta ones you see everywhere? Inspired by my tribulations.

"Annabelle Hadley is a classic American story of redemption, Larry." P.P. slaps the table. "*Annabelle's Children* will immortalize her!" He pauses. "From porn star to angel," he sighs.

"I don't know about 'porn star,'" Carl murmurs. I don't deny it could have happened. Prior to my final visit to rehab, while promoting my Scaredy Cat line of clothing in a Walmart, I'd made lewd gestures with my microphone before propositioning the store manager. Then I'd thrown up and passed out.

"We wouldn't go there," Larry says. But he admits, "She had a hell of a life," and I know he's sold on my show.

"Right," P.P. says. "We start with a documentary. Two hours, Carl?"

"Two parts, one hour each."

"M-hmm. Two hours on Annabelle's roller coaster life. We'll show the couples competing for the zygotes weeping over the highs and lows, the final tragedy. But the winners will have the chance to bear Annabelle's children!"

"The couples' demographics?" Larry asks.

"Like any other reality show: rich, poor, minorities—hey, Carl, gay men would need their own surrogate wouldn't they?"

My former lover shakes his head. "Too complicated. It would be easier to go with a lesbian couple."

There's silence, and P.P. looks up toward the fluorescent lights. His dark glasses are impenetrable. The other men follow his gaze. Carl's brown eyes look sad. I think Larry might see my spider, but he doesn't say anything.

"She was beautiful, wasn't she?" P.P. asks. Carl and Larry mumble assent.

Larry's indentation reminds me of an infant's soft spot—something's pulsing in it. Maybe Carl should have been the one to bring up my beauty. Being dead, I don't dwell on it, but somewhere between party-girl bloat and dying-woman desiccation there *was* beauty. And in the beginning, too, when I was an innocent child with Hollywood dreams.

"Reunion shows," Larry says dreamily.

"And guaranteed spin-offs," P.P. adds. "Maybe decades of programming. Annabelle's children will be the biggest entertainment phenomenon we've ever seen. Think of the merchandising opportunities. It's like we're breeding our own celebrities."

"We will be breeding our own celebrities," Carl says. I look down at the curls I used to run my fingers through. My almost-husband had a diminished sense of smell: he claimed he'd burned out his nostril cilia when he was a boy, huffing hot ammonia gas brewed from a Christmas-gift chemistry set. He had virtually no sense of taste either, and had to fake compliments when we ate at celebrity gourmet restaurants.

A cell-phone chimes, and all three men reach for a pocket, while my host spider dashes into a gap in the dropped ceiling. It's dark. Today is about to end. If death holds form, tomorrow I'll wake up with a new partner. I've got forever to find out what happens to my children.

᪥

I'm attached to a pet ferret. Its nose and eyes are tiny black beads, and it wears a blue collar as thin as a rubber band. We curl around a pink bunny slipper and peek out from beneath a sofa. Running shoes flank our sides like the walls of a fortress. Two adults and two children sit above us. From time to time a popcorn kernel drops, and the ferret darts forward and nips it up, then retreats. Sounds of nibbling accompany the TV voices like static. The television's flickering light paints every surface.

The children are young—a boy and a girl. Nothing has been familiar since Carl and P.P.'s meeting, so I suppose that my presence there was a coincidence and not part of any plan. I can only guess that my experience is the same as everyone who's dead—we're all attached to a living thing. Wouldn't it be something if the entire universe of the dead was attached to the same body—my ferret, for instance? We're a weightless and volume-less population, we overlap, and, in our perpetually increasing numbers, maybe we all switch to a new body together every night. Who can say? I'm already telling you more than you could possibly have known.

My ferret's family is watching a documentary about me, the prelude to *Annabelle's Children*. There are clips from some of my earliest movies. When I was a child, my eyes were

235

wide and green and impish. My hair fell over my shoulders in auburn waves.

"She looks like Cindy, doesn't she look like Cindy?" the mother on the sofa says. No one answers. On screen my child-self makes a sassy quip, and above me the children and mother giggle. Another popcorn kernel falls and my ferret grabs it. Nibble nibble. A solemn voice narrates over photographs of me. I'm not so cute here—makeup blurs my features, and I wear short skirts and low-cut blouses that show my developing breasts. When I smile my mouth is open and my tongue shows. Pose after pose in gown after gown on miles of red carpet. How many packs a day was I smoking? When did I develop the taste for Jack Daniels? I'm in a courtroom. My hair is tied back, and I look sorry. A judge speaks without making eye contact. Police officers usher me away, their hands floating beside my elbows without touching them. Then I'm dancing wildly, my eyes raking across space as I twirl. There's my little red Porsche—and there it is again with its front crumpled. The dad sitting above me on the sofa laughs, low and guttural.

"Rehab" punctuates every other sentence. "Things were to get much worse before they got better," the narrator says. There's a grainy video on the screen—a security tape. That's me in sweat pants and a hoody. I'm at a gas pump next to the Porsche, which has either been repaired or has yet to be damaged. Gasoline gushes from a hose dangling from the car—a puddle expands on the pavement. I've wrapped an arm around the pump, and I'm waving a cigarette lighter and howling. Next, an officer protects my head as I'm plugged into the back of a police cruiser: I grin as if I'm listening to a private joke.

There's M'ling—the vivisected cartoon dog-man from *The Island of Doctor Moreau* who led me back to a righteous path.

"Did we see that cartoon? Can we see it?" one of the children asks.

"It's a horror movie. It's rated R," the mother says. My dog-man cowers in the midnight shadows of tropical trees. The narrator mentions P.P. and Carl. I stand between them in a photograph. All three of us smile. I'd forgotten that I'd buzzed off all my hair while recording *Moreau*. I knew what baldness was like before chemotherapy.

A *PLAYBILL* cover—I'm wearing an apron. My hair is shoulder length. I'm playing a mother. Then I'm standing at a podium, displaying an award.

"Part two tomorrow!" the narrator says. "Recovery and triumph."

I don't know where I'll be tomorrow. My host may not be near a television, and I'll miss seeing my final chapter among the living. They'll say I "battled bravely." This documentary won't show Carl, though he surely helped make it. He held my skeletal hand as I shuffled in loose pajamas to the rooms of doomed children. In my last days I bowed over them, my head as hairless as theirs, and offered what I could. There'd soon be nothing left for Carl. Maybe I owed him *Annabelle's Children*.

❦

Try to imagine an existence without expectations. Without

surprise. Without impatience.

Season One of *Annabelle's Children* is about to conclude: the twelve couples who have won my fertilized eggs will be named. Implantations are to take place during the summer hiatus, and Season Two's opening episode will reveal the successful pregnancies. Viewers are teased by the prospect of a dozen mothers swelling to term with babies due in the spring.

I gather this information while in the company of a speckled catfish. We're suctioned to the glass of an aquarium. Algae and dust obscure the television across the small, dim room. It's a struggle to hear over the pump's hum and filter's bubbling. Other fish waft above, beneath, and behind us. A young man, alone, slouches on the futon beside the table that supports our tank. He wears shorts and a t-shirt. One hand is down his pants, the other holds a beer. The pillow and blanket on the futon suggest it's his bed. I see a sink, a mini-fridge and a counter full of dirty plates; an open door exposes a toilet.

Also on the table with our aquarium is a framed photograph of a bride and groom, which I study during commercial breaks. The groom is a tuxedoed version of the young man on the couch. The bride is—me. I glance away again and again, but each time I look back there's no question that I'm looking at myself. I've been photo-shopped into the picture—I'm almost twice the groom's size. I recognize the silver gown I wore at the Tony Awards. I suspect I'm replacing another woman, someone the young man wants to exclude from his studio apartment. He continues watching television, unaware that he's been found out. Is this what "haunting" means?

Annabelle's Children summarizes with highlights the months of competition that will earn the winning couples my eggs: a young African-American couple stagger through calf-deep mud—the man is heavy, stumbles, and pulls his wife down face first into the muck; another couple, tan and blond, argue over a quiz question I can't hear because of the humming and bubbling—the woman offers an answer with a furrowed brow, the couple embraces joyfully, and the number of points displayed in front of them grows by a hundred; a pair of young women struggle across a rope bridge over surging rapids while carrying a life size baby doll.

The couples who have competed fill an auditorium. The camera sweeps over eager, anxious faces as all await the outcome of their trials. My catfish dislodges from the aquarium glass, drops to the blue gravel, and wriggles and sucks its way behind a scummy rock. Fish cruise over us like space ships. Time passes.

We're back on the glass. A dozen smiling couples stand on the stage—the winners. The host introduces profiles of the last few: here is the blond couple. Their ages, jobs, state of residence (Massachusetts), and income are posted over a video of the pair frolicking with a husky in their suburban yard. The next couple, a black man and his Asian wife, sit on the stoop of a modest Indiana home. Their posted income is a tenth of the blond couple's. The last duo, a pair of healthy-looking young women, is doing as well financially as the blonds—one is a financial analyst, the other a photographer.

They live in an oceanfront condo in San Diego. I wonder which of the two will carry my baby. I missed the profiles of the other winning couples while the catfish foraged. The closing credits roll over a cartoon picture of a red-haired woman in an apron holding a basket of eggs aloft. I assume that's supposed to be me. Carl's and P.P.'s names slide over me and disappear.

❧

"Get to bed!" insists the robed mother to my host, a little girl of about seven who lingers barefooted on the linoleum floor of a narrow hallway. Her mother lounges on a couch. Ashes from the cigarette pinched in the woman's lips threaten the face of the infant she holds like a loaf of bread.

"But the babies are on. I want to see the babies."

"Then you shouldn't have back-talked about your homework."

"But I don't *have* any homework."

"Your teacher says she gives homework every night. That's what she said."

"But I did it in school. I promise! There was time to do it in school today. Can't I see the babies?"

If my host goes to bed, it will be dark, and tomorrow I'll be elsewhere.

"You got your sister Brittany." The mother stuffs her cigarette into a soda can on the table by her elbow. "Get me another Diet Pepsi, and you can stay up," she says to my partner, and the little girl and I scamper into the kitchen. There are dishes in the sink and bottles in a pot on the stove.

A crayon drawing of a pony with a rainbow mane and tail decorates the refrigerator, which contains cartons of milk and juice, Tupperware of different sizes, and a dozen or so cans of soda. We return to the living room, and my little girl hops onto the sofa after handing the beverage to her mom. She stretches her heels to the coffee table. Grime rims her toenails. The baby mews and snuggles into her mother's belly.

"Will Shana be on this one? I like it when Shana's on."

"Shh. How do I know? Keep quiet or you're going to bed."

Shana is three, as are all nine of my children. Ten of the couples winning my eggs had successful, full term pregnancies. One of my babies, Harrison, died with his mother in a car crash last season. I missed the special memorial program, though I saw the commercial for it: Harrison is shoveling Spaghetti-o's into his mouth, but most of the pasta is on his cheeks and chin. He has red hair, like most of my children. His mother laughs in the background as she records her son's messy eating. If the deaths of Harrison and his mother are like mine, maybe they've seen themselves on *Annabelle's Children*.

The first segment of tonight's show features little Veronica. Her parents have separated and share custody of their daughter. Veronica's dad is a construction foreman, and he brings her to work, where she wears a miniature hard hat. She has curls like Carl's. According to the show's host, Veronica "was the first of the children to walk," but there's no video to document the event. I've seen other babies' first words and steps, birthday parties, and Disneyland vacations.

No Shana yet for my little host. Her dirty feet waggle

impatiently on the coffee table during the show's second segment, which features the "scientific" aspects of *Annabelle's Children*. There are statistics and numbers. How many hours are spent in daycare? Who was nursed and who given bottles? Hours of television? Hours read to? Nutritional choices? Doctors in white coats discuss the "likelihoods" of this or that, but no conclusions are reached.

"Shana!" my little girl cries when her favorite appears, briefly, stacking blocks while a technician marks down her progress on a clipboard. My host has tied her pigtails in rainbow ribbons that match the bow in Shana's red hair.

I don't know what I am to these children. I'm not their birth mother, but their skin and hair and feet, their faces and their heart, have grown from my cells. I'm their First Cause. The last segment features Simon. His parents are lawyers. He looks a lot like Shana, and seems to have an eye for the camera—he poses in ways that remind me of photographs of myself in fan magazines. Tonight, while bouncing Simon on their laps, his mother and father discuss "transgendering."

Annabelle's Children's theme song plays while the credits roll. It's a version of my one hit from the only album I recorded. "Who's your mother? Where's your mother?" I'd rasped and ranted punkishly. A children's chorus sings the TV show's rendition, accompanied by a harp. Unless I missed his name, Carl is no longer listed as a "Creative Consultant."

Baby Brittany wails, her mother swears under her breath, and my host rises, pats her little sister's head, and we're off to bed. My TV children have no siblings in their families. Did I miss a rule prohibiting them? I've seen no signs of a male in this house. It's hard for a single mother to care for more than her infant—I learned that in my very last movie, and, since I've been dead, I've seen the truth of it again and again.

∽

I've been hosted by countless dogs, but this is the smallest, some kind of chihuahua. We're tucked between the knees of an old woman. She wears stretch pants and gray slippers that might once have been as purple as the burst veins mottling her swollen ankles. When the dog whimpers to pee its owner's sagging face tightens into a fist.

"Jingles, can't you hold it?" she whines in a pitch that matches her dog's. She struggles with the lever to her easy chair, and Jingles and I hop to the floor of their double-wide. When she pushes open the aluminum door, we skip from a cinder block to the hardpan, and Jingles squats. The woman clings to the door handle while she waits and looks back over her shoulder at her small television. I can't see much in the dark, but from neighboring trailers I hear quarreling TV show voices.

Back between the bony knees. Jingles gnaws on a huge biscuit. It's been many nights since I've seen *Annabelle's Children*. They're calling this special show a "reunion," but the kids have never met. When their parents won my eggs, they'd agreed to keep the children apart, "for the purpose of scientific observation." The boys and girls are eight years old now. Everyone is dressed nicely; children and adults sit at separate daises. Between them is a microphone at which a tuxedoed host and several guests take turns reminiscing and joking mildly about *Annabelle's Children*.

"The kids could have their own baseball team," a speaker quips. I anticipate other jokes about "nine," but all I can think of is that cats have nine lives, and "lives" don't seem appropriate to mention because of little Harrison. In all the time I've been dead, I've never been hosted by a cat. The children have seen their own TV show and understand its premise. They're awkward in the presence of so many biological brother and sister celebrities they don't know. They ignore the host and peek, mouths agape, at the familiar faces of strangers. No two are identical, and together they present a spectrum of resemblance that runs from Carl to me—dark curls to red hair, brown eyes to green. Looking at them is like looking into funhouse mirrors, and I suspect they feel the same way. Are they forming bonds or discovering them? Their parents squint toward the children with clenched smiles and seem to want to rush over and claim their own.

The kids, their parents, and the television audience watch a video montage that begins with swollen-bellied mothers, then shows the children as infants and toddlers, interspersed with clips of my childhood movies, then shots of me receiving my Tony. A final video shows me delivering a speech at a children's hospital shortly before I died. I am bald and hollow-eyed, but I say inspiring things about thinking positively and devoting oneself to a cause. Finally, waiters roll out a grand sheet cake. "THANK YOU ANNABELLE" is printed across it. The host prepares to cut into it with a saber-sized knife and invites the children to gather around with their plates.

Tears sparkle like jewels on the cheeks of Jingles' owner. Have I heard or am I guessing that this is the final episode of *Annabelle's Children*? P.P. Frederico had predicted more than a single decade. While my anthem "Who's Your Mother?" plays, the camera pans one last time across the cake-smeared faces of my children. The song stops as the credits freeze on two names, little Harrison's and P.P.'s, followed by their birth and death years. Maybe P.P., wherever he is, has witnessed this memorial. Maybe he and Harrison are here. Maybe everyone's here. Do you know any different?

❧

If my death follows a pattern, I don't have the distance to interpret it. But I pass fewer nights attached to humans and domesticated creatures. Frequently, I slide through the dark with nocturnal hosts I may or may not see. I have wheeled with bats and lain between crickets' whittling legs. There have been the speed and power and violence of hunting, cries of power or fear. I have burrowed, deep, into loamy soil and rotting hearts.

When I am indoors, my hosts often dive for darkness, and I catch only winks of light. Tonight I hear whispered endearments and murmurs of pleasure: there's lovemaking, but I'm with neither partner. Too dark even for shadows—I must be attached to a dust mite between a mattress and box spring. We rock with the sex, and if by some chance Harrison from Season Four is with us, maybe he remembers that rocking gave him comfort. One of the lovers cries out. Motion stops. Every moment is eternal patience.

❧

I'm coupled with an infant—it seems like forever since I've been attached to a human. His face presses into his mother's breast. He gasps, exhausted and ecstatic from suckling. His mother watches television, but her embracing arms block the screen.

"Shh," the mother whispers.

"Physics means pondering the imponderables," the TV voice says. All television voices sound like the announcer's from *Annabelle's Children*. When I ponder "time," I picture the lines a prisoner scratches on a cell wall—four lines and a cross hatch, four lines and a cross hatch—five and five and five and on and on, until everything is shaded into darkness.

My host-baby coos and frets, reconnects to his mother's nipple.

"Mmm," his mother sighs.

"Paul Dirac," the television voice continues, "theorized that whether light is composed of waves or particles depends on whether you ask it a wave-like or particle-like question."

❧

Don't tell me that *you* understand!

On this endless day I can't tell to what or whom I'm attached; time no longer seems to be something that moves. There's light, but I don't ask it questions about particles or waves. The light illuminates the bookshelf I face and have been facing forever. I focus on a book with a glossy paper cover; it's surrounded by dusty, title-less volumes. Studying the spine of this newer book is all I do.

I haven't lost the sense that I'm attached, but either the dynamics of connection have changed (were *due* to change?), or I'm hosted by something imperceptible to my understanding. What could be so small? A microbe? A malignant cell?

The book I stare at is titled *My Life as a Child of Annabelle: the End of Reality TV*. Below the title and unreadable author's name, a sweep of auburn hair spreads over the book's spine from a hidden cover photo. It might be my hair. It could belong to one of my babies. I've looked at this spine so long I can't imagine not seeing it. Concerning the title, I can ask one kind of question if "End" means "death," and a different kind of question if "End" means "goal."

As far as you know, you're hosting all of the dead. And maybe that's the end.

Acknowledgements

"Queen of the Waves," Georgia Review, winter, 2015

"An Oofy Baby Sees Fortunato's Side," Tahoma Review, spring, 2018

"Doctor Moreau's Pet Shop," PANK, December, 2011

"Interstate Nocturne," Surreal South '11, 2011

"Refugees of the Meximo Invasion," Roanoke Review, 2013
"Cherish the Muffin Top," Literary Orphans, 2015

"Obligates," The Pinch, winter, 2016

"Demi-Christmas," Grey Sparrow Journal, winter, 2013

"Blue Madeline's Version," A cappella Zoo, spring, 2012,

"Snow Angels Sans Merci," Prick of the Spindle, spring, 2011

"Smooth," Prime Number, summer, 2011

"Fiji Mermaid," Madison Review, spring, 2014

"Lactophilia," A-Minor Magazine, 2014

"X," Zymbol, issue 7, 2016

"Annabelle's Children," Altered States, 2014